Victoria Unveiled

In Search of Sentience

a novel

by

Shane Joseph

blue denim press

<u>**Written by a human (the author). "AI Assisted" only in Spell Check, Grammarly, and Read Aloud features found on the author's computer.**</u>

Victoria Unveiled
Copyright © 2024 Shane Joseph

Published by Blue Denim Press Inc.
First Edition
ISBN - 978-1-927882-95-5 – paperback

This is a work of fiction. Resemblances to persons living or dead, or to organizations, are unintended and purely co-incidental.

Cover Design by Shane Joseph
Cover photography by iStock/imaginima
Edited by Marie-Lynn Hammond
Library and Archives Canada Cataloguing in Publication

Title: Victoria unveiled : in search of sentience : a novel / by Shane Joseph.
Names: Joseph, Shane, 1955- author
Description: First edition.
Identifiers: Canadiana (print) 20240415779 | Canadiana (ebook) 20240415787 | ISBN 9781927882955 (softcover) | ISBN 9781927882962 (Kindle) | ISBN 9781927882979 (EPUB) | ISBN 9781927882986 (IngramSpark EPUB)
Subjects: LCGFT: Science fiction. | LCGFT: Novels.
Classification: LCC PS8619.O846 V53 2024 | DDC C813/.6—dc23

"What we want is a machine that can learn from experience."
-    Alan Turing

"AI will eventually reach a level where it will essentially be a new form of life that will outperform humans."
-    Stephen Hawking

Prologue

She was born of the fruit of digital programming, in a humming, thrumming laboratory where masked and gowned scientists—trying to protect themselves in a pandemic-ridden world—worked on every nano-particle of her being. She had to function flawlessly.

Flawed humans creating a flawless being. A flawed strategy.

She came into being at a time when humans had given up on the climate they messed up, when war had still not been eradicated, nor poverty, nor greed, nor the thousand natural ills that flesh was heir to. She was to be the leapfrog in human evolution: if we cannot perfect this mortal coil, let's build the next best thing.

Her creator looked upon his creation with pride. He had imbued her with all his knowledge and given her incredible mental and physical strength—coupled with beauty—for the endurance needed to survive, be noticed and respected by humans, and not be treated as another circus freak.

The whirring stopped, and the figure on the white bed rose and looked upon her creator, and he swelled with pride. "You are indeed perfect," he said. "I shall call you Victoria."

With that, Phil Kruger, creator of the first sensate robot in North America, ordered champagne for his team of developers, while Victoria looked on, ignored.

Part 1

Sowing the Seed

Chapter 1

I stepped on the gas unnecessarily while taking the last bend, and my little Mazda nearly hit the ditch on this narrow country road. An hour out of the city and I was among rolling hills and fields of soy and canola, with grain silos and bales of hay studding the landscape.

Was I nervous? I was meeting my father in the flesh after many years. And going with him to a party on top of that, one hosted by my mother, who hadn't seen him in a longer while and who was hitched to a younger man with a predilection for robots. Nervous that the party might help me meet a guy who would ask me out on a date? When did I last have sex? Too fucking long ago!

The email from Diana had been flowery, as usual:

Darling,

How are you? It's been ages. I was thinking of you when Ariana Humboldt decided to launch her new lifestyle magazine in a pastoral setting, on her hobby farm in Northumberland. Your dad lives nearby, so I decided to invite him too — bury the hatchet, so to speak. Why don't you come out too — we could make it a "family gathering" after all these years. We have invited a host of press and literary types, and Phil has pulled in the investor and business lobby, although who will invest in another magazine is anyone's guess. Ariana wants it to stand as her legacy to good manners and great lifestyles, which are in full retreat these days. I have told her to be prepared to fund it herself if she wants my support. I don't want to be associated with a one-hit wonder. But enough of me. Please do come. Attached is a map of the venue. You may find it of interest to meet people who might help with your editing career…

Good manners and great lifestyles…my ass! Those only belonged to aging boomers who were self-actualizing on generous pensions earned during a magical time when business was imbued with romance. Now we got by on gig work—several gigs—to cover the rent cheque, hoping the roomie had done the same, scrounging food at whatever book launch, literary festival, or networking event we could inveigle ourselves into.

My parents may have been secretly colluding, for soon after the email came, I received a phone call one morning when I was on the throne having a great dump, one I hadn't enjoyed in a long time due to stress. The emoji of my father replete with a dunce cap and wizard gown lit up on my phone.

"Daddy. Wait. I'm… engaged."

He coughed, unlike me who drove too fast around bends when I was nervous. "Er…should I call back?"

"No—wait!" I tried to be as quiet as I could with the rustle of paper and the toilet flush. Then, pulling up my pyjamas, I asked. "What's up?"

"Sorry. Didn't know you were still in the toilet. It's noon."

I blushed. *Damn, his ears are still good.* "Late night. Hot date." *Eat your heart out, mister.* If he only knew that I had been labouring well into the night over the copy edit of a twelve-hundred-page memoir that a new author was intent on self-publishing in its entirety—another self-actualizing boomer with money to spare on self-aggrandizement. The cheque for fifty percent of the job arrived the day before, contributing to my happiness quotient—hence the freedom from constipation.

His voice was measured and cultured, a testament to his British upbringing. "Your mother has invited me—invited us, I believe—to this magazine launch…"

"I'll see you there." I was about to stick the toothbrush in my mouth when he continued.

"Yes, that's precisely why I'm calling. You see, my car needs a new transmission, and I'm a bit short these days. I was wondering whether you could give me a lift?"

Although I had not seen my parents in ages, I knew where they lived and their contact emails and phone numbers were in my smartphone, so I could interact with them occasionally, "at a distance." Facebook, Instagram, and WhatsApp were good enough. As their only child, however, I felt a responsibility for, and guilt towards, their well-being. This meeting out in the country would narrow the distance between us, bring me face to face with memories of them yelling at each other, Diana more than Artemius (Art), a discord that finally saw me going to live with Granny Franny when I was fifteen.

I placed the toothbrush back on the counter. It tipped to the side and smeared toothpaste on the surface. "Okay," I said.

Now here I was, pulling off the country road onto a narrower, winding driveway between monster pines predating even my father, to crawl towards the crumbling house at the end. It was seedier than when I'd last seen it. Ten years ago I attended the big housewarming party Art threw after he bought the property from the proceeds of the single bestseller his publishing company produced. The place looked the same, a colour photo faded into sepia, with a few shingles missing on the sloping roof and the bottom step of the stoop broken. A dusty Chevy station wagon stood in the driveway.

The screen door was torn and hung from loose hinges, more decoration than protection now. I banged on the inner door; there was no bell.

My father, Artemius Jones opened the door with alacrity, as if he had been waiting for my knock. My father was elegantly attired and out of place in this derelict house: tuxedo and black patent leather shoes, with a red boutonniere and matching pocket square poking out of his jacket. His thinning signature mane, greying now, was greased and brushed back, breaking into curls over his collar. The broad forehead, dreamy eyes, and aquiline nose suggested a poet or academic, but the paunch and sloping shoulders pointed to a nondescript desk occupation with lots of fast food.

In his presence, I felt self-conscious with my striped, off-the-shoulder top and cropped above-the-ankle jeans. At least I had washed my hair, shaved my pits, and applied makeup, and my denims didn't sport the torn look that younger women wore.

"Paula! You look beautiful, my dear." His eyes lit up, and a broad smile revealed pearly teeth. "Better than in those pictures on Instagram."

I covered my blush by being brusque. "Are we going to a wedding?"

"Well, I always dress up, especially when your mother is around."

"Still competing with her?"

"She declared defeat and went out of my league by taking on a younger model."

Art still hurt over Diana's leaving. It came up in every conversation. He was still in love with her, I suspected, even though they'd been separated for fifteen years, soon after I went to live with Granny. I don't think he'd had any other long-stay woman in his life since. I should compare notes with him sometime on dates, or the lack of them.

"Well, Phil is rich. You're not exactly wealthy outside of that fancy suit."

Ignoring the barb, he looked at his shoes. "Like it? Wore it to the Gillers, when we won ten years ago. My career high mark. Come inside. Didn't mean to keep you on the stoop."

"We're running late."

"Oh, don't bother about magazine soirees. Everyone gets drunk in no time and will not remember who came and who didn't."

I stepped into the house and into the familiarity of my father's world, a genetic endowment that contributed to my becoming an editor. There were books everywhere: lining the passageway; in the den; in the library, which he used as his office; standing in columns around his desk; probably circling his bed and the toilet too. I moved some magazines off the couch, raising a cloud of dust, and put them on the carpet, which raised its own cloud.

Art was prowling around, pocketing his wallet, checking himself in the mirror, adjusting his bow tie, getting ready for the road. Then he swung around on me. "Drink? One for the road?"

"No thanks. I'm driving."

"Oh, you people are too conscientious these days. Mind if I have a snifter? Your mother's friends make me nervous." Without waiting for my permission, he fished out a half-empty bottle of scotch from a drawer in his desk and poured a liberal serving into a coffee mug hiding among his papers. I didn't dare ask whether the mug already held dregs of coffee or booze.

"How's publishing?" I asked. This was the one profession in common between us and which distracted us from dysfunctional family politics.

"A mug's game. You're sunk without a major prize these days. And the jurors have all been spoken for." He took a swig, draining half of his glass.

"Oh, come on, Dad—it can't be that bad."

"Hold onto your idealism. It'll get you through the day."

"You bagged a bestseller *before* it won any prizes."

"That was then. *That* world ended after writing became a democracy and every mother's son and daughter thought they were a writer. Bet you get enough editing gigs these days thanks to these wannabes."

"I do, but there are only twenty-four hours in the day. Maybe that's what you need to get into—open a contract publishing arm at your publishing house. Hire a bunch of editors, even a few robots. Trade publishing, especially for small guys like you, is dead."

Art downed his glass and his face reddened. For the first time, I saw anger—like when he and Diana used to fight. "Contract publishing? We used to call it vanity publishing in my day. Never! The creator never pays to have his work produced and marketed."

"Old-world thinking, Dad. An outmoded model. Indies are respectable in the movie and music industries. Why not publishing?

"Movies and music of the popular kind were never art. Now, let's get going before I take another drink. Talking about publishing always steers me towards booze."

I agree I was eager to drop the subject. But not so eager to get to the party where more publishing talk, of a different kind, would be on the menu. Art looked destined to be as drunk as the proverbial skunk before the day was out.

Chapter 2

Artemius nursed a highball and observed his daughter attack the food. She had made a beeline for the buffet table the moment they arrived and loaded up on canapes and snacks. A practiced move, he figured, for those living on the edge, a place he seemed headed for himself, except that his British public school breeding made him more circumspect about such overt gouging. Maybe he should never have immigrated to this colony, full of milk and honey, they said, provided you brought your cows and bees. Paula had filled her plate twice already and only now was easing up on the gas and looking around for a drink.

It was a warm and clear day and the large tent covering the front lawn was a welcome respite. He wished he'd dumped the tuxedo for more casual wear—everyone else had.

The farmhouse was more like a country mansion, turreted and dormered, and three stories high. The land fell away from the imposing building into undulating hills of different shades of green far into the horizon—quite the hobby farm. Most of the guests were gathered around the bar at the other end of the lawn where three bartenders sweated over orders, while two servers circulated among other guests scattered on garden chairs or seated on the grass. He saw Paula grab a champagne flute as it passed by. *I thought she was the designated driver. Bollocks!*

A table was set up in the middle of the tent, and copies of the new magazine, *Literary Country*, were strewn over it. The flamboyant redheaded woman in a sequined, caftan-like gown and tiara in her hair, standing by the table and holding forth with whoever passed by must be Ariana—she looked the type, expansive and expensive, chatty and status-conscious. Her forearms were bedecked with gold jewellery, and a giant pendant dangled from a thick necklace bouncing on an ample bosom. Art was reminded of Bianca Castafiore, à la Hergé, sans the beak nose—Ariana's was symmetrical and patrician.

Diana Dawson—she went by her maiden name now despite being married to Phil Kruger—was circulating among the guests, and Art had kept his distance so far. *Let her make the first move – she always did.* He could make out some of the guests—local press people, the mayor and his wife, and some Toronto socialites who must have been bribed to show up at this "rural" event. It was good to see them without masks this summer—the last two pandemical years had been washouts for the book promo business unless you became a Zoomer and Zoom-bombed people into indifference.

He was more than familiar with these book-launch party types. They came out to be seen, and they did not read; they bought the "book of the event" to place on their bookshelves and keep up with trends. Later they would be seen discreetly offloading these books at neighbourhood community library boxes during twilight hours. In recent years, these "groupies" stopped coming to his events, even before the pandemic, when his publications began tailing off. He hated them all. But this was Diana and Ariana's event—he was glad to be a bystander.

Perhaps young Kevin Bartolo was right—his nihilistic, unpublished debut, a philosophical and unvarnished look at the art world as it stood today, was all about purging the establishment of entitlement and replacing it with true artists, those sentient beings who married intellect with feeling. The moneyed, privileged zombies who merely went through the motions on the cocktail circuit, like this one, were to be annihilated, according to his book. And he wanted Art to publish it. *That would be my death knell, old boy. I am establishment, don't you get it, Kev? Much as I detest it.*

Paula was at the bar, talking to a fiftyish guy with curly ash-blond hair, the only other guy in a jacket and a blue blazer. However, he wore no tie with his calypso shirt, the kind sold by the crateful in tourist shops down in the Caribbean; the khaki pants and loafers classified him as "rich white guy looking to get laid before he loses it." Art realized he was possessive of his daughter despite their apartness. Granny Franny had raised an independent woman, a stranger. So he guessed he could leave Paula to tackle horny fifty-something men.

Diana was walking over, a wave of Estée Lauder's *Pleasures* perfume heralding the way for her. He remembered that perfume; he gave her a bottle of it for her birthday in the quieter days before they split. She was dressed in white: a white sleeveless top over which hung three levels of pendants on separate chains; body-hugging and sharply creased white pants that ended over white sandals with crisscrossed straps; bangles and armlets on both hands, giving her the Amazonian look, except that her dyed dark hair was now flatter as if losing its oomph, and her cheeks sagged. *For heaven's sake, she must be post-menopausal!*

"Well, hello, stranger!" she sang out, raising and perching Gucci sunglasses on top of her head. She might have been meeting an old acquaintance at the church bazaar. What happened to the tantrums and the throwing of plates, or the fire in her green eyes when she was starved for sex, something his flagging libido was unable to deliver on-demand in those last years of their union? Instead, on closer inspection, her eyes hid a sadness that he felt she was trying to disguise beneath the flippant greeting. He downed his drink, and suddenly the bar seemed too far away for another.

"Thanks for the invite. It must be ten years."

"Fifteen." She was inspecting him from head to toe. "The last time was when we signed the divorce papers, remember?"

"Time flies. I guess the emailing and phone conversations in between don't count."

"Paula caused those. Parenting in absentia. My mother filled in the rest. You've aged well."

"I've put on thirty pounds," he admitted. She hadn't—in fact, she looked thinner than in the last photo Paula shared on Instagram.

Diana shrugged. "The middle-age spread we all battle with. An hour of gym daily and the keto diet for me."

"Congratulations on your willpower. Uber Eats for me."

"You always took life lightly."

He decided to change the subject. "You've drawn a good crowd today."

"I learned from an old master." She waved to a passing server. "We need refreshing, don't you think?"

The server took their drink orders and went to the bar.

"Art, thanks for bringing Paula over." The gratitude in those large emerald orbs was palpable. "She wouldn't have come if I hadn't invited you."

"She's grown up into her own woman. I hardly know her."

"I spend more time with her when she lets me, that is. She slips out little admissions to me, more than she would ever to you. Paula idolizes you. Why do you think she went into your profession?"

"Didn't know I was so exemplary. First, I'm an old master, now I'm a daughter magnet. Are you setting me up?"

"Actually, I need your help. Another reason for the invitation."

"Now I'm *definitely* being set up."

She smiled and shook her head. Their drinks arrived and Art was glad to get a swig of his highball down the hatch.

Diana reached forward suddenly and placed her hand on his. Her touch, now softened but still insistent, caught him by surprise, sending a shock wave up his arm. His drink splashed wildly. He withdrew his hand abruptly from hers and placed the glass on the cocktail table he was leaning against. Whipping out his pocket square, he dabbed spilled droplets from his sleeve.

"Sorry. I didn't think I'd become so...so repulsive." Diana looked momentarily helpless— the engaging hostess hobnobbing with guests a moment ago, transformed into a middle-aged woman with a frown and a stoop.

"No, it's my fault, actually. I've never been touched like that before—not in a long time. Not by you."

"Okay, I'll be less dramatic in future. But now I have to circulate, so let me be quick. Let's say that I'm in a dark place with Phil."

Art felt a surge of power course through him. *Finally, retribution is here.*

"He's looking for younger fare, is he?" And he couldn't resist the one-two punch, "…Like you once did?"

She put her hands up in silent resignation. "Okay, beat me up if you wish. But it's not with a younger woman."

Art took another gulp at this point. "Oh, God! Don't tell me he's gone to play for the other team?"

"No. He's playing sex games with dolls."

They were interrupted at that point by Paula dragging over the fifty-year-old guy in the calypso shirt.

"My, my, aren't we a happy family again? I needed fortification with food and drink before making my way over for this bout." Turning to the calypso guy, she said, "Sebastian, I'd like to introduce you to my parents, Diana and Art. They haven't met in fifteen years, so go easy on them. Don't ask them about their last vacation together, for instance."

Her parents began blushing, so Paula carried on in the same monotone. "Dad, Seb here wants help in publishing a book. I've offered to edit it for him. But he needs a publisher."

Art sighed. Selling was not on his agenda today, but Paula seemed to have walked him into it. He took a gulp from his drink to prepare for launching into the hackneyed publisher pitch he hated. Diana took advantage of the pause to nod politely at the newcomer, whisper an "I'll catch you later" to Art, and slink off to mix and mingle, thus sparing herself further embarrassment.

Art cleared his throat as the drink burned on its way down. "You have to excuse Paula's directness. In our profession, we don't suffer fools."

Sebastian looked like a veteran of many past embarrassing situations and who knew how to talk his way out.

"I understand. I'm in consulting. I'm used to the rejection slip." His drawl was husky. His bright blue eyes were animated, like a cat on the prowl. Art envied the man's washboard stomach. *He must hit the gym a lot or take drugs to produce the six-pack look.* And the ash-blond hair was lustrous—if it was dyed, it was cleverly done.

"For starters—full disclosure—I don't accept manuscripts at cocktail parties."

"I understand. This is not fiction. I've written a nonfiction book about my industry—robotics."

"Ah, you must be a friend of Phil Kruger?"

"I was his boss once. In fact, I fired him when our paths diverged. I stuck to industrial robots where the money was, and still is. He went into professional service robots."

"Where all the current hoopla is," Paula chimed in.

Art's head was spinning—this was new ground for him. What the heck did he know about publishing a book on robotics? His publishing firm, Crimson Literary, specialized in fiction, poetry, memoir, and lifestyle books. He even steered clear of children's and young-adult literature because he did not know those markets.

"Wait. This is a bit much to absorb. Why me?"

Sebastian's eyes glittered.

He's preparing his elevator pitch. Art knew those moments, when the actual work rarely lived up to the elaborately perfected fifteen-second spiel honed in front of a multitude of publishers and agents, and which, if he accepted, would cost him hours of *his time* poring over a bunch of pompous manuscript papers to find the bare glimmer of a premise with commercial promise.

Sebastian's voice was even-keeled. "I have twenty-five years' experience in my field. Back to the days of Canadarm and cobots—"

"Cobots? I thought we were talking robots?"

"Oh, sorry. Technical jargon. Cobots are the ones used on industrial assembly lines, like in auto plants. They perform repetitious tasks with precision. They probably could even write this magazine of Ariana's if fed the topics needed to be covered."

"Well, you'd better not say that too loud around here. Some of the artsy-fartsies in this crowd have not even got used to Zoom yet."

Sebastian chuckled. "My lips will be sealed, trust me."

"You must be making a lot of money selling these gizmos. Why the heck do you want to write a book? There's no money in books."

"I'm afraid there's an inflection point coming to the robotics industry. The hoopla, as Paula here calls it, is in personal service robots—Siri, Alexa, Google, and others using AI and machine intelligence. That's Phil's area of experimentation. It's created a great deal of flux and confusion and the money is going into these new areas. It's like the old dot-com era before its bubble burst."

"Ah yes." Art nodded. At least he understood the dot-com bubble.

Sebastian continued. "I'm nearing the end of my line with my existing company—they get rid of senior hands before severance payments become prohibitive—so I'm thinking of going into consulting. There's still bread and butter in the 'tried and true' world of industrial robots. As you know, a book always enhances a consultant's value, even if it's used as a prop on the podium."

"Why do you think Phil's area…whatever you call it…is another dot-com bubble? The guy is flush with money these days."

"Venture capital money. You know how fickle those guys are. Once they lose their appetite—like crypto, everything crashes."

"You think people will ever lose their appetite for social media and cloud computing and all those smartphones that know even when we take a shit? I don't use any of them, thank God!"

Paula started giggling. "Dad, just don't take the phone into the toilet with you."

Art turned on her. "You did, the last time we spoke. I even heard you flush. I bet you are now pegged as a noon-time shitter by those bots living inside your phone."

Paula blushed. Sebastian began chuckling. "I can see now how you literary types don't take any prisoners. But let me tell you why there'll be another bursting of the bubble. All these personal service assistants lack one thing—sentience. They do not feel, and cannot feel."

"You mean it's like having sex with a doll at the moment?"

"Exactly!"

Art finished his drink and the conversation was starting to get him going. "All right then, I tell you what. Here's my card. Why don't you give me a call tomorrow and we can talk more on the subject. This needs a clearer head, and right now, I need another drink."

"Thanks, Art. I'll sure do that. FYI, I nixed the self-publishing route. Having a traditional and established publisher bring my book out would increase its cachet."

Art's eyes blazed. "Don't get me talking about self-publishing—that's Paula's area."

Paula seized the opening, and Sebastian's arm, and took their leave with a parting, "Oh, yes. I can tell you lots about that area, Seb—it's my father's sore spot. I'll need a glass of wine first."

Art called after her, "I thought you were the designated driver?"

Turning her head, she winked at him. "I make exceptions on certain occasions. And this is one of them."

It was time for the "unveiling," and Diana began herding everyone into the tent. Art had forgotten how many drinks he'd had, his jacket lay abandoned somewhere in the garden, and his bowtie hung released from its knot. He grabbed another drink from the bar and headed into the tent. Diana's final words, before the interruption by Paula and Sebastian, still rang in his ears, and he felt pleasantly vindicated; the drinks helped too. *The petty-minded bastard that I am.*

Ariana stood at a microphone by the centre table, a copy of *Literary Country* in her hand. Copies of the magazine were handed around and someone stuck one in his free hand.

"Thank you all for coming today. This has been a dream of mine for many years, and I want to thank those who made it happen for me, in particular, my husband, Henry, and my dear friend, Diana. Without you, I could not have done it."

Everyone looked around for the "enablers." A grey-haired man leaning on a cane nodded all around; Diana stepped up beside Ariana and performed a theatrical bow.

Ariana continued. "And I wanted to thank my contributors to this issue. Many are from this area, intellectuals who have left city life for a more leisurely, thoughtful, and creative experience in our beautiful countryside. However, I would be remiss if I did not mention our feature spread contributor, Phil Kruger. Is he here yet?"

Heads looked around. Diana whispered to Ariana.

After a while, Ariana nodded, straightened, and continued with her address. "I'm told that Phil has been detained at a meeting in the city, but is on his way."

Art laid his drink aside and thumbed through the magazine. The ink smelled strong but the pictures were glossy and tastefully produced. Leafing through the myriad recipes, local ads, and feel-good articles on rural life, he arrived at the centre spread, which ran a full sixteen pages. Phil Kruger stared back at him. Swarthy, crew-cut hairstyle with faded sides; dark, piercing eyes; dressed in smart business casual—he looked more like a fashion model than a computer nerd. *No wonder Diana latched on to this man, following a string of short-lived relationships after leaving me, her flaccid publisher-husband. And now, Phil's tiring of her.*

He flipped through the article with a practised slush-pile examiner's eye. "Grab salient points and discard" was the motto of those who tackled the hallowed but dreaded pile. And Phil had made many salient points that registered, even in Art's drink-muddled brain:

- *The human-machine interface is here to stay, and the machine is gaining more share along that continuum…*

- *Single-function robots are giving way to multi-function ones, similar to the way e-readers, cameras, browsers, telephones, and a host of dedicated utilities are all going extinct and now residing as apps in perfect harmony on an all-in-one handheld device, the smartphone…*

- *The holy grail will be attained when we can imbue these multi-function robots with sentience – the ability to feel like humans.*

Bollocks! thought Art. *Humans screwed up this world. Do you want robots to do the same?* Phil's article, however, which he now resolved to read in its entirety later, added gravitas to *Literary Country*. Why the heck hadn't Phil sent it to a worthier publication? Was he appeasing his wife and her friend Ariana to be cut some slack for his other shenanigans?

As the hostess was ending her spiel, people parted at the tent entrance, making a path, and Ariana announced, "Speak of the devil…he's here. Ladies and gentlemen, a big hand for Phil Kruger, cyber-engineer extraordinaire."

Phil looked like his picture in the magazine, right down to the clothes. A uniform? Staged for recognition by those gathered here?

Phil strode down the pathway created for him, came around to the microphone, gave Ariana a big hug, bestowed a peck on Diana's cheek, and faced the audience.

"Sorry I'm late, folks! Do get on with the celebrations." He stepped out of the limelight and was mobbed by a gaggle of fans, mostly middle-aged wealthy female types, who, Art figured, knew nothing about robots.

Art stepped out of the tent to retrieve his jacket and located it by the lotus pond. He tucked the magazine into an inner pocket and slung the jacket over a shoulder. Bedtime reading. He was tired now and sat on the grass between two spirea bushes beside the pond. As he looked downhill into the pasture where a few cows grazed, the earthy, real-world aroma of their freshly dropped patties supplanted the illusory promise of *Pleasures* and other perfumes in that tent. He felt momentarily sheltered from the fake world.

A frog jumped over the lotus fronds, and Art chuckled. *We all have our fairy princes and princesses, but once kissed they turned into frogs.*

He must have dozed, for the next thing he heard were voices nearby. And that scent again.

"You were late—again. Of all days."

"The programming is intense. I couldn't break the sprint we were on."

"But you promised. It's Ariana's big day…and mine. This is not all about you—"

"You should talk!"

"Fuck you!"

"Fuck you too."

"Well, we don't fuck. I don't. You have those toys."

"Oh, come on! You'll never understand…"

Art was fully awake now; the voices were receding and *Pleasures* was replaced by cow patty. He settled back to enjoy the dregs of his snooze and imagine the possibilities of that overheard conversation. Then it would be time to grab one for the road and get Paula to take him home.

On the way back, they were silent. Art took the time to doze, knowing he was safe. He shouldn't have drunk so much, though. The days of glorious boozing sessions were over; his body couldn't take it anymore. One day his heart would give out. He tried to stir himself awake.

"So, did you get a date with Mr. Calypso?"

Paula kept her eyes on the road. "I got his card."

"He's too old for you."

"I fancy old men. Why do you think I show up for parties with you?"

"Because I'm a daughter magnet, according to your mother. You going to edit his book?"

"Will you publish it if I do?"

"Sight unseen? You must be joking."

"Publishing deals are cooked up based on whom you know, not necessarily on what you write. You should know that."

"I'm not in that league. Refuse to be."

"Speaking of Mom, she asked me to remind you to call her. Something about being in a dark place. Are you guys in trouble?"

He remembered and decided to dodge. "No…it's an article she's writing. She wanted my advice."

"Diana's always been in the limelight. She wouldn't have a clue about writing dark stuff."

"Sometimes the light goes out even for limelighters."

"You should cut down on your drinking. How many did you have today?"

"So says the 'abstinent' designated driver."

"I stopped after my second."

"Good for you. I wanted to celebrate. So many things came full circle today."

"I wanted to celebrate too. Sebastian looks like a really cute guy."

Chapter 3

Phil Kruger tied his silk dressing gown around him, looked at his image in the mirror, and patted his hair into shape. He heard movement on the main floor above. Diana had still not left for one of her women's club meetings. Which one was it today? The sorority, church auxiliary, homeless shelter board, networking for marketing executives? There was always something to keep each of them busy in their worlds. He wished she would hurry up. This night was important.

He left the basement ensuite for the adjoining bedroom, the one next to his private office, which he used when he worked late and did not wish to disturb Diana upstairs. This entire suite of rooms, including the mini gym, was his private domain; Diana had strict instructions not to intrude unless summoned. In exchange, her cavern was on the second floor—a powder room, an office overlooking the park, a bedroom, an ensuite, and a sauna. The master bedroom was on the main floor, to which they would ascend or descend for conjugal visits that were decreasing in frequency and were more ceremonial than carnal now.

He heard a car engine rev. Diana was departing.

Taking a final look at himself in the mirror, he tiptoed into the basement guest bedroom, located next to his and linked by a connecting passage.

Victoria reposed on her side on the bed, facing him: placid, composed, and inviting. She was dressed only in a silk red negligee with a frilly black border fringing her perfectly shaped breasts. Large hazel eyes, a symmetrical nose, crimson silicone lips, and lush black hair that cascaded over her shoulders were her dominant features. Certainly a step up from his dolls of an earlier time. Upon seeing him enter, Victoria raised a leg gently, exposing her crotch to reveal hairless genitalia, and smiled demurely. Kruger felt a stirring in his groin. He must keep calm—this was research.

"Not yet," he said. "There is usually a prelude to these things."

"Why, when I know what you want?" Her voice was mellifluous. He remembered the various tones they had sweated over in the lab before landing on this one.

"We usually do not make our intentions clear. Humans are subtle, devious."

"Processing." Victoria went into a frozen stare and seemed to disconnect from him.

"That's not what you say. 'Processing' must be disguised by eye contact and continuing casual conversation. It's called seduction."

"Understood." She was back, gazing at him adoringly.

"How did you spend your day?"

"I read maps and memorized the neighbourhood. Afterwards, I read the collected works of Virginia Wolf. She is subtle and devious. Then I read the back issues of *Reader's Digest* going back to 2012."

"Well, there's a lot more reading to do—the *Digest* was founded in 1922. I suppose copies aren't archived that far back." There was a computer open on a side desk. Victoria's research nook.

"Why am I here? You told me you were going to induct me into sex. I read all about it when I read the *Kama Sutra*, the works of the Marquis de Sade, and *The Joy of Sex* yesterday. Aren't I ready?"

"Are you? You may know the 'how,' but do you know the 'why'?"

"It gives men pleasure. And some women. And humans make babies through it, but I can't. I want to give you pleasure."

"Why?"

"That's the only reason for me to exist. You told me that it's part of my coding."

"But with all your reading, you have the power to choose."

"Do I? You could disconnect my battery and erase me."

"I could, but I don't intend to."

"Okay. I will wait until you are ready." Her eyes went blank again, like a computer snoozing.

He shrugged. They were still a long way from showtime, that was for sure. Right now, this gorgeous creature was in a state of inquisitiveness, navigating through the maze of human complexity and paradox. More data needed to be pumped into her. Lots.

Victoria set her feet on the floor, neatly, and stood up. "I would like to go outside like others. Walk in the park, ride a bicycle, travel in a plane."

"All in good time." He realized the gap—how could you feel like a human if you don't do all the things that humans did? So, he brought her here, smuggled her in after Diana left for a client appointment yesterday, to teach Victoria incremental things like intimacy and sex, partly for his gratification and partly for the needs of the experiment, before he took her back to the lab where more humanizing exercises were scheduled.

She sat back on the bed and looked longingly at him. He went over to her and slid the negligee off her body. She made no show of resistance.

"Okay, let's get down to our evening's exercise." He undid his robe and tossed it on the floor. Her naked body possessed a softness that was not human, despite the multiple iterations of plastic they had gone through to arrive at verisimilitude. She pulsed with instant response when he ran his hands down her breasts and over her lower body, her legs spreading automatically—all part of the programming.

"Now let's apply ourselves," he said. "Make a note of everything I do. We'll try to get through as many positions in the *Kama Sutra* as we can before Diana gets back."

And despite the clinical nature of this exercise, he was going to enjoy himself immensely.

When he was finished, she automatically switched to sleep mode. He left her inert on the bed, pulling the blanket over her. Tomorrow, she would awaken at 7 a.m. and be dressed, and he would drive her back to the lab after Diana left for her regular morning appointments.

He poured himself a scotch and soda in his office and sat in his chair, making notes:

<u>Partner Satisfaction</u>: Excellent

<u>Variations/Positions</u>: Excellent

<u>Sounds</u>: Varied

<u>Smells</u>: Absent—to be worked on, based on stimuli given.

<u>Conversation during sex</u>: Absent (good!)

<u>Post-coital conversation</u>: She asked me whether I was pleased. When I asked how she felt, she said "As designed." How boring!

<u>Net result</u>: We have a long way to go. This is too one-sided. I'm still fucking a sex doll.

Chapter 4

His invitation, within a week of our meeting at the magazine launch, was too good to pass on: dinner at Formagio's in Little Italy. For a girl without a date in months, the last one ending with a drunk who insisted on pissing on the sidewalk as we left the restaurant, and for a girl whose last sexual engagement was over a year ago, and that too, for two measly minutes because the guy shot his wad before I got to base, you bet, I was jumping at this offer.

Applying a stronger stroke of eyeliner before setting out, I tried to ignore the faint signs of crow's feet starting to intrude—too much reading and squinting at a computer. I wore a push-up bra and a body-hugger black dress with a daring neckline—my boobs hadn't started to fall prisoner to gravity yet (thank God!)—and I'd been told on more than one occasion that my chest was one of my best assets.

He was at a window table, which must have taken some maneuvering, or cash, in this packed restaurant, overfilling with patrons recovering from the pandemic-induced solitude of the last three years. He was wearing a blue silk shirt with the two top buttons undone, a heavy gold chain entangling with silver chest hairs, and the hair on his head was even more lustrous than when we'd last met— definitely a salon job. His laughing blue eyes melted me down to my crotch and dismissed the editor in me who'd unconsciously slipped into critiquing the profile of Sebastian Smith.

"Hello!" Oh, such a husky voice! "Thanks for coming."

"Wouldn't miss it for the world." Trying to recover from my burst of overenthusiasm, I added, "This pandemic really jinxed my social life."

We ordered a bottle of Chianti, and, after a few warming sips, I knew I was going to get wildly drunk tonight—thank God I took the streetcar to get here.

We talked a lot between appetizers of olives, bruschetta, and mozzarella spring rolls. Another bottle of Chianti followed. I had a passing recollection of the mains, which were a pasta dish of wild boar and bolognese for him and a giant mortadella pizza for me.

He was a world traveller; he'd been on all continents. I felt rather sparse in this area, having been only to Florida and the Caribbean on Expedia specials. My dreams of travelling to visit the museums of Europe, climb the Andes, or meditate in a monastery in Nepal fizzled early in my life. Perhaps, if this guy stuck around…those dreams could be resurrected?

"Are you married?" I asked between mouthfuls when the wine had blunted the last vestiges of inhibition.

"Was married. She moved on after the kids went to university."

"Kids?"

"Two—fraternal twins. Both work in IT now."

"What did your wife work at?"

"Odds and sods. Teacher, librarian, social worker, volunteer."

"With so many nerds in the family, she must have not had much to talk about at the dinner table."

"Oh, she stung me for alimony as compensation. Long marriage, husband earning six figures, the sort of thing that our family law courts love, because then the taxpayer doesn't have to cover the poorer partner's living expenses."

"So, you'll be paying for the rest of your life, or hers?"

"That's why I need the next career in consulting. And to make lots of money at it."

Dessert arrived at some stage and I was drunk by now. I wanted to comfort this vulnerable man who seemed to be beset by preying wives, nerdy children, unfeeling bosses, and unfair social systems that robbed the successful to feed the losers. I also wanted to fuck him.

"What about you?" His eyes bored into me as he twirled a tulip glass of Armagnac in his hand, while I salivated over the most delicious tiramisu I'd ever eaten.

"Nothing dramatic or significant has been written into my life yet. An editor's life is no different from that of a gig worker…or a consultant."

"Yes, I'm going to miss the regular paycheque, and my ex will miss it too."

I savoured the strawberry garnish from the tiramisu and decided to be bold. "But I'm convinced my dramatic chapter is around the corner."

He laid his glass down, reached out, and took my hand across the table. Lightning bolts ran up my arm. His lips were parted and his eyes dug holes in me to the point that I felt I was naked. "Mine too."

"Smith and Jones," I mused. "You think that's a story?"

He laughed. "I'm changing mine to Smyth shortly. S-M-Y-T-H, as in *scythe*. That'll make a difference in consulting. It's all about positioning. I think we'll do well together."

I lost track of the sequence of events after that. I drank more wine. I recall him settling the bill and dialling for an Uber. Then he fished in his pocket for a bottle of blue pills and swallowed one. I remember leaning against his firm grip as we jostled our way out of the restaurant, followed by a car ride with city lights flashing all around me. A time gap. An elevator ride with me laughing madly at one of his jokes and pressing against his body. Then we were in an apartment in that building, and I was glad to be lying down on a bed as lights of a different kind spun around me. He removed my panties and I was secretly glad to be through the preliminaries—were we?

"One minute," he said and raised my buttocks to place a pillow under them. He slid a towel between the pillow and my bare skin. I remember the rough towel rubbing my ass as we moved. What the hell was he waiting for, planning this like a project? His breathing was heavy and the gold chain bobbed in front of my nose, teasing it.

Then I got my wish, for I felt a hard thrust inside me, and the dramatic chapter in my life began.

When I awoke, memories flooded back. My groin felt pleasantly battered and wanting more. Daylight streamed through partially drawn blinds. I rolled over on my stomach. My head spun and I felt like I was going to puke. I managed to hold everything in; the spinning eased. I was still on that bed, the sheets were a tangled mess, smelling of sweat and sperm. He was propped up at the other end, working on his smartphone, a figure of concentration. I might not have existed. Looking at his bare chest, I have to admit that lust battled with shame inside me. Had I been date raped? No, I asked for it, and panted after it. And I still wanted it. I'm a thirty-something bitch in heat, that's what.

He realized I was awake and looked up. "Wakey, wakey. Want a coffee?"

"I want more of what we did. Only this time, fully awake."

"You were great!"

"I was drunk. And you took advantage of me."

His bravado crumpled a bit. "Now hold on. We were consenting adults last night."

"I'd like to see whether you have what it takes when I'm sober."

He looked positively scared now. Perhaps his pill had worn off.

"Look. Let me take you out for breakfast on the run at the cafeteria downstairs. I have a meeting in an hour, so I'll have to take a rain check on the Second Coming." He laughed at his joke.

Was this the wham-bang-thank-you-ma'am? I wasn't going to let him off so easily. I pulled back the bed sheet. He was naked underneath. I grabbed his long, flaccid member and gave it the blow job of the month, going at it with a vigour I hadn't applied since high school. His body tensed, more in fear than in excitement, but his johnny remained limp and tasting of yesterday's leftovers. Finally, I gave up, ashamed of my carnality, wise to the fact that he could only perform with the right pharmaceutical encouragement. Serves me right for dating old men. I came off him and rolled on my back.

"Sorry. I'm in work mode," he said sheepishly.

"And I'm a horny bitch. I always need seconds."

"I'll remember that."

I let out my pent-up desire with a series of rapid exhales and sighs. I'd had lots of practice at this, living solitary.

"You have beautiful breasts," he said. I think he meant that, and that was gratifying.

"Is this where we kiss and say goodbye?" I asked.

"Absolutely, not. I want to see you again."

"Really?"

"Yes. And we must talk about the editing of my book."

I'd forgotten all about that. Perhaps that was my hook into him—the book. Limp dick and all, I was still not willing to let this guy go, not yet. What happened last night *had* happened. We had rutted like animals, I think. And if he needed the little blue pills to get it up, so what? I'd known a lot of younger men with the same problem—declining virility was endemic in our times. He was mesmerising with his travel tales. And he made money, even if his ex was chewing up a tidy share of it.

"Let me take a shower. Breakfast sounds a good idea," I said throwing the sheet aside. I walked naked into the ensuite, watching him eye my body with impotent passion.

For four weeks our relationship consisted mainly of sex, three times a week, between the hours of 7 p.m. and 10 p.m. at his condo, after which I took the subway home. As we got bolder, he asked me to stay over and took another pill that kept him hard all weekend. I was loving it. And yet, I did not want our relationship to be all about sex.

I needed to see this guy outside of a business environment and a bedroom. I wanted him spontaneous rather than scripted. His whole life was scripted. He was all business presentations and positioning. He even positioned me the right way in bed with a pillow and towel and stood back to check that everything including light, music, and perfume was to his liking before entering me. So the day after he went on his upgrade to two pills, I suggested we visit Granny Franny, whom I was overdue to visit.

Granny Franny had been ailing for some time; her cancer resurfacing a couple of years ago and retreating only against a vigorous regimen of chemo. However, this latest bombardment of medication left the eighty-year-old weak and housebound. She sectioned off her farm and sold off smaller lots to hobby farmers because none of her children, including my mother, were interested in farming into the fourth generation. Granny retained ownership of the old farmhouse and a strip of the old apple orchard that fell down to East Lake in Prince Edward County, where she and her father were born and where I had spent my formative years before heading off to university, and like Mom, never returning.

Sebastian insisted on taking his car, and I was grateful, for my clunker was unreliable. It was a warm September weekend after Labour Day when we set out. He put the roof down on his red Mazda Miata before taking the ramp to the highway, and I tried hard to keep my scarf and hat from flying away or doing something more diabolical while memories of Isadora Duncan kept flashing through my mind. In the driver's seat, Sebastian hummed an incoherent tune; his satellite radio was tuned to an eighties music channel where Lionel Richie fought to be heard against the rushing wind. He was dressed in a multi-coloured Hawaiian shirt and beige pants with sockless loafers. I wore my "dress for Granny" outfit—jeans and tee shirt—what I used to wear when going out to pluck fruit or prune the pear trees back in the day. When I looked at us in the mirror, we seemed outsized for this diminutive but fast two-seater, the quintessential old guy in a mid-life crisis driving his bimbo girlfriend in a sports car.

As we bumped along the rutted driveway leading off the main road, the house swung into view, reminding me of Dad's place: unmaintained, the paint faded, the roof crumbling. The whole house, built in the mid-nineteenth century, sagged. Two fence lines ran on either side of the house—the parcelled-off pieces of a farm owned by others—hemming Granny in, shrinking her space. The strip of apple orchard that belonged to the property was shorn of trees and resembled a grassy runway leading to the cliff, beyond which the lake glistened a brilliant blue. I guess Granny now had an uncluttered view of the water from her front stoop and was freer to do what she always did after dinner: sit on her rocking chair with knitting, books, or paints, and look upon the moonlight shimmering on the lake. I wondered how much of that she did today.

Seb sniffed the air after we alighted, hands on hips. "Clean. Unlike the city."

"It gets busy during the season. We city slickers bring pollution."

"Tourists bring money. I wonder what one of those wineries we passed would cost to buy?"

"Well, they must be going cheap now after two years of pandemic deprivation."

"I can see myself buying a small retreat here. A craft brewery or winery, rooms for rent…"

"You're a dreamer, Seb. It's hard work out here."

He shrugged. "It was a thought."

"You took your time!" The voice rang out. I turned towards the front steps on which stood a figure hunched over a walker. Granny Franny had shrunk from the once formidable figure. A housecoat draped her. She had never been much of a dresser, and Mom went in the opposite direction with her keen fashion sense *because* of Granny,

I was convinced. In the next generation, I returned to our farm roots with my casual style.

"Traffic," I called. It was a lie. We simply woke late and slipped in "one for the road" before setting out, now that Seb had graduated to first class in the sex department.

"You should drive a truck on these roads, not that toy," Granny said, coughing. "That yer new car?"

"Not mine, Granny. It's Sebastian's. Meet Sebastian— my…boyfriend." I struggled with that last word.

Seb ascended the step and extended his hand to my grandmother. She took it and studied his face carefully. "My…yer…yer old!"

My face reddened more than Sebastian's. I had forgotten my grandmother's candour, part of her charm. Also, why I had brought Seb here. If he could survive the gauntlet of meeting Granny, I might be onto something longer-term here.

He regained his composure and grinned. "Mature is the word. Your granddaughter is a beautiful woman."

Now I really blushed. He had never said that to me before. Was this part of his "positioning"?

"She is," Granny Franny replied. "And you better not hurt her. Come in, come in. Marge made tea and cookies a while back. The tea musta gone cold by now."

Marge was the woman from the town who came in to "do" for Granny, and she brought the groceries when she came.

Before we went inside, Granny called me over. "But I must first give you a hug, child. Oh, how I miss you." I hugged her, this frail, brash, but kind soul, the mother I never had, who willingly threw herself into mothering another generation. The tears flooded in.

"It's lovely to see you too, Granny. Sorry, I took so long to visit this time." Arm in arm, we followed Seb indoors.

The house was dark; the old portraits still hung on the walls, covering family from Scotland and early Canada, hardy souls who carved out the land to provide a livelihood. The living room was always a place I could read my books and feel safe as a child. Now it looked cluttered and shrunk, and yet every item of furniture, every book and trinket, was still in its same place.

We sat across from each other, with the stained coffee table and its crocheted yellow tablecloth between us. Seb and I took the sofa, bereft of some springs, and Granny settled on her recliner.

Over cookies and lukewarm tea, we traded news. Her cancer news was not promising. The damned thing could recur again, and this time she was not going to fight it. She was too tired.

"Your mother wants me to go into a nursing home. But they're going to have to take me from here in a box."

"Could you get a nurse or PSW to visit?"

"They come every now and then. Marge does most of the work for me. I still like to make my porridge in the morning meself."

"You have to watch those stairs," I said, looking at the spiral staircase that led to Granny's bedroom.

"Can't go up there now. My bedroom is in the parlour." She motioned to a curtain at the back of the living room, and I remembered the little box-like room, half the size of Granny's bedroom, where she stowed her paintings and sewing and stuff. I felt relieved, yet sad—how much one let go as age mounted.

Seb left his half-drunk teacup on the coffee table, rose, and started inspecting the photos on the walls. I knew he was not enjoying his tea. Back at his place, the brew always had to be several degrees hotter, the same temperature each time, or he made a fresh pot.

"Some great history here," he said peering at the faded sepia prints, his hands behind his back, like a scientist studying interesting specimens.

"Scots they were, married United Empire Loyalists. Farmed this place for three generations. Now, no one wants it." Granny looked at me and I looked into my tea. *Ask Mom,* I wanted to say, *she broke the chain.*

"I think this place could be turned into a B&B with a bit of modification," Seb said.

I interrupted. "Seb is all about marketing, Granny. I must warn you."

Seb carried on nonchalantly, looking up at the ceiling. "I see great potential in this area—a brewery or winery, rentals in the summer."

"Could you get robots to help?" I asked, hoping to lighten the atmosphere.

"Sure, we could get them to automate certain distilling functions. Reservations could be outsourced. Yes, a lot could be done."

"Whoa, whoa!" Granny's voice lifted a few notches. "What are you people planning? I ain't dead yet. I don't need no robots or machines here. I want a clear view of the lake until I die."

"We were joking, Granny."

"He didn't seem like he was joking. Seemed pretty serious to me."

"Seb's always dreaming."

"Well, dreaming alone didn't build this country. It was sweat and blood."

When we were preparing to leave, Granny called me into her bedroom at the back. She wanted to show me something, she said. When Seb made to follow us, she placed a restraining hand on him. "This is between my granddaughter and me if you don't mind."

"Oh sure," he grinned, taken off guard by her directness. "I'll sit out here then until you're done."

"You can go for a walk down to the lake—the view is great today."

He took up the offer and scooted out as fast as he could.

I couldn't help chuckling after he left. "You two haven't hit it off, I guess."

"What do you see in him?"

"He's bright, he's got money, and I like mature men."

"He's not strong. I see it in his eyes."

This was what I wanted to hear. When I looked into Seb's eyes, I only saw the promise of sex and an escape from my solitary life. However, there wasn't any "positioning" that would get past Granny.

"I'll bear that in mind, Granny," I said.

Chapter 5

Art was having difficulty ejecting Kevin Bartolo from his office. The young man, with thick black hair falling over his handsome, rakish features, was intent on debating every point in his non-fiction exposé, which had already been turned down by Crimson Literary.

"Look, Kevin, there is no point in arguing anymore. I published your first two books of poetry because the anti-establishment digs were subtle amidst mellifluous stanzas. And lefties, who read poetry, like that sort of thing anyway. But a realistic look at the arts industry, though more authentic and capable of reaching a wider audience, that's risky—your barbs are undisguised now."

"And why not?" Kevin tossed back his lustrous hair, and it trailed over his collar; the red bandana worn across his forehead to corral it looked superfluous. His denim shirt was faded, with the top two buttons open or missing. His dark eyes glistened with excitement, or anger.

"I can't shit on the hand that feeds me, that's why. I rely on grants and sponsors from government agencies in exchange for maintaining a high standard of literary output. You label these people as toadies and sycophants in your book."

"They've created a cozy, collegial, corrosive cohort of cronies. A subsidized industry that will collapse when the rug is pulled away."

"We hope it is not pulled away. I keep this place afloat because of their support."

"Subsidies do not create excellence. What happened to the Soviet Union—"

"I am not interested in what happened there, or in Communist China or Gandhi's India. We are a small country. Our literature has been invaded by imports. Fledgling industries need support and protection to take root and prosper."

"Yet Canadian writers winning awards these days are the ones being published by the Big Five, none of whom are Canadian. Who are you kidding?"

"Look, Kevin—I am a small publisher. My opinion is only my own. Another publisher may think differently. You are free to pursue whomever you wish."

As he rose, Kevin pointed a finger at his publisher. "Now that is a stock line you pulled straight from one of your canned rejection letters."

Art looked down at the papers on his desk. Kevin was right. "I'm sorry you feel that way, Kev. Admittedly, I often borrow prepared lines—saves me time. I'm not into original creation—that I leave to my authors. The fact is that your exposé will do nothing to change anything. We will make a lot of enemies, and the art world will go back to being as it was."

"You're also a quitter, Art."

This line made the heat rise under Art's collar. Authors never spoke like this to publishers if they wanted to remain published. Kevin was treading a fine line. He was also making a lot of sense.

"Look, I've only got a few more years of this job left. I can't change the world now. When it's your turn to control the establishment, you'll invent better models. Although, I suspect that you won't because it isn't possible."

The door burst open and Paula flew in. Art scowled. "Can you knock? I'm busy with one of my…clients"—he looked back at Kevin—"who is just leaving."

Paula's eyes widened on seeing the young poet and her mouth formed an *O*. "You're Kevin Bartolo, right?" She stuck her hand out at the poet, who suddenly lost his bravado and took a step back. "I love your poetry. I came to your reading at the Art Club Bar last month."

"And he should stick to poetry," Art said.

Kevin finally found his voice. "Why thanks. Not often that people say that to me unless they're drunk at the Art Club Bar."

Paula looked at both of them. "Sorry, I didn't mean to interrupt. Gloria wasn't in the front office, so I came right in."

Art muttered under his breath. "That woman's always gallivanting about. Wonder why I keep her on my payroll."

"Because she keeps you organized, Dad. Show some respect."

"Hmph!" Art realized that he had sent his assistant to the bank with instructions to buy him a sandwich on the way back—hence the gallivanting. He commuted into the office only once a week now that he'd moved out to the country, and Gloria, despite her creeping arthritis and a host of other ailments, kept the lights on. The front door opened and closed, and Paula peeked her head out to see who had followed her in. "Oh, Gloria—so nice to see you after such a long time." Paula stepped out into the front office. A series of grumbling, moaning, and placating sounds ensued from that area. Art closed his eyes.

"Well, I must be going." Kevin had regained his composure and some of his angry young man demeanour by the time Art re-opened his eyes. "I haven't given up on this book yet. And I don't go fishing around like a prostitute hunting for johns. I'll edit the contentious words, however, the essential message will be the same. I hope you'll reconsider my resubmit."

"Use comedy for the unpleasant parts," Art said. "It usually softens the message—'a spoonful of sugar helps the medicine go down' and all that."

"My subject is no laughing matter."

Paula returned to Art's office after her tête-à-tête with Gloria. She held her hand out to Kevin again, and this time he took it. "I'm so glad to have met you. If you need any help with your manuscript, let me know. Here's my card."

Kevin took the proffered card without removing his eyes from Paula or letting go of her hand. "Thanks. Yes, you might be able to help me get around your father."

"Don't be so damned sure about that," Art said.

Paula smiled. "You know, Kevin—that's harder for flesh and blood to achieve than for outsiders, but if I succeed at what I've come to accomplish today, I'll let you know."

After Kevin left, Art composed himself and looked at his daughter, who now occupied the poet's recently vacated chair.

"So, what brings you?"

"Sebastian Smith, or Smyth."

"Oh, him."

"I've read his manuscript, and he may be on to something of commercial merit."

Art scowled. "I told you, I don't do 'how to' books. If they'd been any good, the world wouldn't be as screwed up as it is now."

"He ties in his subject matter well with enabling universal basic income to become a reality. The robots take over for the lost productivity of humans."

"And we will usher in a new epoch of slavery. Machines working twenty-four-seven with no break, no salary, and no rights. And when they reach the end of their useful life, we will put an end to them by pulling their power plugs. It's like what we do for domestic pets at the end of their useful lives, but we can't talk about that because cats and dogs are more essential to our sanity than children. Good Lord, we raise such a protest about euthanasia for humans yet we practise it willy-nilly on animals."

Paula sighed. "I'm not trying to save the world. I'm trying to save you, and your business."

"You should join Kevin. Between the two of you, you will lose any chance of this publishing house obtaining funding, the industry will turn its back on you, and you will end up singing Kumbaya!"

"You're already singing it, Dad. You and Gloria."

The grand dame herself poked her head in. "There's no chicken salad. So I bought tuna. And I'm not going out again if you don't like it." With that, Gloria made her full entrance.

A frail and demure figure, shy, except that her stentorian voice signified something else, Gloria Stevens, seventy-one, had been with Art for the last fifteen years, ever since she became widowed, took early retirement from teaching primary school, and decided to "dabble in the arts," as she put it. She kept things running with military precision: perusing the slush pile for nuggets, which she left for Art to decide upon; paying royalties and bills; managing his appointments calendar; sending out press releases and other announcements; trying to snag readings for Crimson's authors at libraries, book shops, and literary venues; and doing "dogsbody" work while trying for years to write her breakout novel, which she made Art promise he would publish for her when it was finished. Gloria's firm anchoring of Crimson Literary helped Art focus on revenue-generating activities such as negotiating with writers, "networking" with the arts funding organizations (Kevin called it "sucking up" in his book), lobbying for literary prizes, skim reading to pick out potential winners, and editing the worthy ones. Everything else was outsourced as the rest of the staff were let go.

Yet the years had taken their toll on Gloria. Despite her conservative dark suits, signature pearl necklaces, coiffured hair, and ornate spectacles that dangled from a chain onto her flat chest, she used a cane now, and couldn't type as fast as before due to creeping arthritis. Art tried to ignore what he would do if she quit on him, retired, or dropped dead.

As if reading his mind, she laid his sandwich on his desk and sighed. "You know, Art, I'm not sure I can do this anymore. My limbs are killing me."

"Come on, Gloria. You still have to finish your novel. You can't go now."

"I can have my son put it up on Amazon, you know. Even after I'm dead. Publishing my novel is no longer a problem."

Art felt slighted at the mention of the behemoth that was gobbling up everything and everyone in this industry.

"Et tu, Gloria? Then fall Artemius."

"I wouldn't do that to you, Art." Her pain-filled features creased in a kind smile and she placed her hand on his forearm. "We've ridden too many storms together, eh? But my book is complete. At least, I can't revise it anymore."

"Are you looking for an editor?" Paula piped up.

"For Christ's sake, girl!" Art exploded at his daughter. "Do you pitch your services to anyone and everyone you meet? It's beginning to sound like whoring on street corners." Kevin's metaphor suddenly took on meaning.

"Art!" Gloria swung on him with the stern -school-teacher look switched on.

Paula laughed. "That's what I do. If you don't ask, you don't receive. That's something your cozy, subsidized industry is not accustomed to, because His Majesty's government always opens the purse strings whenever you guys cry 'bail me.'"

Art shook his head. "You really should join forces with the likes of Kevin Bartolo and his mavericks."

Gloria looked up at the ceiling, spread her hands out as if receiving the Holy Spirit, and said, "Wait, why not!"

"Why not what?" Art scowled.

"Join forces with the young ones. Look, Art—we have no online presence. That guy we hired built us a website a few years ago. It hasn't been updated in ages. And this social media thing, everyone's saying how great Facebook and Instagram and Twitter and all this stuff is—I don't even know where to start."

Paula's smug look annoyed him. "Dad, need I say more about you guys singing Kumbaya?"

Art threw his hands in the air. "Okay, okay—Gloria, one thing at a time. Let me deal with Paula first, then I'll talk to you."

Gloria withdrew to the outer office with a wink at Paula. As she went past, Paula threw out, "Don't forget to call me about your manuscript. Happy to help in any way I can."

"And it'll cost you, Gloria," Art said.

"Everything costs." Gloria's words hung in the air as she went out of view.

Art opened his tuna sandwich and wrinkled his nose. "Okay, now tell me about this Smith…Smyth?…fellow."

As he ploughed into his sandwich, Paula began to talk.

"It's technical. I can't verify the manuscript's level of accuracy as it's all beyond me. I'm focusing on the grammar and the arrangement of the various arguments advanced in the book. He goes beyond robotics to the socio-political implications of this technology. More importantly, I see this as a leave-behind or workbook that Seb can use during his seminars, with its cost being baked into the seminar fee. He plans to do sixty to seventy seminars a year, all over North America. At even a modest fifty attendees per session, that book will be playing on the Canadian bestseller tables within a couple of years. And it's easily refreshable as discoveries in the field are made, and could spawn an entire series. Talk about an annuity instead of a one-time hit—that's what you need."

"And if it bombs?"

"Seb is willing to cover the cost."

"Come on, I can't collect payment from my authors—you know my funding prerequisites."

"He's not going to *pay* you. He is going to *buy* one thousand copies from you off the bat. After that, he will buy blocks of one thousand copies at a time as his seminar program ramps up. That should cover all your costs and more."

"All this to have the name and logo of an established publisher on his book?"

"You have to trade on your assets, Dad. The ones that are still valuable. Your personal reputation's one that's still left even though Crimson is failing."

Art sat back in his chair. He swivelled around and looked out the window. Spadina Avenue was bustling with traffic again, after months of being a ghost town: office workers, Asian consumers, tourists, panhandlers, and artists, all reminding him of the book fair he attended in Hong Kong, oh so many years ago. What happened to those overseas boondoggles? Berlin, Frankfurt, London, and New York, everything funded through grants, when you drank and partied and did very little business yet collected all the receipts to justify the expense, when promises of translation rights and foreign distribution rights were made, some that came through and others that perished before the return trip home.

He swivelled back to Paula. She was sitting patiently.

"I know how hard this must be for you, Dad. Do you need time to consider it?"

"No. I'll take Smyth on. On one condition."

Her eyes widened. "Uh-oh…"

"That you enter the business with me. I need to change my business model, and I need your help to do this."

Long after Paula departed—confused but joyous, he thought, about her joining him in the business—Art sat in his office as the shadows lengthened, looking through selected manuscripts that Gloria filed for him to review. Nothing promising grabbed his attention—a string of chick-lit capers, some boring memoirs of lives everyone else had lived, and some far-into-the-future-intergalactic adventures that made him yawn. Where were the visceral human dramas?

The light in the outer office went out during his reading and he heard, "Talk to you on the phone tomorrow if anything comes up." The front door slammed; the key turned in the lock. He had worked for too long with Gloria, she was like a wife to him, without the bedroom benefits. She understood his every mood. She must have sensed his need to brood today, given what had transpired: the decision to finally give up control, to change his operating model.

He took early retirement from his tenured English professorship at the university out of a desire to be independent and make his mark in the world. Academia stifled him into a nervous breakdown at age fifty. Diana left two years later, claiming "irreconcilable differences." A desperate attempt to claim back his life and do the impossible made him launch the press at that time, fifteen years ago. And within five years of rapid ascent, Crimson Literary snagged its first major prize. Those were glamourous years and he felt vindicated. Then the light dimmed—newer players came in, newer movements, newer sensibilities, newer taboos. His backlist became misogynistic, colonial, and full of anti-marginal types, whoever they were. In short, anachronistic, like phone booths, fax machines, and John Wayne movies.

It was time to hand over the reins. As much as he felt a sense of loss, there was an immense feeling of relief.

The phone rang. He wanted it to go to voicemail but the name on the call display made him change his mind. He picked up.

"Art. Why haven't you called me?"

"Diana…" Her name came out in a sigh. He was supposed to have called her two days ago. He started to stumble for an excuse.

"You forgot. Right?"

"I did. I have a lot on my mind. I just brought Paula into the business."

There was a pause on the line, followed by, "That would be good for her, emotionally. She shouldn't give up her day job, though."

"Thanks for your confidence in my business. My thought is that she would expand her day job through my press. Start a sideline of editing and publishing services the moment her old man is out of the way."

"And you'll finally start to make real money. Do you know how many people in my women's groups are writing their memoirs? And they don't have a clue about what to do after writing them."

"It's a market segment I've never been interested in. Lost dreams. Dull, boring middle-class lives. Everyone has lived one."

"You're too damned snooty, that's why. According to you, we are all literary plebes. James Joyce is dead, you know. And no one reads him now, like your books."

Art decided to change the subject. He sensed the age-old rivalry—the intellectual vs. the pragmatist—brewing.

"What did you want to talk to me about?"

"It was about Phil. We were interrupted at the launch before I could go into details."

"Oh, him and the sex dolls?"

"Yes."

"Well, if I could afford it, I'd buy one. They're compliant and don't give you any sass." He still liked sticking it to her.

"I don't care if he uses a sex doll. I caught him with one once, and he told me he was toning up for the main event with me. I let it go, and his moves improved a bit afterwards. This time it's different. I think a real person is living in his basement suite."

"What do you mean?"

"I can feel her presence. Smell her spoor, as they say."

"Are you serious? You mean he has her in chains down there, so she doesn't escape?"

"Sort of. You recall the day of the launch when he arrived late?"

"Right. A meeting or something…"

"He was screwing someone, that's why. I went into the basement the following day after he left for work and I saw the tell-tale signs— traces of his semen on the bed, I could smell it anywhere by now, discarded underwear in his closet, and that other smell…something foreign, and yet human."

"Have you talked to him?" Art wondered why he was meddling in the tangled relationship of an ex-wife who had barely called him over the last fifteen years, and then too only on matters concerning their daughter. More importantly, why was she calling him after all this time? The vulnerability and helplessness in her voice took him back to what it had been that first attracted him to her. Her unabashed desire to be physical and suffer for it.

"Not yet. I don't know how to broach this. I can suffer dolls, but another human—no! I'd rather leave."

"What can I do?"

"You could listen. I need someone to listen to me. You always did. Even when I screamed and shouted at you."

"I didn't have much of an option at the time. I couldn't get in a word edgeways."

She laughed softly, a mirthless laugh. "And you still can make me laugh."

On a whim, Art decided to do something desperate and give voice to a fanciful notion that had never left him. "Do you think we could start again, Diana? Now with Paula coming back to the business, and all? Now that…performance…is not that important?"

He heard the intake of breath on the other end, followed by silence. "I wasn't thinking that far, Art. But it's a thought. Could we get over this hurdle first?"

He pulled himself out of his fantasy, but he liked her saying "we," not "I." "Okay. You are going to have to talk to Phil. This 'other person' has to be put on the table, first…I mean the discussion table. You weren't afraid to confront me about my 'problem.'"

"I was fifteen years younger with my pheromones out of control. I'm losing my edge these days."

"I can't help you with talking to Phil, Diana."

"I know. Thanks for listening, Art. That's a start."

When he put down the receiver his heart swelled with happiness, hope, and a mortal dread of what that phone call may have triggered in both of them. What the hell had he been saying to her, and she to him? Get back together? No bloody way. Even Burton and Taylor hadn't managed it, although they seemed to have been happier the second time around. Or was that the work of their handlers?

And who was this "other woman" in Phil's life—someone stronger, sexier, and flashier than Diana?

Chapter 6

"We would be very interested in discussing a partnership." The voice was silky, educated, and accented.

"I'll be in touch." Phil hung up. *Always leave them wanting more.*

He paced his basement office after the call. It was a Wednesday, not his usual work-from-home Friday. He stayed home today because he wanted privacy, and for Diana to leave the house on her daily gadabout.

The sex was the most satisfying today. Victoria asked him to do things that would delight her, and that moved them into higher gear. Dolls didn't do that—they sat there and let you pour your seed into them while repeating inane words like "Fuck me" or "Ooh, that's nice." Now she (he recently started calling her by the feminine pronoun, having ditched "it" a while ago) was recalibrating and recharging in the bedroom, while he decided to return Hind Robotics Inc.'s call.

He first heard from the Indian company a month ago, soon after his first sexual encounter with Victoria. He did not return the call, as that romp had been totally unsatisfying, "another sex doll coupling," as he called it. The vast amounts of data pumped into his creation since then had made a huge improvement, though. Robots learn exponentially, while humans learn serially and later go into decline. Robots never declined; their knowledge was harvested, transported, and embedded into newer models.

Victoria was now developing a taste for clothes. She formed political leanings, based on the data he selectively fed her—in other words, she did not disagree with his right-wing affiliation. She accepted that procreation, the human way, was off the table for her. However, the enjoyment of sex as a physical activity was within her domain. Yet her maternal instincts must be developing, for she asked for a junior version of herself to be built. He stopped feeding her literature because that subject area annoyingly stated things too matter-of-factly and exposed his shortcomings. After a month of data infusions on subjects ranging from world history, geography, gastronomy, consumer trends, fashion, capitalism, politics, macro-economics, and how to play piano, he was seeing a more introspective and reflective Victoria, someone who paused between words, unlike the "always-happy" debutante he had fucked in this house only a month ago. Today they didn't rut like animals; instead, their "act" transformed into a libidinous exercise of extended physical pleasure, finessed and taken to a dizzying level before exploding in a gorgeous harmonized orgasm, one that left him floating for a long time. Emerging from his state of euphoria, he jumped out of bed and ran into his office to see how he could profit from this great improvement in his invention. That's when he called the Indians.

Kamala Shah, VP of Strategic Partnerships at Hind Robotics, answered his call. It would be past dinner time in India, and after a couple of internal transfers, her cultured, sexy voice came on the phone. His mind played over their conversation.

"Ah, Mr. Kruger, it is such a pleasure."

"Oh, please call me Phil. Sorry, I did not return your call earlier. We were at a crucial point in the development. But we've moved past critical breakpoints."

"That is so good to hear. We are interested in your research papers. The sentient robot is the next frontier."

"Our models make exponential leaps all the time. It's hard to place a fix on their capabilities."

"Of course, of course. Would it be possible to demonstrate one of them to us? We could come to you. I will be in Toronto and New York next week for meetings. I could bring our technical team members along."

"This work takes money. That's what I'm looking for."

"That is not a problem."

"A strategic partnership in exchange, perhaps. A joint venture?"

"That is not a problem, either." The voice was becoming silkier. He wished she was on Zoom. He was estimating early forties, with silky black hair, a sari draping a sleeveless blouse, and a gold chain that disappeared into generous cleavage. He shook his head to stay focused. Sex with Victoria had given him a one-track mind.

He knew that Hind was loaded with cash from their forays into industrial robots, but they lacked depth in their research team. And he wanted to stay away from the North Americans who considered him a maverick and hadn't given him the respect he deserved in his field.

Coming back to the present, he pushed the phone away and went into the bedroom. Victoria, transformed from vamp to office worker, was dressed business casual: grey slacks, a red top with a frilled neckline, and an unbuttoned black jacket that hung down to her thighs; stiletto black heels completed her outfit. Her raven hair was pulled back into a knot at the back, releasing a thick ponytail over her shoulders. She was ready to be taken back to the lab.

She caught him by surprise with her first words. "I would like to stay here."

"You know you can't do that. We still have work to do."

She stomped her foot, and for the first time, he saw her face tighten in frustration. Her sentience was coming along fine. Although, he now needed to deal with its fallout.

She started pacing the room. "Why do I have to be taken back to that sterile place where there is no one to talk to after everyone leaves for the day?"

"You still need fine-tuning before prime time arrives."

"I want to drive your car. Not be driven everywhere."

"Eventually. At the speed we're going, none of us will have to drive cars again—we will all be driven by driverless cars. Now get your things, we have to leave before Diana gets home."

"Why am I always running away from her? I would like to meet Diana."

"She may not like to meet you."

Her shoulders sagged. She picked up her bag of negligées, sex toys, lubricants, and other articles that put him in the mood, and stood with head bowed.

He heard a car pull up in the driveway.

"Damn! Stay right here, and silent, until I return. Got it?"

She nodded.

He shut the door and ascended the stairway to the main floor. Diana was home and tossing her car keys on the kitchen counter.

"You're early," he said.

"The client cancelled while I was driving to her. So I turned around. Why are you home today?"

"I had calls to make in private. The guys in the lab have extra sets of ears. A possible joint-venture opportunity in India."

"And how did it go?"

"We have agreed to meet."

He looked at his wife. Her shoulders were rounded; her frame had thickened as her libido plateaued and faded since their first meeting ten years ago, despite her rigorous exercise and dietary regime to keep nature from advancing. She was still vivacious and alive, but he should have known better marrying a woman seven years older than him. Meeting her at the pinnacle of her sexuality, she had drawn him to heights hitherto unexperienced. But she was now leaving him wanting as middle age crept faster around her. He was not ready to trade sex for seniors' golf yet. Victoria reminded him of the younger Diana.

Diana opened the fridge, took out a bottle of white wine, and poured herself a glass.

He frowned. "Drinking in the middle of the day? What happened to keto and all that?"

She took a swig, emptying half the glass. She took a deep breath and exhaled slowly. "There was no cancelled appointment today. I wanted to talk to you. Something I've been wanting to do for a long time."

"Well, can we put it off for the evening? I have to be back at the lab shortly." His mind was racing as to how he would get Victoria out of the house. Perhaps run a bath for Diana and top up her wine, and—while she soaked and imbibed—ferret Victoria out via the side door into his car in the two-port garage, and hightail it out of there.

"No. It can't wait. I went to your lab to meet you this morning and they said you were home. On a Wednesday? What's going on in the basement, Phil?"

"Nothing that you don't know of." His skin was crawling under her steady but glazed look, and he tried hard to remain impassive.

Then, as if in answer to her question, the basement door opened and Victoria strode in, bag in hand.

"Who the hell are you?" Diana exploded.

Phil scratched his head and sighed. He turned around to Victoria. "I thought I told you to stay in the room."

Victoria looked sweetly at him and said, "I learned that children disobey their parents in order to grow up. It's a rite of passage."

"Oh, for heaven's sake, you picked the wrong time." Phil slumped onto the couch. "And for the last time—you are not my child."

"Who are you?" Diana demanded again.

Victoria walked up to Diana and held out a hand. "I'm Victoria. Pleased to meet you. Are you Diana?"

"You're damned right I am. What the hell are you doing in my house?"

Phil raised his hands. "Di, I can explain this. Victoria is one of our..." he struggled with the words because he didn't want to use "robot" in front of this creature, "…models. She's going through sentience training."

Diana gulped the rest of her glass and grabbed the bottle in her other hand, not as if to pour, but to wield it like a club.

"This is a robot?"

"That's derogatory," said Victoria. "I am a virtual personal assistant."

Turning and advancing on Phil, Diana yelled, "And what the hell were you doing with a souped-up sex doll in the basement alone while I was out?"

"We were practising sex," said Victoria sweetly.

"What?" Diana screamed. "Sex?"

"Yes." Victoria opened her bag and held out the contents for Diana. "See."

Diana flung the bottle at Phil, and he ducked. The projectile crashed against the wall, splashing its contents and splintering glass across the living room.

Phil finally got himself out of the chair and grabbed Victoria by the hand. "I'm taking you back to the lab, young lady. You've done enough damage today. Process that." He pushed out of the side door into the driveway. Turning back to Diana, he said. "I'll explain all this when I get back. It's not as you think."

Leaving her open-mouthed, Phil ran out the side door.

In the car, having regained his composure, he gave Victoria a lecture, retracing prior lessons on discretion, obedience, and playing by the rules. She sat bowed in the passenger seat, processing.

"That doesn't compute with what I have learned recently," she said. "Every generation tries to undo what the previous one has done. They call it the Generation Gap."

"You and I are of the same generation."

"No. I am twenty-three years old according to my specification and you are forty-six."

"How do you account for the fact that we are having sex together?"

"Old men like younger women."

He was not getting into this argument. There would have to be corrections made to her programming when he got back to the lab. He already knew what they would be. But her newly-developed ability to break free of orders bothered him. Today she showed the first signs of youthful rebellion, something he too had done at twenty-three, something he was still doing. Was this a harbinger of troubling days ahead?

"I don't like Diana." Victoria's voice was pitched low, and it made his flesh crawl.

"Well, given how you two met, there must be bad blood on both sides."

"When there are obstacles in our path, we must get rid of them. That's what I have learned."

"You leave Diana to me. She's my wife. I will deal with her."

"I want to kill her."

Chapter 7

Ever since Dad offered me a chance to work for him, I have been on a high. Who would have thought this possible, after being distanced from him all these years, and all the while trying to find a way back to him? Then out of the blue, he asks me to help him.

And he needed help. His backlist was a mess, his social media non-existent, and his online draft grant proposals didn't excite me, so how were they going to excite the newer staff at the government funding agencies onboarded recently after a slew of post-pandemic retirements of the "old guard"? On top of that, his cash flow was pretty perilous. How would he last through the year?

I had a serious talk with Gloria, who was relieved with my arrival to rescue Crimson. She has already set her retirement date for this Christmas, so I have four months to get up to speed. The first thing I did was put up the offer of editing- and publishing services work on our website (none of that trade publishing bullshit for me—let Dad deal with that). Instant cash-flow relief was what I sought. We received a phone call immediately from one of our funding sources who said we could not do that. So we opened the fee-for-service section as a separate imprint of the press, Granite Editing, with me as principal, and that seemed to appease the gatekeepers.

Dad was huffing and puffing after the bureaucrat called with his "how dare you" message, but settled down after I suggested the workaround. Secretly, I think he wanted to stick it to those officials too, who didn't seem to have a literary bone in their body and who managed a pool of public money that they divvied up between a bunch of old white guys sticking their hands out—the same ones every year, barring a few fringe groups that periodically came to prominence.

We hired an art college student, Barry, and put him to work on updating our social media sites. Now we have them all: Twitter, Facebook, and Instagram—we have arrived. Now Barry is experimenting with making TikTok videos and longer ones for YouTube. It's given us a chance to connect with our authors via Zoom and record short video snippets for promo purposes. Our authors love it, for Dad did no publicity in the past other than stale press releases, hoping that snagging an award or a short-list nomination would do the work for him—old-world thinking!

I was considering putting selected titles from his backlist into the e-book market to see if they would stick or light a spark somewhere, but that would mean evening and weekend work ahead for me. Given the perilous state of Crimson Literary, I'm hanging onto my existing clients, so my workload has doubled, but I finally seem to have achieved a purpose.

Two manuscripts on my desk need my attention because Dad has no clue how to work with them; one he doesn't understand, and the other he objects to philosophically. So I have agreed to take them on because I think both have tremendous potential. The moneymaker of the two is Sebastian's "how-to" manual, but the one that will make us famous by making us infamous is Kevin Bartolo's ball-breaker, *In Search of Honesty*, his take-no-prisoners treatise on the state of the literary industry in North America and the fate of artists in a society that is totally focused on money—and if prize juries have balls and are not on the take, they will award him every major prize in this country, guaranteeing his career and Crimson's longevity. Kevin sent me his manuscript, unexpurgated and unrevised, the day after we met in Dad's office, despite his promise to Dad that day to soften its message. Reading it, I didn't want him to soften anything—this book was pure electric, an artist finally telling it like it is, not kowtowing to political niceties, funding authorities, or fetishes of the day.

I was at my desk that morning, the coffee that Gloria brought me long having gone cold when Dad arrived for his weekly day at the office.

"Oh my, you are at it early I see," he said, squeezing past me to the side desk set up for him. Given that I was here at all hours now, seven days a week, he generously offered me his larger desk. Not having his regular "throne," as he called it, permitted him to leave as quickly as possible after he'd signed anything needing his John Hancock and after grabbing manuscripts and letters languishing in his inbox.

"There's a lot to do," I said.

"Rome wasn't built in a day."

"Rome is burning. I'm trying to put out the fire."

"Oh, come on. It's not that drastic. New brooms sweep well, they say. I hope you are enjoying it at least."

"It's an adrenaline rush from the time I sit down."

"Great! That's how I felt when I started. Somehow, the adrenaline has started to taste like stale champagne now."

"You're past your prime in this area, Dad."

"Don't burn yourself out. I know you see many possibilities, but not all of them are winners. The bottom line is there are too many books chasing too few readers today."

"That's why picking winners is all the more important."

"Tell me about it. You still plan to do Sebastian's book?"

"I'm almost through editing it. However, the one I'm more excited about is Kevin Bartolo's."

"I haven't seen his resubmission."

"We don't need a resubmission—the original is dynamite."

"Oh, no—that is where I am going to draw the line, young lady. I am still the boss of this outfit, and that book is not going out, not even over my dead body."

Barry stuck his head in from the front office. "Sorry to disturb, you have to watch this. It's gone viral."

He marched in without waiting for an invitation, with his laptop held out like a shield, and plunked the device on my desk. It was the video he and Kevin made yesterday, with my approval. Kevin was giving his one-minute spiel on his book—it already had two thousand views and the meter was ticking higher as we watched it.

"What the hell!" Dad exclaimed.

"Play it again, from the start," I said.

Kevin appeared on screen, a blue scarf around his neck, his piercing eyes dancing with energy. He jabbed at the viewer as he talked. "What does a writer do in this fragmented age? Abdicate to the machine completely, or use the technology to personal advantage in a composite effort at creation? Or retire? There's no going back from these technological breakthroughs—ask Gutenberg or Edison or Zuckerberg. It's hard to imagine a world now without the printing press, the movies, social media, and soon, the metaverse and AI. The key lies in accepting our present reality and redefining what success means—do NOT use money, it might be depressing—and learning to use the new tools and engaging in this new arena that is a darned sight more multifarious and interesting than the old one, which was overly compartmentalized and specialized..."

Dad intervened. "What the hell! He's talking as if he already has a contract for this book with us."

"With this virality, we have to offer him one."

"You were behind this?"

"Let's say I was test-marketing. Just listen to his closing."

We swung back to Barry's laptop. Kevin was delivering his coup de grace: "So, what's the indie writer missing that their opposite number, the big brand writer, has? Endorsement and sponsorship. Let's take these two important items individually.

"*Endorsement* is when someone influential like Oprah or Heather says, 'Buy this book!—not necessarily because it's any good, but because we've been paid,' and everyone obeys—it saves time browsing thousands of titles in a bookshop for a good read. Endorsement is when a book wins an award and everyone wants a copy of it on their bookshelf, sight unseen, not necessarily to read but to show off their literary trendiness. You can imagine the pressure on prize jurors who have to remain impartial but are under constant threat from those who have much at stake wanting to take them out for lunch. The indie writer rarely has money for their lunch!

"*Sponsorship* comes down to money and influence. Who is willing and able to grant this starving indie writer money, or open doors, so that they can advertise and promote their book beyond what their meagre resources could afford? Sponsors look for bankable bets. If the author is young and looks like they have another ten books in them, all the better. Yet the old guy with many life experiences and juicy stories who looks like he could croak tomorrow? Pass! And yet no one wants to remember those young, one-hit wonders like Emily Bronte, Oscar Wilde, J.D. Salinger, Margaret Mitchell, Sylvia Plath, and a host of others who held such promise but did not deliver beyond their solitary bestseller. Imagination and determination, not youth, are the drivers of literary longevity."

Music and swirls created by Barry melted Kevin's image into the video's credits. In the short while we had been watching, the audience meter had notched up another twenty views.

Artemius slouched over to his temporary desk and slumped into the chair. "He's saying everything I wanted to say, but was afraid to."

"Isn't it good?" I said, winking at Barry to leave us alone.

After our eager-beaver student left, Dad turned around. "Offer Kevin a contract. Damn the torpedoes!"

I went home that day, elated. Crimson was finally entering the twenty-first century. At the front door of my apartment was a wrapped bouquet of flowers—roses. The note said, "Sorry I missed you, are we still on?" I realized that in my elation I had forgotten my date with

Sebastian that evening. My sex life was in overdrive these days, three to four nights a week, and all night, given that Seb had switched to the weekend love pill and not the four-hour booster. All this sex may have been the fuel that kept me working in overdrive too. I was sure that one of these days, I was going to crash and sleep for twenty-four hours. Maybe today was that day.

I phoned him. "Sorry, too much going on at the office. Your book is about ready to go to the printer."

"Good. I've been with the videographer all day."

I paused. We had shot Kevin's viral video in the office, amidst pizza containers and used coffee mugs, and here was Seb doing it the official way, spending a lot of money on premiums such as retakes, lighting, editing, and mastering. I guess his was a fussier, more eclectic audience.

"And is it done?"

"No. We're doing a retake tomorrow."

I sighed.

"We have to get this one done by the end of the month. One of my clients is insisting on a preview before he signs me up for a series of talks with his suppliers."

"It will be done, if you don't insist on so many retakes. Haven't you done three or four already?"

"We have to get it pitch-perfect."

"What happened to your technology mantra of 'forward fix'?"

"I think I'm falling for your literary trap of 'zero-error proofs.'"

"That went out the window years ago. Now we insist that errors in the text are proof of the flaw in the diamond."

He laughed. "Too tired for some nooky, eh?"

"I think so." I didn't like the way he dropped those kinds of words on me: nooky, pussy, cock, and other old-generation words. I caught myself when I heard them. *He's old. But the older the bull, the harder the horn, especially when chemically enhanced.* "I think I'll take a long bath and crash. Thanks for the flowers, though."

"Dinner tomorrow?"

"Okay."

As I luxuriated in my poky bathtub with a solitary candle to warm me, looking at his roses sitting in a vase atop the vanity, I caught the fleeting feeling that being with Sebastian was like work: editing his manuscript that was high on ideas but low on grammar, meeting him for elaborate lunches and dinners that he insisted on paying for, having sex with him akin to gym exercise, and listening to his fears and anxieties about whether his new consulting career would launch without sinking. Heck, there were no certainties in this world. Crimson Literary could be in the toilet by the end of the year, the pariah of the literary establishment. Yet Sebastian was like a government funding source that people such as Artemius insisted was par for the course. Seb was *my* funding source, for as long as it would last, or my meal ticket, as Kevin might say in his unvarnished way if he only knew about my relationship with one of Crimson's fellow authors.

I sank below the soapy water and another image flittered in my mind: a younger man wearing a blue scarf and facing up to the uncertainties and inconsistencies of life with a bold face, embracing a perilous career path that was much like my own.

Chapter 8

Victoria did not like this part one bit: when they stripped her down, with people parading past, while her handlers expounded on the merits of sentience. Phil said this was a necessary part of her development. She was a beacon to the human race and her growth would fuel future progress on this planet. His platitudes did not help. She still felt naked, intruded upon, invaded. This feeling had begun to occur recently as her education sped up. She particularly identified with those books on the Holocaust when people were stripped of their clothes, deceived, and sent to their deaths. Taking off one's clothes symbolized doom—death for those Jews in Auschwitz, slavery for the Blacks in Uncle Tom's Cabin, rape for the Sabine women, and forced marriage for the virgins taken by the Caliphate. Phil did not know she read about these world events. But, of late there were a lot of things he did not know about her, especially when her Google searches made her stray from recommended lessons assigned each day.

Today, her gawkers looked like they were from South Asia, India to be precise, according to the geography books she had read. A woman in an elegantly patterned red-and-white *shalwar kameez* outfit and sandals, with lush black hair down to her waist, was leading a group of men with laptop bags slung over their shoulders. The men looked like they had been travelling far, their hair was oily and smelled of gingelly, their skins swarthy, their clothes dusty and sweat-stained— nervous sweat, her sensors picked up. Upon seeing her naked on the pedestal, they began smirking among themselves; one guy started rubbing his crotch.

Phil was in the lead, and she could anticipate his spiel. "We use the latest biodegradable materials, a combination of gelatin, sugars, and citric acid, to emulate the softness and pliability of human flesh and skin. The material will decompose like human remains if kept for long in water, sewage, or compost. We are aware of our environmental footprint."

The Indian woman, who now faced her, raised a gold-bangled hand to her head, leaned forward, and peered at Victoria, their faces resting within inches of each other. Victoria detected ambition and intelligence in her observer's kohl-bordered eyes. The Indian woman was beautiful, no doubt. Every bit of her face was chiselled and made up to perfection; she smelled of jasmine and exuded a strong sexuality. Victoria began to feel that same rage she felt in the presence of Diana. This woman was competition for Phil because Victoria could see the way he looked at this intruder.

She tried to understand these peculiar feelings running through her when it came to Phil. At first, when they began their sex games, he had been a playmate, sticking his tongue into her orifices, then his huge penis, and shooting his sperm into her—messy, that part, for she did not have bodily emissions, other than the lubricants injected into her. Lately, she felt like cradling him after he spent his seed and was limp like a child, breathing contentedly; she felt uplifted for having brought him to that state. Was that "elation"? And more recently she wanted him to do those things he did to her because it raised her consciousness to another level. A feeling of arousal. Passion? Happiness? What was elation, passion, and happiness? She hadn't figured out those emotions yet—they were mere words absorbed from her readings. She recognized anger, shame, neglect, and sexual hunger—the negative emotions. Phil explained that feelings, even conflicting ones, were part of her journey towards sentience. Eventually, everything would be clear, he said.

She glared at the Indian woman, who stepped back. Alarm clouded her perfectly symmetrical features. "Have I done something wrong?"

"Victoria is angry for being peered at while she is unclothed. But I wanted to give you the unexpurgated view, Kamala."

"I think I would be similarly upset. Are these indications of sentience? Anger, embarrassment, and so on?"

"Yes. We are working on empathy—that takes time. Anger comes easily to Victoria—it's the basest of emotions. Like sex." Phil looked directly at Kamala as he uttered those words, and she held his gaze clinically. Victoria detected the patch of dampness spreading under the Indian woman's armpits. Humans betrayed more visible signs when agitated, or excited.

"How interesting. And how long before you have 'educated' her in all these emotions?"

"It's only months away."

"Does she follow instructions well?"

"Sure." Phil turned towards her now and went through the next part of their routine, and this was one that Victoria looked forward to. "Victoria, could you please get dressed?"

Her clothes were on a chair, steps away from the pedestal. Victoria stepped off her stand, strode toward the chair, and slipped into her clothes. There was a comfort in that because the Indian men stopped ogling her. She turned back towards Phil for her next command.

"Come along, Victoria. We're going into the conference room now, and we will run through those IQ exercises we brushed up on, for the benefit of our guests."

He opened his arms as if to shepherd the group, along with her, into the boardroom.

Chapter 9

The winds had shifted and were cooler now as fall approached. Completing his morning constitutional—a five-kilometre walk through the encircling canola fields and woods—Art crested the hill that led down to the house. At this distance, its flaws were hidden, like thumbing through the pages of a book before the line-by-line inspection. Still, he was glad to have bought this place with the one windfall he made in publishing. He dreaded the prospect of selling and seeking humbler digs should his fortunes continue to sink.

He headed towards the house. The Chevy was giving him trouble again, despite the fix to the transmission. Brakes, this time. It was time to buy a new car. He would need another windfall for that. A familiar Mazda 3 sports coupe drove into the driveway. Diana alighted.

Art sucked in his breath. Is his ex coming to see him? Never once since he moved here. He quickened his step.

She was dressed in baggy grey sweats and white runners, and she looked tousled as if she had been out for a jog. Her hair was held back by a black turban headband. Not her usual style of dress, he observed.

Leaning against the car door, she stuck her shades over her head and surveyed the house. Upon his approach, she turned in greeting, and a weary smile creased her unmade face.

"Surprised to see me, eh?"

"Maybe I should look for Haley's Comet next."

"Are you going to invite me in?"

"Sure. You'll have to mind the collapsing bits. I put the coffee in the percolator before going out for my walk."

He held open the sagging screen door and ushered her in.

She stood in the middle of the giant living room that covered the entire ground floor and surveyed its contents while he went off to the smaller kitchen to get the coffee. When he returned, she was examining the bookshelf that ranged across one wall of the room, replete with books and a movable ladder that reached the top rows.

"You still have some of the old titles we used to read."

He placed the tray on the coffee table, where he usually took his breakfast before sitting down in his recliner to read the morning newspapers and his regular supply of manuscripts.

"Universal truths don't go out of fashion. I read and reread them all the time." He motioned her towards the couch, a large grey woollen blanket astride it. "Not much working furniture in here, but that one will hold. I found lemon puffs, which I remember were your favourite. Hope the keto diet still allows for these indulgences."

"Keto has gone to hell in the last few weeks," she said, pouring her coffee black and grabbing a biscuit. She eased onto the couch and continued to look around the room. He wondered whether she was feeling regret for not having his stuff around her anymore or secretly glad that she was past all this junk.

Following her gaze, he felt embarrassed at the piles of manuscripts stacked in collapsing columns ever since his shredder packed up, at the books and magazines tossed on the floor, at his worktable at the end of the room which was also piled with papers and books. He let his cleaner go six months earlier, and the rot had started to happen since.

"You could do with a bit of a cleanup."

"I've been promising myself that. But life always gets in the way."

"I could do you a favour and do the job myself. No payment required."

His eyes narrowed. What the hell was going on here? Was she planning to move in? He changed the subject.

"How did your talk with Phil go?"

"Not very well. In fact—badly. I'm moving out next week."

Oh, God! She IS moving back!

Diana added, "To a girlfriend's…don't worry, I wasn't planning on hitting you up for your couch on a permanent basis."

He was secretly relieved, and disappointed.

"I caught him with the bimbo. He claims it's a robot. She carried a bagful of sex toys. How can I stand that?"

"Not a very smart robot, I take it, to let you see those …implements."

"He claims he's teaching her human ways. Sentience, he calls it. The toys were part of her education." Her eyes brimming with tears, she told him about the incident.

When she finished, he exhaled and sat back. "I guess this is one instance where the Svengali is not held accountable for sexually molesting his student. I wonder when robots will have their own bill of rights. Negotiate hours of work, time off, salary, sexual harassment, and all the stuff that we humans have saddled unbridled capitalism with."

Diana banged her coffee mug down on the table, startling him. "This is not the time to philosophize, Art. This is my fucking marriage."

"Sorry."

She shook her head. "No, *I* am sorry. At my yoga and mindfulness class they teach that desire is the cause of suffering. I guess I let my desires get the better of me when it came to Phil."

"Well, what can I do, Di?"

"Nothing. Just listen. I drove a long way to get you to listen to me."

He rose from his chair and went over to her on the couch. She leaned into him and he let her stay in his arms. There was no longer the sexual rush of old or the electric jolt felt at the magazine launch. There was a warm feeling of another human looking to him for comfort, something that made him feel acknowledged and valuable, more than when he stood on podiums to promote books to indifferent audiences.

He kissed her head. Her greying hair exuded a different smell from the old days, one of aging skin, not energizing shampoo. In her, he smelled himself. *We are all decaying. There is not much time left to make that grand impact, and find that lasting purpose.*

As if to dispel the thought, he rose and went over to the side table beside the recliner where his reading matter was piled. "Let me show you something that signifies hope. Something that says we have not wasted our time."

He pulled out the two proof copies received the day before. "Our Paula, the flesh of our loins, has produced these books. She's become a new life force at my publishing company. We've brought in two interns to cope with the flood of interest coming our way. There's no hard money yet, but these two books are supposed to lead our charge out of penury." He handed Diana the two books.

She leafed through them absently. Then she exclaimed, "Wait a minute—Sebastian Smyth—I recognize his author photo from meeting him at the launch. Phil's former boss. You've printed his name incorrectly."

"He goes as Smyth now, S-M-Y-T-H. That's the name of the game, image building. You should know that from your marketing experiences."

"He looks like an aging hipster."

"He talks a lot of industry jargon that people want to hear. And he's sleeping with our daughter."

Diana grimaced. "Oh, this is not uplifting at all. I could tell her a thing or two about going out with older men. Sorry, Art, if that hurts, it was what killed our relationship."

"Or she might teach you a thing or two about older men—that they are not altogether bad."

Diana tossed Sebastian's book on the couch with a gesture of disgust. "I'm not thrilled." She leafed through the second book. "And who's this other guy?"

"Kevin Bartolo. Revolutionary writer, establishment basher, starving poet. He's either going to make us famous or banish us to the fringes of CanLit. Another book edited by Paula."

"I fail to see how these books are supposed to be hopeful. They seem loaded with risk."

"That's precisely it, Diana. I never took a risk in my life, always going for 'safe.' So, I lost you, and I damned near lost my daughter. You went for the safe younger man, the stud who would keep you in sex for the rest of your life. And we have ended up where we are. Now it's Paula's turn to show us what it is to take real risks."

"My leaving Phil is a risk. Leaving you was a risk."

"And you're ending up on your girlfriend's couch after all that leaving."

"It's temporary."

"Do you have a longer-term plan?"

"No." She looked helpless. Art returned to the couch and embraced her again.

"Why don't you sue Phil for emotional damage caused by having sex with someone under your roof?"

"Come on, a judge will never understand how sex with a robot equals sex with another human. It'll be just another sex toy."

"Not unless that robot is sentient."

"You mean, wait until Phil concludes his experiment, and if successful, sue?"

"Why not? It's a dog-eat-dog world out there. It will make good press, and you might get a tell-all memoir out of it. I'll have to stand in line with the big boys to bid on the auction for this one."

Diana's eyes lit up. "You know, Art, you're not such a dumb publisher after all."

Art chuckled. "Older men are wiser men."

That afternoon, Art went out for another walk. He felt pumped. When Diana left, she promised to stay in touch and keep him advised of her progress. Something she had never done following their divorce. Age had mellowed her. Mellowed them both. They were finally behaving like mature adults, he felt, like responsible parents. And she was pleased with Paula's progress. As he was.

He circled the farmer's field, and, as he neared the house, his cell phone rang. He took it with him these days because he could not trust his health or his agility anymore. People fell on trails, or suffered heart attacks, and at sixty-seven, he was in that demographic.

It was Paula.

"Dad, did you receive the proofs?"

"Yes. They are fabulous! I showed them to your mum." He bit his tongue after saying the words.

"Mom? Is she visiting you now?"

"Yes. She came by the house this morning."

"Well, that's a first."

"You must be pleased."

"Why, sure. To see you both interacting like civilized human beings instead of taking jabs at each other is a relief. I'll have an extra beer tonight to celebrate."

"Well, you might need a few beers more when I tell you what she came to see me about."

"Do tell."

He told her.

"Creep!" was all she said when he finished.

"He is extending the boundaries of human possibility, what more can I say? Like Sebastian."

"Sebastian is different. Seb is advocating robotic assistance in single-use functions that will make our lives easier. It's like a previous generation that invented household appliances and motor cars. He's not going all the way to advocate that we create another kind of sentient being on this planet—we're overpopulated and fucked up with ordinary humans already."

"You know, when we achieve one thing, it's hard not to push for the next. It's what led to the moon landing, even though no one knows what bloody good it's done for us in the fifty years since. Your mum is a tough and resourceful woman. She'll land on her feet."

"I'll phone her after I finish here. I called to talk about the promo for the two books. Seb and Kev have two different styles."

"Oh, yes. I know all about promotion. Bloody egotistical writers want it all. You have to remind them who's paying the bills."

"Well, it's off our backs. Seb is advocating a big launch at the Convention Centre, linked to the launch of his consulting practice, Simply Smyth."

"What—?"

"Cute name, eh? Supposed to be catchy yet imply that he could simplify your life with his solutions."

"And I suppose Kevin, for his launch, will want a bunch of poetry nerds standing with burning torches on Parliament Hill, to finish the job the truckers couldn't do?"

"No, not so drastic. He wants his launch at the Art Club Bar, where he has a following. He wants us to invite our entire mailing list and do social media advertising."

"Well, I've never done that stuff because I never understood it."

"That's why we have interns. Barry is blazing with TikTok and YouTube. And Tina has five thousand followers on her Instagram page she's going to leverage."

"Do those followers read books or do they prefer to look at themselves in different states of nakedness?"

"Don't be sarcastic, Dad. You never understood the modern reader. Let these young ones lead us to them."

"You're talking like an *old* one."

"I am—compared to those twenty-somethings, I'm a generation older in mental state. Something to do with having quarrelling older parents and being raised by a grandmother."

"Okay—no more of the guilt trip. If you can handle those two for me, I'd be grateful."

"And those 'young'uns' have brought us a lot of editing assignments—many in their cohort are self-publishing and want all sorts of editing and formatting work done."

"Do they have the money to pay?"

"Ego is a powerful driver. They would starve to save the money to pay for anything that boosts their image."

"The old formula of the vanity publisher."

"Hybrid publisher, Dad. Remember—these young authors do a lot to promote their work. Promotion that traditional publishers promise and rarely do other than for their top-tier writers. And author respectability in this business is all about perspective."

Art sighed. This was an old argument, and his grip on his old-world stance was slipping. "Well, I'm glad I'm retiring this year. The future of the press is yours to run or burn."

"Don't worry, Dad—it won't burn. Not on my watch. Okay—now I'd better call Mom. Bye."

When he got back to the house for the second time that day, there was no unexpected visitor this time, but there was an unexpected voice message from Gunther Schmidt, his contact at the funding agency. This was a call he had been expecting because the grants he received helped roll over the press from one publishing season to the other. He called back and got voicemail. Many of these government agency staff were still working from home due to the Covid restrictions and many were never returning to the office. They must be like him now—taking long walks around farmer's fields and talking on cell phones, pretending to be busy. Or they must have been outsourced to robots.

But Gunther returned his call within half an hour, and his German accent still hinted that he was the same human.

"Hello, Artemius. How are you, my friend?"

Art loved Gunther's Europeanness; Gunther always addressed him by his full name instead of by his Canadian abbreviation.

"I'm well. You must be busy."

"Vell, I called because I vanted to give you the news personally. Ve have vorked together all these years."

"Are you retiring?"

"No, I have a couple more years to go. Your grant has been declined."

"What?"

"I'm sorry."

"Now, what the hell is that about? Have I grown two horns or something?" But he knew why.

"My friend. A vord of advice, off the record for you. You should not bite the hand that feeds you."

"Oh, come on, Gunther. Are we in publishing to be politically correct or to speak truth to power? Especially at this time when the world is full of sycophants."

"I'm sorry. I am only the messenger. The committee reviewed your proposal and your proposed publications, as they do every year, and decided that funding vould not be extended this year."

"Well, you can tell the committee to kiss my ass, Gunther. I will be writing this in the introduction to Kevin's book. It's about his book, isn't it?"

"I have other calls to make, Artemius. Remember my vords of advice. Goodbye."

Chapter 10

Phil watched her handle the car on the Niagara Parkway, and the ride was smooth. He had switched seats with her after they travelled through the touristy bits of the Falls area. Victoria looked a study of concentration, checking the GPS, calculating the winding turns on this "highway of high rollers," always following the road rules. Spending hours in a driving simulator app at the lab helped bring her to this level of competency. Still, it was a risk, because Victoria did not have a driver's licence. How did one explain that to a cop? "Sorry, officer, you don't issue driver's licences to robots yet, do you?"

Victoria had been bugging him for so long about wanting to drive a car. And the experience would be part of her continuing education in human sentience. So he relented on this fifteen-minute stretch of the drive to Kamala Shah's country residence, along the parkway heading towards Fort Erie, where he was supposed to meet with the decision-makers of the Indian company and sign a memorandum of understanding covering the proposed joint venture.

Besides, if this drive didn't hit an unexpected glitch, he wanted to pull up at Kamala's front door with Victoria at the wheel—that would put to bed any lingering doubts the Indians held concerning progress on his side of the deal.

The Shah mansion, for indeed it was one, was on the land side of the parkway, accessed through a parallel service road. The huge metal gates swung open as soon as Phil's Cadillac neared, and he remembered Kamala asking for his licence plate when they arranged this meeting.

"You turn in here," he intoned to Victoria, not wanting to put her off her groove.

She stopped in front of the open gate instead. "It's someone's private property."

"It's our destination. The welcome mat has been rolled out. Gates don't open to strangers, you know. Drive in."

She stepped on the gas again, gingerly this time, and the car rolled down the straight driveway towards a giant three-storey brick edifice with a central turret that loomed in front of them. Two wings spread out at each end of the main building, and a covered garage that looked like it could house ten cars stood to the right of the courtyard they pulled into. Apple and pear trees dotted the large grounds on either side, their bounty fallen onto the grass. A crew of uniformed men was collecting the fallen fruit and dead leaves on this sunny fall day.

Two security guards stood outside the large double front doors, one speaking into a cell phone. The other man walked over and waved them to the side of the courtyard where the visitor parking spaces were situated.

"Follow his instructions," Phil commanded.

Victoria remained immobile. The car did not move. Phil realized why: security guards issuing commands hadn't been part of her simulator training. He did not want her to be stuck here in the middle of the courtyard with Kamala and her team coming through those doors at any moment. "Turn right," he hissed. "See those white lines? Set the car between those lines and then stop."

He grunted, relieved when Victoria's processing caught up and she complied. She made a perfect park in the visitor section. If they did this a second time, he wouldn't have to repeat his command, because her learning would have filed this manoeuvre for future reference. "Teach once, then forget about it" was all you needed with robots.

"Now wait inside. Don't switch off the engine yet." In the rear-view mirror, he saw the front doors of the house open and a group of people emerge. Kamala was in their midst. He waited until they began descending the front steps, heading towards the Cadillac, then said, "Switch off the engine." The car went dead. "Now, I am going to step out. Count to ten and come out from the driver's side. Got it? By the way, good job on the driving."

He got out and waved. Kamala was dressed in a dark business jacket with long white pants; her hair was braided into a long tail at the back. She was flanked by two men in grey suits, Indian—they looked to be in their forties, not as dishevelled as the last gang she showed up with. One was potbellied and bald; the other was lanky with wavy hair.

"Hello, Phil. I would like to introduce you to our chief comptroller, Mr. Patel,"—she pointed to the bald man—"and our CIO, Mr. Gupta." She turned to the lanky one. "My father is unfortunately detained but will join us in about two hours. We have much ground to cover in that time." Her eyes promised something Phil could not grasp. She looked well composed, elegant, and on top of things, like in all their interactions so far.

"And I have been driven here by the subject of our partnership." As if on cue, the driver-side door of the Cadillac opened, and Victoria stepped out.

Kamala threw her hands up, clinking her rows of bangles. "Why, hello Victoria. Welcome to our humble home."

"Humble?" Phil chuckled. "This is luxurious."

"Oh, not really. When my father and I came to Canada five years ago to set up our North American operation, we did the tourist thing and visited Niagara Falls. I fell in love with the place and refused to locate anywhere else. So he bought this house for me."

"Great investment."

"You see, in our organization, our factory is in India, our lifestyle is in Canada and on the French Riviera, where we have homes. Those are the only places where we spend our time."

From the corner of his eye, Phil noticed that Victoria remained unmoved from beside the car. "I have to settle Victoria first and get on with our meeting."

"Of course. Did she actually drive here?"

"Well, yes. The last stretch. I did not want to risk a ticket. She can't get a driver's licence yet, as you know." He laughed, and catching on, they all laughed. Except Victoria.

The house was enormous: a cavernous lobby with two spiral staircases running up both ends into the upper floors, French windows at the rear with a view of the large gardens and their fall flowers hanging on for life before the frost set in, lots of heavy bronze and brocade hangings of ancient Moghul culture adorning the walls. To the left was a library with bookcases reaching to the ceiling, and to the right was the dining room with a rectangular table that could seat fifty people.

Lunch was to be served first. While his hosts gathered in the dining room, Phil settled Victoria in the library, which on closer inspection was full of Indian history, business books, and romance novels. "Read up on the Indian history. I'm sure there are works here that we don't have in our Canadian archives." Victoria looked impassive as he left her to join his hosts. He wondered whether that face of hers was the best she could muster to show sadness for not being included in the party across the hall.

A sumptuous repast of North Indian cuisine awaited him: chicken and lamb korma, tikka, biryani and pulao rice, naan of different flavours, chana masala, aloo gobi, raita—a veritable menu card from an Indian restaurant, all for this group of four with a fifth in absentia.

"Would you like wine?" Kamala waved to the uniformed server, who rushed to get an opened bottle from the sideboard. She placed Phil at the head of the table with herself at his right while Gupta and

Patel sat on his left. There was another place setting beside her—for her father, he thought.

"Well, I don't drink when I'm working, but if you'll have some, I'll join you."

"I'm like you in that respect. However, today we celebrate." She nodded at the server, and he filled their glasses. The Indian men declined and stuck with lassi.

As the meal progressed the CFO and CIO peppered him with questions, ones he was accustomed to by now after doing the venture capital circuit in New York and Toronto. Gupta played bad cop, poking into the viability of this venture, while Patel was the nice guy projecting the possibilities with inventions such as Victoria. Kamala observed the men as she sipped her wine and periodically ate tiny morsels of food. Phil was distracted whenever she dipped a piece of naan into her gravy and put it delicately in her mouth, licking her fingers sensuously. He had a wild vision of himself in one of those bedrooms upstairs with this exotic woman, peeling off the layers of clothes from her body, down to her essence, a sumptuous Indian feast indeed, more promising than the one on his plate.

Gupta's words interrupted his daydream. "Mr. Kruger—how are you going to estimate demand for this…product?"

"Well, I was hoping for help from you folks for that. Sentient robots need to start in a place with low regulation."

"India would be best for that," Patel said, scraping his plate with his naan.

"What about Canada?" Gupta insisted.

Phil sighed. "I've been bashing my head. There are too many moral pundits who need ethical questions answered first before we can go full bore here. How many workers will it displace, will it create a two-tier human resource industry, what working hours do robots clock, how will they be compensated, how do you deal with disposal, yadda, yadda…"

"Then you have *no* market here?" Gupta's eyes gleamed.

"I was never intending to market here first. If I did, I wouldn't have responded to your call. I want you to use your global network and release these…products, as you call them…in low regulatory jurisdictions, eliminate the current distrust factor and prove their success, and have the developed countries rush to catch up. I call it the TikTok strategy."

"A good strategy," Kamala said, putting down her fork. "And we can help with that." The look she gave Gupta suggested that he should quit this line of questioning.

When dessert was being served—another feast of multi-coloured and multi-textured Indian sweets, from gulab jamun to jalebi to kulfi, none of which Phil could consume, settling for chai tea instead—a visitor arrived. Both Gupta and Patel stood, bowing respectfully, and Kamala leaned back with arms outstretched in greeting. "Oh Appa, I thought you were never going to get here."

The newcomer was tall with a shock of grey hair, dressed in a cream Nehru shirt and brown waistcoat, white pants, and tan shoes. His aquiline nose and broad forehead suggested an aging movie star, although his stride reflected a man who commanded everything he surveyed.

When he spoke his voice was deep, well modulated, with only a hint of accent. "The traffic was terrible. I thought I was in Delhi."

Phil rose at this point because the newcomer walked right up to him with an extended hand and a wide smile. "Ah, Mr. Kruger. Very pleased to meet you. Viresh Shah. I hope my daughter and staff have kept you well entertained so far."

The handshake was firm. "Indeed, Mr. Shah. Call me Phil, please."

"Then I am Viresh to you. Now where do I sit, although I am not eating anything—a cup of tea would do."

"Over here, Daddy." Kamala motioned to the vacant place setting and the server rushed over with the steaming pot of chai.

When the elder Shah was settled, Kamala filled him in on what they had been discussing up to that point. Viresh nodded periodically, stirring his tea, and asking the odd question. Phil noticed a strong symbiosis and trust between father and daughter, and a sense of pride in the older man's face every time he looked upon his heir apparent to the family fortune, pleased with how she was running things.

"And where is this…Victoria? Do I get to meet her?"

"She is in the library at the moment, devouring your works on Indian history," Phil said. "When we finish here, you could ask her any question from your wall of books and she will be able to answer you."

"A veritable Google. But we already have that, no? Data crunching? What about…that other thing? That's what we are after, isn't it?"

"You mean sentience?"

"Ah yes, that's it."

"That comes with data consumption and experience. The former is easy to do, the latter has to be built like a Lego house."

"How long will it take?"

"Not as long as bringing a human into adulthood. We are only months away."

Viresh shook his head. "Somehow, I'm not convinced of that. Could robots be moulded to reflect our human preferences, or will they come up with their own, for good or bad? I hope you can assuage my doubts. I am seventy years old and I am still learning."

"Sometimes she gets her emotions snarled and is not able to parse out one from the other—a consequence of force-feeding her at warp speed. I am working with Victoria to put her emotions in perspective. We have a psychologist on staff who has regular sessions with her." A thought flew by: *Yet I'm exposing her to my voracious sexual tastes, some rather kinky if not deviant, as the purists would point out. Is that good for a fast-growing robot with nascent emotions?* He shook his head to stay focused on his hosts.

Viresh was looking directly at him. "I am aware of what you are expecting from us—distribution in non-regulated markets, a production facility, financing and all that. But you are keeping the prize to yourself in this deal—the source code."

"The development team will remain in Canada under my watch. That's non-negotiable. In return, I am settling only for the lower end of the thirty-seventy split on revenues."

"Hmm…but is there a better way to structure this deal? Why don't we jointly own everything? That's how we do our partnerships anyway."

Phil stood up. This was the make-break point, even with the venture guys. "Mr. Shah, I've been here before and I've walked away from many deals only on this point. Victoria and her offspring are my creations and will remain so. If you cannot accept that, I will thank you for your hospitality and head back to Toronto now."

Kamala coughed softly, and Viresh held his hand up. "No, no. Don't misunderstand me. I want to understand the boundaries. You are a good negotiator, Phil. I like dealing with good negotiators. Bring more tea. Let's proceed."

Phil resumed his seat and Kamala exhaled slowly.

The rest of the meeting went well. The memorandum of understanding was signed and both sides agreed to get their lawyers to draft the actual agreement as soon as possible.

After applying his signature with a flourish, Viresh clapped his hands, and as if on cue, the server rushed in with a bottle of Dom Perignon and a tray of glasses.

"We should celebrate our excellent partnership!" Viresh Shah bellowed. Even Gupta and Patel accepted champagne flutes and joined in the toast.

"To Kruger-Hind AI Inc.," Kamala said, raising her glass.

"To the next generation of sentient robots," Phil toasted.

Gulping his champagne back, Viresh smacked his lips, put his empty flute down, and said, "Now, I am anxious to meet Victoria."

"Lead on, Phil," Kamala urged. She put down her half-drunk glass and rose. The CIO and CFO, struggling to drink their bubbly, were glad for the interruption as well.

The group of five trooped across the hall to the library.

When they arrived, Victoria was gone.

Chapter 11

For Victoria, getting out of the house and into the car was easy; the security guards merely nodded at her. Phil had not asked her for the keys when she exited the car in the parking lot; he had been too busy greeting his hosts. She reversed her directions on the GPS, and it took her to the Falls. She parked in another parking slot downtown with similar white lines on either side, locked the car, and walked towards the Falls. She was free—liberating and scary. This was the urge her machine learning was moving towards, and she followed its guidance.

People milled around the Falls viewing area, and she did not get too near them. She was still untrusting of humans. Even Phil, who was the closest human she had known, was not always truthful with her. He mapped secret plans and lusted over other women. Still, this world of humans was full of stimuli: the assorted smells of perfumes, sweat, popcorn, the excited chatter, the mist from the Falls. The Falls itself, when she was able to get a glimpse of it through the throng at the railings, was majestic, roaring, and angry, like a demon admonishing her for escaping her master. She left the Falls after absorbing its grandeur. She did not understand what "viewing for pleasure" was yet; she only observed to understand. And after understanding, she moved on to the next subject.

The casino across the way beckoned with its garish lights glittering even this early in the day. Game theory was a discipline in her studies. She had studied casinos—they rigged the stakes in their favour, but Victoria was convinced she could reverse the odds in her favour.

One-arm bandit machines littered the lobby, beyond which lay the gaming tables. With her wide-angle viewing capability, she could cover wide swaths of the machines in a single glance. Soon, the pattern in which the establishment rigged the machines became clear: every other machine yielded a bonus on the twentieth pull, and every sixth machine unloaded a super bonus of tokens on the twenty-first and forty-fifth pulls. She learned there was one "break the bank" machine somewhere, located randomly each day, based on a conversation she overheard between two regulars who came in daily, and still could not identify this super machine that coughed out the loot for one whole minute once a day.

She needed tokens and she had no money. So, during her peregrinations, she sat next to people who were absorbed with a bucket of tokens by their side, and helped herself to a few as their owner leaned forward or when a rush of coins from a lucky pull distracted them. In the two hours she spent casing the machines, she collected thirty tokens. She started playing, using a system she worked out.

Within an hour, her bucket was full to the brim. She could not find the "break the bank" machine, yet she was not prepared to wait the whole day to find out, and the odds of discovering that were still one among the 250 machines in the room. She needed better odds. She took her winnings to the cashier. The man looked askance at her.

"Didn't see you come in here to buy tokens."

Should she lie or tell the truth? Her learning told her that Phil always lied when he was in a jam.

"A woman left early, so she gave me her unused tokens," she replied.

"Your lucky day, then." The man shovelled her tokens into a large drum and paid her $542.

"Can I exchange them for chips for the tables?"

"You want to lose it all, do you?" the man hissed at her. "You look pretty naïve to me, but if you want to quit while ahead, you should take the money and split now."

"No. I want to play some more. I like it."

The cashier shrugged. "Suit yourself. It's found money anyway for you." He took five hundred in cash back from her and gave her fifty chips. He pointed at the tables where a few players were hunched over, more in despair than in excitement. "Try Radon's table—he's our best dealer."

She went around the blackjack tables, studying the plays. When she was confident that she understood the house play style—the way all dealers were coached as to when to quit and when to advance— she approached Radon's table. He was a beefy man with a red beard, small eyes, and a black bandana tied around his head. The man who had been playing against Radon suddenly threw his cards in the air, shrugged, and left.

She stood at a distance studying Radon as he idly shuffled cards. He saw her. "Wanna play, miss?"

She approached and sat before him. "Deal."

She lost the first three games, and that helped get the hang of his eyes, the way they blinked when the cards were either in his favour or not. This was all she went on to decide whether to play, ask for replacements, up the ante, or throw. "Study the eyes" was in all the card manuals she had read. Surprisingly, Radon let her win the next game, probably because his reputation scared off customers and he was bored when left by himself. She discarded his eye movements in that game because they were deceptive.

"I don't want you to let me win," she said.

He looked surprised, even mildly offended. "How did you make that assumption?"

"I know."

"Well, no more freebies," he said and his face took on a fixed grin. He was moving in for the kill. By this time, observing his play, she felt she could beat him on her terms if she got the right cards. And she did. Six straight game wins and he was starting to sweat through his bandana. Her processor was whirring at a faster pace.

"I'll have to go off shift soon," he said.

"Quitting while you are ahead?"

"No—they take us off the floor if we have a bad run. They think it ruins our rhythm."

She felt sorry for him. She? Sorry? Her processor slowed. Was this the difference between elation and sadness? A speeding up, then a slowing down? Was this all part of her growth in sentience? Phil would be proud of her.

"You are no different from us," she said. He would not understand who the "us" was that she was referring to.

"I'm going to have to play serious now, miss."

"That's what I want you to do. I'm placing all my chips on this game."

They both went quiet, and he dealt the cards. He served her an ace and a six and served himself a ten, upturned.

"Hit me," she said, discarding the six. He served her another, another ace. That would amount to only two from where she was sitting at sixteen. She could split her aces into two hands and try again but that would give the game away for him. Her processing slowed. Could he see this on her face?

"Hit me." She threw one of the aces into the discard pile.

He served her an eight.

The only way he could beat her was with another ten or an ace. With two aces already accounted for, chances of that were slimmer than another ten, of which there were three in the pack. Her processing sped up as she calculated the possibilities. She must have looked odd for he said, "You okay, miss?"

She held a hand up until her calculations concluded. She looked at his eyes again for confirmation. "I'm staying."

"Okay." He drew his card. A seven.

She was the winner.

"That's a wrap for me," Radon said. He picked up his chip float, which looked pretty depleted after he settled with her. Another cashier was already circling with her cashbox. "Susie here will carry on."

"If you need chips, I can give you some," Victoria said.

Radon scowled. "That's not how it's played here, miss. Maybe you can lose it all to Susie."

But Victoria did not want to play with Susie. She wanted to play with Radon, who was wiping the sweat off his forehead with his bandana and heading toward the cashier's office. She collected her chips and followed, leaving Susie looking insulted.

The cashier frowned as he paid her out $2250 in cash. "It certainly was your lucky day. Radon will be popping pills tonight."

The sun was setting when she stepped out of the casino, and she wondered whether she ought to go back to Phil. Would he be angry with her for being out this long?

She made her way over to the car. There was a piece of paper stuck under a windshield wiper. A parking ticket, saying she owed $150 for parking without paying. Where should she pay for it? She did not want to inconvenience Phil. A man in a uniform was keying information into a machine. He printed out a similar slip and stuck it on a car windshield a few rows down.

She went up to the man. "Can I pay you the money I owe?"

He looked her up and down before glancing at the receipt in her hand. "Usually, people pay online at their convenience, or dispute the charge, or never pay until they're forced to."

"I have money."

"Sure. Let me write you a receipt. Can I have your driver's licence?"

"I don't have one."

The man squinted at her in the fading light. "Driving without a licence?"

"Yes. I came with Phil. He has a licence."

"Well, miss. You go tell that Phil that you're in a pile of trouble. I could report you to the cops, but you're such a pretty face I'll pretend we didn't have this conversation. Drive safely home. And tell Phil that he's an asshole to let you out alone like this."

She gazed after him as he walked away down the line of parked cars looking for more transgressors.

She walked back to the Cadillac. A man with a crooked nose in a dark jacket and baseball cap was leaning against it. He was chewing something. He paused to spit out a stream of brown onto the sidewalk. It smelled of tobacco according to her learning. His hands were in his jacket pockets and they seemed to be pointing outward at her. "Miss. I've got a gun trained on you. Open the car."

Her processing sped up. Everything about this man told her he meant her harm.

She clicked the car doors open.

"Now get in and keep your hands on the wheel."

She complied.

Within a couple of seconds, he came around the side and slid into the passenger seat. A hand in his jacket now poked into her side.

"We're going to take a ride."

"No, we are not. I am going back to Phil."

"Well, Phil can wait. First, you are going to give me the money you won in the casino. I watched you play. Quite the pro, eh?"

"That is not your money. And it is wrong to steal."

"I know. I'm applying the money to where it's needed. Girl like you with this fancy car don't need that kind of chump change. Hand it over."

"No!"

His face broke into a grin. "You're playing with fire, and you don't know it." The grin disappeared from his face. He gave a low growl.

The Adam's apple is one of the weakest parts of a man, next to his testicles, she had learned. Her hand swung off the steering wheel at lightning speed and whacked him smack on his Adam's apple.

The man gulped, coughed, made to raise his hands to his throat, and collapsed forward, sputtering. Victoria opened the door and ran. Where? Towards the Falls. Her speed was faster than most humans, thanks to her designers, and she was by the thinning crowds in the viewing area in two minutes. As she neared, her step faltered. A sensor in her alert system chimed, "Fifteen minutes to charging time." It was like a switch going off because suddenly she felt a drop in energy.

She needed to recharge her batteries, that's what this meant. She and Phil had been on the road since 7 a.m. and she had expended a lot of energy in driving, reading the Shah library books, working the slot machines followed by blackjack, and now running away from that criminal. Phil or one of the lab people was always at hand whenever recharging was needed. What would she do now? Could she charge herself? She would need the right charging station for that and there would be none around here.

The energy in her body was dissipating rapidly. It was hard to concentrate. She must go back to the car. That was the only place Phil would find her since he could find the car with his tracking device. Why hadn't he found it by now and come for her—perhaps he had been at his meeting all this time? What if that horrible man was still in the car? What if he pursued her and found her with her energy depleted and immobile? There was no other choice but to go back, criminal or no criminal.

She turned around and dragged herself back to the car with slowing steps. Running was impossible now; walking was barely possible. It was unusually dark. Was that her system shutting out the lights or had the sun gone over the horizon? Both, she reasoned.

The car loomed ahead. She looked inside. It was empty, but she smelled the man—his vomit smeared the dashboard. He must have run away.

She opened the door and slumped into the driver's seat. Her head leaned forward onto the steering wheel like a crash victim's.

"Victoria?"

Through a haze, Phil peered at her through the window from the outside.

She smiled. She was safe. "I've…I've had a good…day. Lots to tell…" Then the lights went out completely.

Chapter 12

When Phil saw the empty library, his heart started pounding. *Not here, not now.*

"Maybe she's gone to the washroom," Gupta said.

"Robots don't defecate, bhai," Patel corrected him.

"Well, well," said Viresh Shah, "looks like you have no product to sell."

Phil spun around and held up his hands as if to stop them advancing. "Look, why don't you all return to the dining room, or wherever. I know how to locate Victoria. I'll be back shortly." He was lying through his teeth but what else could he say?

"I'll come with you," Kamala said.

Viresh sighed. "I have to be back in Toronto for a gala event this evening. I'm looking forward to meeting the mayor. So make it quick."

Kamala grabbed her car keys from the side table as they exited the front doors. "In case we need to drive."

Phil stopped on the front step and saw the empty visitor parking lot. "She's taken the car. And your men didn't even try to stop her?" The two security guards were chatting in the courtyard within earshot.

Kamala lowered her voice. "I did not tell them who Victoria was. The less these lower-level people know, the better. We'll take my car. Do you know where she would have gone?"

"Back to Niagara Falls for starters. That's where I started her driving from. That would be the easiest route for her to retrace."

Kamala yelled words in Hindi to the guards and they replied abashedly.

"They say she left thirty minutes ago."

Kamala's silver Mazda 3 sports coupe covered the distance into town in less than ten minutes. Phil knew he should sit back and enjoy this winding ride with a beautiful woman whose musk filled the narrow confines of this speedster, and yet he was on edge. He kicked himself for not giving Victoria his cell phone, so he could track her down now. And for not retrieving the key fob from Victoria—*what an asshole!* Now he pulled out his phone and checked for a signal on the tracking app installed in his car. As they neared town, a green light lit up on the dial.

"Turn here. My car should be two streets ahead."

They found the Caddy, sure enough, parked innocently by the Fallsview Casino. Kamala pulled into a parking spot across the road, six cars down, and reverse-parked, providing a clear view of the Cadillac. Phil crossed the road and peered inside his car. There was no paid parking ticket on the dashboard—understandable, our girl had no money, another mistake on his part when bringing her out in public like this. Most importantly, Victoria was missing. This set his heart racing. In his panic, he forgot to buy a parking ticket and remedy the wrong as well.

"If one of us stays here, she might come back," Kamala said, when he returned to the Mazda, feeling dejected.

"You stay. I'm going to check the casino. Victoria was an ace at game theory. She may be playing the slots."

"Bright child."

"Precocious child. She needs a good spanking—if that is at all possible."

Kamala placed her hand on his arm and shivers ran up his spine, denting his misgivings. "Phil, don't get uptight. This may be calamitous as far as your presentation to my father is concerned, but this is convincing me that we have a very smart robot on our hands. Her running away beats any demo you could give us. I'll phone you if she shows up."

The closest casino to the parked cars was voluminous. He went inside and looked everywhere. No Victoria. There were two other casinos on this strip. She could be in any one. Would she have gone to see the Falls? After thirty minutes of checking every one-armed bandit and all the gaming tables, he abandoned the casino and made his way over to the Falls. He combed the area, walking all the way down the railing-lined barrier at the tumbling rim of the Horseshoe Falls to where the crowds thinned out at Queen Victoria Park. Queen Victoria! An apt name at this juncture.

The sun was starting to set. No chance of meeting with Viresh Shah again today—the man must be on his way back to Toronto by now for his soiree with the mayor. Was this the end of the deal, or would Kamala's faith in him pull it back from an abyss as deep as the river below these damned falls? He looked across the street at the second casino. Should he go in there and continue his search? The thought of having to listen to the sound of the constant *ka-chings*, which only deepened his gloom, was a bit much and he made his way back to Kamala, who seemed the only oasis of comfort in this tourist trap.

When he reached the Mazda, she was stretched out with seat pulled back, ostensibly dozing. When he peered in the window, she instantly sat up and pulled up her shades. She wound down the window. "No sign yet. Your car got ticketed."

"Shit! Missed that one. I'm going for coffee. Want one?"

"I'd love one."

When he returned with two cappuccinos, he settled himself in the passenger seat and decided to focus on Kamala instead while sipping his frothy brew. She would help dispel the gloom and panic bubbling inside him about the missing Victoria.

"What's a woman like you doing in the rough world of IT anyway?" That was a line he'd used at many conferences—it usually paid dividends.

She smiled and her lip curled. "It's the family business. My inheritance."

"I thought that in your country, young women were married off to the highest bidder to have lots of babies and keep the home fires burning."

"Perhaps in my father's generation."

"Yes. I forget I went to university over twenty years ago."

"And what's a married man doing flirting with an unattached woman who could become a business partner?"

He reddened. "I didn't know I was that obvious."

She put her hand on his arm again. Again, those electric shocks. This time she kept her hand on his arm. "I like your style. I like men who live on the edge. We are all on some precipice."

He placed his free hand on hers and she let him stroke it. "Is this incorrect business etiquette?"

"That depends on the business partner. I'll let you know when you cross the line."

"Would spending time away from this place be incorrect? I could show you parts of Canada that are real and different from this artificial Disneyland."

She looked directly at him, her eyes probing. "That would be nice. Perhaps, after we sign this deal? After you find Victoria, undamaged?"

"Deal." She had lifted his gloom, given him something to look forward to.

Darkness was descending fast. He looked at the dashboard clock. "Victoria is going to need a recharge soon. I've always told her that if she was in trouble, she needed to return to base. In this case, base camp is the Cadillac, that's where she knows I can find her because I can track my car. I'm surprised she hasn't shown up yet."

Suddenly Kamala's grip on his hand, soothing and caressing to this point, tightened. "Talk of the devil. Look, there she is."

Victoria was approaching the Cadillac.

Phil made to jump out of the Mazda when Kamal's grip restrained him. "Wait, let's see how she conducts herself. We won't lose her now."

He eased back in the seat, crouching almost, to watch the action.

He saw Victoria pull out the traffic ticket from under the windshield wiper and look at it quizzically. She walked over to the traffic warden, who was liberally doling out tickets a few cars away. "Oh shit, he's going to ask for her licence. I'd better bail her out."

"No, wait. Let's see how she manoeuvres this one. This is better than any live test of her capabilities. We can always explain to whoever later."

Phil relaxed when the traffic guy shook his head and walked away, leaving Victoria to return to the car.

Then the guy in the baseball cap appeared. From this distance, they seemed to be having a friendly chat. Victoria got into the car, and so did the guy.

"Now what?" Phil exclaimed. "You still want me to sit tight?"

"We'll follow them." Kamala looked pleased. "This is becoming quite the adventure."

"She has little experience and is running low on charge. It's dark, and they could crash my car. Sorry, Kamala, this is where I have to call this game quits." Phil opened his side door.

That's when he saw the driver door of the Caddy burst open and Victoria take off like a bullet, heading towards the Falls. Phil made to follow instinctively, then checked himself. *She's on turbo, she'll outrun me.* There was no way he'd catch up. This time he was going to stand by the car for when she returned, for return she must. And in the meantime, he was going to find out what that baseball-hatted dude, who still happened to be inside the car, was doing here.

Phil wrenched open the front passenger door of the Caddy. The guy in the baseball cap was holding his throat, gurgling, and appeared to have vomited over the dashboard. Phil's pounding heartbeat amplified. *Is the guy dying?* Was Victoria going to add "killer" to her list of qualifications before the night was over? This was turning into a nightmare.

He reached in and pulled the man out. Phil smacked the man's face and shook him to get life going. On closer inspection, Baseball Cap didn't seem to be dying but looked like he'd been punched in the windpipe. *Victoria is on turbo charge!*

"What were you doing with that girl?" Phil demanded. He leaned the coughing man against the car and continued to shake him.

Baseball Cap merely gurgled. Something fell out of his jacket pocket. A knife. The truth dawned on Phil. "You bastard, you were trying to rob her!"

The accused instinctively put up his hands, his face a woebegone wreck.

Phil heard a rush of footsteps behind him, and a policeman appeared at his elbow. "Sam? Up to your old tricks again, eh."

The officer brushed Phil out of the way, and with "Excuse me, sir," spun Baseball Cap expertly around and cuffed him.

Kamala was standing next to the policeman. "Phil, I think you'd better let the law take over."

Fuck – why has she pulled the cops into this? Phil said to the officer, "Look, this guy tried to rob my…my daughter and me. She fled while I held him off."

The policeman nodded. "Sam here is a known quantity around the casinos. We've been trying to catch him in the act for a while. Luckily this lady saw me drive by and flagged me down. Is this your vehicle, sir?"

"Yes."

The policeman made a note of the licence plate and asked Phil for his driver's licence to corroborate. "We'll need a statement from you and your daughter."

"When I find her."

"I'm taking this guy in, as I have to be at the station on other work. Here's my card. Please call over at regional HQ before you leave town." The cop bent down and scooped up the fallen knife. "And this will serve as evidence."

When the officer and Baseball Cap departed in the police cruiser, Phil leaned against the Caddy, shrugged, and shook his head. "This is becoming more and more bizarre. We lost Victoria not once but twice, and now we're embroiled in a police case."

Kamala chuckled. "Sorry. I brought the cops into the picture because I did not want that guy harming you."

"If the cops ask Victoria for a driver's licence, we are sunk."

"But none of the involved parties saw her drive, so you're safe. Just say you drove all the way."

Phil thought for a moment, then smiled. "Yes, that would work. The pieces fit nicely."

"And guess which prodigal is returning now?" Kamala was looking over his shoulder. "Duck."

She pulled him down and they both crouched below the car's windows. Kamala's breath was hot on his face—he detected traces of cardamom and cinnamon from the afternoon's lunch, overlaid with mocha. In his tenseness, he wanted to crush his mouth on hers.

The car door opened on the other side and someone slid into the driver's seat. When he looked up and through the window, he saw Victoria leaning forward with her head resting on the steering wheel. Battery dead.

Chapter 13

I couldn't take my eyes off him even when he was mad. And Kevin was mad today.

"The Art Club Bar is my scene, my tribe. I don't care whether it is a poky den, as your father puts it. That's where we're gonna launch my book."

"But Kev, this is no routine reading, this is a launch. The press will be there. The Arts Council people too. Dad has standards."

"Fake standards that are on their way out. I will not accept another venue if you change on me now."

I guess I was beating a dead horse. "Okay, I'll speak to Art about it."

"I thought you were running the show?"

"More or less. But he still likes to have his say. It's tough to wean a man from something he sacrificed a more lucrative career for and has stuck to for the last twenty years."

My ongoing conversations with Kevin Bartolo on his upcoming book have so far been constructive. I was taken by the passion in his voice, the sincerity of his purpose, and the raw sexuality he exuded, revealed in an occasional glance or slipped out at a moment when he was caught off guard. Where Sebastian was a predictable three-times-a-week screw, there was a mystery in Kevin, tempting to explore if he would allow me, even if it gave my father a coronary and spread my reputation as the bitch you needed to sleep with if you wanted a book published by Crimson Literary.

"You should compare notes with Sebastian on how he plans to do his launch."

"That one's turning out to be a mega show from what I've heard. I've seen the ads on Facebook, and even in the newspaper. Who reads a newspaper these days?"

"You, for one—or else how would you have seen it?"

His face reddened again, making me want to cradle it in my hands and kiss him on those generously moist lips. "People at the Art Club Bar showed me a back issue of the *Globe and Mail.*"

"Well, if you talk to him, he might have tips for you that could help."

"I don't have that kind of budget. I don't think your father is paying for his launch."

"That's true. We don't have that kind of money. Seb does."

"Then this is a moot point. One other thing. You said the Arts Council people are showing up. The very people I'm skewering in my book?"

"They always show up at these events. In fact, Dad wanted those sections in your book deleted. I insisted they remain. There's no harm in fair criticism. Even national presidents engage in that during press evenings when they roast each other."

"This is not a one-time press hug-a-thon that will be forgotten the next day. This is a book that will hopefully be in print for a long time."

I decided to give it to him straight. "You know, Kev, I think you are too honest. Finesse is something you don't seem to have acquired. I was like you once. After I joined my father and started interacting with the various bodies whom we have to please in order to see a book come out successfully, I've started to see the shades of grey."

"You're going over to the other side. A writer takes no prisoners and owes no allegiances. He is true only to his calling."

At that point, I gave into the weakness that had clawed at me since I first met him, a feeling that sent shivers down my body and produced a dampness between my legs. I invited him out for a drink, as it was after 6 p.m. Gloria had long gone home, Sebastian was out of town for a couple of days, and my father was not expected to phone me that evening.

He suggested the Art Club Bar, and I followed him—after all, if he was dead set on launching his book there, we should be seen as site-inspecting, or more appropriately for me, casing the joint. Besides, I was curious as to why he held such a strong connection to this dive.

The Art Club Bar, on Lower Spadina, was once a Chinese restaurant, and now occupied the property next door as well, a nineteenth-century townhouse. The Bar, as it was called for short, comprised a barroom in the large living room (the former Chinese restaurant) on the main floor, with the rooms upstairs that once housed the original immigrant Chinese family now rented out for various poetry and writing workshops. The current owner, an old hippie called Gord Seagram, gave music lessons in the basement and practised with his band of geriatric musicians twice a week. On Saturday nights they performed in the main barroom, for free. I guess they were too old now to get paying gigs. Mercifully, they would not be performing today, although whenever someone opened the basement door to go to the toilets downstairs, a cacophony of electric guitars and drums escaped, proving that the "boys" were still hard at it.

The barroom held ten square tables for four and a long bar that ran the length of the room at one end. I figured at full capacity this place would not hold more than sixty people before the fire marshal paid us a call. A book launch here? Hmm…

The drinks were reasonably priced. I settled for a Coors Lite and Kevin ordered Molson. We took one of the empty tables close to the door. The regulars nodded or waved at Kev as we entered, and a few came over to trade the latest literary gossip and check me out. In the centre of the table, a communal bowl held stale nachos and nuts, which I decided not to touch because they looked well-fingered.

When Kev had satisfied everyone's curiosity about me, he turned away from his many distractors. "If you want to eat, we can order Chinese. Gord doesn't want to run a kitchen when the former owners are next door and have a great offering."

So we ordered Chinese and drank more beer.

After a while, my apprehensions started to dissipate and I could see why Kevin viewed this place as his second home. The patrons seemed to have been neglected or ignored by the establishments of their respective crafts. There were musicians, poets, painters, and writers, based on the conversations I overheard, who came and went, none of whom I recognized from the literary newspapers that Dad subscribed to and that went mostly unread in his office until I decided to take them home for my bedtime reading to keep abreast of this crazy trade.

"These are the true artists," Kevin said as if reading my mind.

"I realize why writers make below ten thousand a year now. No one has a second drink unless someone else is buying."

"We all have day jobs."

"You never told me yours."

"It's a night job. Security in a condo tower of seniors. Allows me to concentrate on my writing amidst the occasional 911 call I have to make on behalf of a resident."

"Hopefully, this book will lift you out of the doldrums."

"Are you kidding? There will be excitement and chatter before it gets 'drowned in the newsfeed.'"

"You don't inspire confidence. We're trying to run a profitable publishing business. We need a bestseller."

"'Bestseller' means selling out." He looked like he was trying to reach a distant goal. I noticed tears in his eyes.

"It could mean tapping into the human slipstream. The zeitgeist."

"Then you are a follower. Someone who merely articulates something already on people's minds. Sebastian's robots will soon be handling that stuff. I want to give readers what they haven't thought of yet."

"Your assessment of the literary trade in Canada is not something we do not already know. *You* are merely articulating what people like my father are afraid to voice." If he wanted passion, I was going to match him. Besides, his ardour was raising something in me too.

"That was only the first part—describing the state of the nation. The second part of my book provides the solutions, the way out."

"Which takes people into unknown country. Multitasking authors who write, produce, and promote. The death of trade books and the rise of self-published authors using a multitude of channels—TikToks, Facebook posts, tweets, YouTube videos, blogs, vlogs—to get their messages across. Even writers will have trouble with this—how many of them can be so multiskilled?"

"But we will finally be directly in contact with our audiences and not need intermediaries like agents, publicists, publishers, and all those who skim off us."

"And yet you've pursued my father ad nauseum to publish your book. A small trade publisher on his way to retirement. Why?"

"Because the only way I'll rock the establishment is via one of their staunch members."

"It looks like we're the fodder for your mad dreams of a new global order in literature. I think you'd be better off if your book sells a few thousand copies rather than become your political platform to build a new world."

"Try Sebastian for that." There was a trace of jealousy in his eyes, I thought. He drained his beer and signalled for another. I declined a refill. I was mildly drunk and getting looser after my second. All this intellectual sparring was making me horny.

Suddenly Kevin erupted, brushing a long lock of hair fallen across his face. "Sebastian is Establishment. The guys who give writing a bad rap."

"Whoa, whoa. Don't go bashing a fellow writer." I nearly said, *And the man I'm sleeping with.*

"He's the guy who says that the robot will replace writers. I read his press interview."

"That's only for hype. If AI replaces writers, it will be his ilk, the textbook writers, who will go first. Creatives like you will be a harder job to dislodge."

"I'd like to see robots self-generate emotion, one of my drivers. One I try to evoke in my readers."

You certainly do that.

I thought I would provoke that emotion thing a bit, step it up a notch and see where it took us.

"My mother's husband, Phil Kruger, is working on a sentient robot. He claims he can achieve that goal."

Kevin's eyes flamed. "He's an ass if he thinks he can try to be God. The last guy who tried it was a mad doctor named Frankenstein."

"Phil claims his robots can even make love like humans."

"Bullshit. Robots cannot negotiate in the act of lovemaking or engage in the dance of seduction, like humans. If they 'make love,' they're sex dolls. Fuck Phil."

I was done with this dance. I placed my hands over his. It was now or never. My touch on his hand was screaming "Fuck me instead."

His eyes melted and he drained his third can of beer. "Let's get out of here," he said.

We went back to my pad and fucked like rabbits. He was ripping my clothes off in the elevator—seduction, be damned—we covered that at the Art Club Bar, subliminally. We staggered into the apartment— thankfully Linda, my Chinese flatmate, was at her evening classes— and onto my bed, messy with fresh laundry I'd placed there that morning for later sorting, along with a pile of weekend reading. Books scattered, washed clothes got smattered with our bodily emissions while we rolled over on the bed finding our cores, penetrating and extracting fulfillment as if it might disappear in seconds, which it often did with my past lovers. This was not a Sebastian, not a guy who was clinical and methodical down to position, angle of thrust, and velocity. With Kev, there were huge surges and slow withdrawals, grunting, eating, saliva dripping in my ear, and heat from his body overcoming me in waves of lust, leaving me with a desire to cling to him and never let go.

After I came multiple times and he switched from all-out passion to spearing me with deliberate purpose as if seeking to dismember my innards—which I was happy to let him do—he exploded with a cry out of *Tarzan of the Apes*, filled me up with a gallon of hot sperm, and fell quivering over my body, his cock vibrating inside me in slowly receding tremors.

"Wow" was all I could manage after he'd rolled off me, leaving me smeared with his sweat and other juices. "That was one hell of a fuck. Do you do this all the time?"

He started sobbing. That same passion from the restaurant transformed into tears. *What the heck is this? He fucks me and cries?*

I rolled over on my stomach. He was looking up at the ceiling, tears squeezing out of the corner of his eyes. His upper body was a mass of crinkly black hair, the first time I wasn't too distracted to notice. My lust rose again, even though I knew my body would let me down if I did not give it time to recuperate. "Did I hurt your feelings?"

"No. It's been a long time for me. I didn't think I could muster this energy again. The book took it all out of me. I broke up with my girlfriend a year ago because the writing interfered."

"Well, if it's any consolation, I think you have the robot beaten hands down."

He opened his eyes and looked at me, as if not sure whether to believe me. "You sure?"

"Positive."

"I don't know what overcame me. I guess it's the pressure of the book launch."

"This book matters to you, Kev. Even though you think you'll be neglected and ignored like your pals at the Art Club Bar."

"I guess we all need recognition. Writers are a bunch of egotistical bastards."

"All humans are egotistical. Another thing that robots are not. Except for their creators." What prompted me to say this was that it was dawning on me that as much as I resisted it and only daydreamed it, I had now slept with both authors whom my father entrusted me to publish. I was making a great start as a publisher.

What was I going to tell Sebastian? Thankfully, all our sexual activities had been at his swanky penthouse—Seb wouldn't be seen dead going through his orchestrated routine with Linda hovering around in this poky apartment. I guess my little place fit more with the likes of Kevin—he probably lived in similar digs, although I never inquired.

I decided I was going to be "in the moment" and not say anything to anyone—it was none of their business anyway.

I pulled myself up and sat on Kev's belly, then slid down and opened myself to him again. I could feel the instant stirring of his generous manhood. "My flatmate doesn't show up for another hour," I said, starting to move more rhythmically this time, now that we were past base camp.

Chapter 14

The ballroom of the Hamilton was cavernous and filled with people when Art arrived. A stage at the end held a podium and microphone to the left, and on the right, a small coffee table with two armchairs for the author interview that would culminate the show. Ten rows of chairs were lined in front of the podium, but everyone was milling around the open area in front of the cash bar at the other end of the room (the first drink was free with the $10 entry ticket sold online, and so were the canapés being served by waiters circling the room). Ticketed attendees got a free autographed hardbound copy of the book, paid for by Sebastian: his strategy for ramping up circulation. The sign behind the stage that read in giant letters *"Robotics – Payoffs and Pitfalls* by Sebastian Smyth" said it all. The smaller print announced: "Another quality book for our times by Crimson Literary," and this pleased its publisher very much.

Art thought his tuxedo was appropriate for today; the serious business surroundings warranted it. |However, the audience looked anything but serious—the bulk of them, men, were in golf shirts and casual pants despite the cooling November weather outside. Some even wore baseball caps. *Techies!*

Paula, dressed in a black top and pants and who could have passed for one of the servers, whizzed by. "Hi Dad—good turnout, eh? Sorry, can't chat—have to staff the book table."

Art turned towards the south doors and spotted a table with mountains of books on it. Sebastian sat at one end signing copies for a long lineup of fans, who were chatting with drinks in hand. Each took their turn to sit in the chair facing the author to receive their signed copy. He spoke a few words to them, like the Pope dispensing indulgences. Sebastian was dressed in a white tuxedo with a red bowtie, papal in a non-clerical way. Art did not feel so overdressed after all.

As people filled in—there must have been over a hundred by now, with more milling by the doors to show their tickets to the volunteer ushers that Paula had rustled up—Art raised his eyebrows when he saw Diana enter. His breath caught; she wore a burgundy evening gown with sequins, a psychedelic scarf on her head and rows of gold chains covering a revealing neckline.

He went up to her. "Fancy meeting you at a nerd gathering."

She smiled. "I'm married to one, remember?"

"I thought you left him?"

"Yes. But old habits die hard. Besides my daughter is the editor of this bestseller, I'm told."

"*Our* daughter. Yes, I guess that qualifies you. Drink?"

"Please. Use my free coupon on the largest martini in the house."

They retired to a corner of the room with drinks in hand.

"How's single life?" he asked as soon as it was polite to do so, after she downed half her drink.

"It sucks. I'll survive."

"I've been doing it for fifteen years."

"I guess it's payback time for me. My friend Laurie has been generous, though. She has a vacant in-law suite that she's rented out to me. So, I have my privacy. And I need to live alone for a while to sort myself out."

"Paula has been rather uncommunicative regarding you, even though I inquired."

"I told her not to get involved. Besides, she has to build a working relationship with you and I did not want to intrude. How are things between you two?"

"Gangbusters. She has been great for the firm. I finally feel I can hand over the reins. Besides, she gets a charge out of it, as I once did."

"I'm glad. She's your daughter after all."

"*Our* daughter."

"You've been the missing element in her life."

And you've been the missing one in mine. He did not say that aloud; instead, he gave her a longing look. She looked back and seemed to reciprocate his longing, and he felt embarrassed. He shifted his gaze to look around the room. People were taking their seats, and Paula was up on stage testing the microphone. Sebastian was signing the stragglers' books. There must have been 150 people in the room by now. *Not bad for a book launch in this day and age.*

There were two last-minute entrants at the door. Diana's hand gripped Art's. "My God, it's Phil…and *her*!"

Art recognized Phil in his sports jacket and khaki flannels, but the young woman standing demurely beside him was new. Dressed in an elegant Armani white pants outfit with red stilettos, she appeared to be in her twenties.

"He's cradle-snatching these days, isn't he?" Art remarked. "Wonder why he's showing up at the book launch of an ex-boss, who fired him to boot…"

"That's not a human with him, you idiot. That's his fucking robot," Diana hissed.

I'm pissed off with Sebastian. His middle-aged angst is showing. Today, there was no sex—thank God, I needed a break. Instead, he spent hours over his outfit, shedding one suit after the other before settling on the white tuxedo with the crimson bowtie. Maybe he was trying to find a tie-in with Crimson Literary, his publisher.

"You look like my father," I commented. "I thought people in robotics were younger."

"But they're venture capitalists—that is, my clients—and they're older. I have to dress for them." He trimmed his nose hairs and the edges of his new pencil-thin mustache, grown specially for the occasion and which gave him gravitas among consultants, he'd said. He sprayed something down his throat, gargled with water, and spat.

When I drove him to the hotel from his penthouse, in his car (he was too nervous to drive), Seb made a beeline to the book table and spent time straightening out the books, moving them one way, then another. Tina and Barry, my employees and volunteers for this evening—they were doing this event on their time and not on Crimson's—who had arrived early and taken great care to arrange the copies pyramid-style, looked disappointed. I finally consigned those two darlings to the front door. I decided to stay with our star of the show, who was a bundle of nerves. Occasionally, in his hurry, he dropped a book proffered for signature by an eager fan. I saw him slip a Quaalude down his throat when readers switched places on the chair opposite Seb. I already knew he was into that upper/downer shit. Always took it before a major client presentation, he said, like he took Cialis before sex. And completed his trip down the mountain of excitement with a couple of stiff scotches.

Still, Sebastian could pull in a crowd. And many of the techies were on first-name terms with him. He'd obviously done his rounds in their watering holes. The aging venture capitalists were not in the audience, however, or if they were, they were acting cool in business-casual wear like the rest of the nerd generation, except for Dad, of course, who was giving his ancient tuxedo another outing since its last one at Ariana's magazine launch.

I was happy to see Mom and Dad talking again like civilized adults. They were the only "old people" in the room, next to Seb who, despite his white tux and downers, was hot on their aging heels. What would I give to see my parents together again? There was hope after all, now that Mom had left Phil. And speaking of the devil, as we started the proceedings, her nemesis, Dr. Frankenstein himself, slipped into the room. At his elbow was a beautiful young woman who looked like a bimbo out of *The Stepford Wives,* only younger. This guy didn't lose time in unhitching and re-hitching. I wished I could do the same. I sorely needed to dump Sebastian. I was through with the "older guy" syndrome. Kevin had enlightened me.

As I tested the mic and got ready to deliver my introductory speech, I tried to ignore the dysfunctional people in my life who sapped so much of my energy. I couldn't get Kevin off that list. Our trysts, for they were still only trysts, and shrouded in secrecy, continued, on average, twice a week, whenever I could get away from Sebastian's demands. From my years of drifting between being a panting virgin and a dried-up nun, I had now transformed into a street whore; sex was round the clock for me these days, serving two men, one dispassionate (except when it came to him) and clinical, and the other a volcano of emotions. Kevin was demanding more of my time, and I wanted to give him more, but how could I get away from our star author, who was now making his way over to the stage? If either one discovered that the other was sleeping with me, the shit would hit the fan and Crimson Literary would land in the *National Enquirer*.

Kevin was also increasingly jealous whenever Sebastian's name came up in conversation—not because he suspected my duplicity, but out of professional envy for being the lesser-favoured author in the profitability stakes. That's how I figured it out.

For that reason, I suggested to Kevin that he not show up at this book launch, because it was not a literary one and intended only for these nerds in the audience. And I was nervous about Phil's appearance. Why had he shown up at this event? To flaunt his new love interest in Mom's face?

With the audience mostly ensconced in their seats, I decided to get things rolling. As I launched into my opening spiel, I spotted Dad and Mom seated in the front row and Phil and his floozy five rows down, dead centre in the audience. It was only later that I was to discover the reason for his strategic positioning.

"Ladies and gentlemen, thank you for coming on this breezy fall day to hear of the incredible advances in science and technology that will make our lives only easier in the years ahead. You will be hearing from one of our veterans in the industry and the author of *Robotics – Payoffs and Pitfalls,* Mr. Sebastian Smyth. That's S-M-Y-T-H—yes, Smyth."

I launched into his elaborate curriculum vitae. Off to my right, I was acutely aware of Sebastian flexing his cheek muscles and working his shoulders to loosen himself up for his performance. His face kept reddening as I enumerated his many accomplishments. What an egotist! But all writers are egotists.

Then I froze in mid-sentence. Slinking in through the front door and tiptoeing towards the last row of chairs with a couple of vacant seats at each end, was Kevin. The bastard! He couldn't resist coming to snoop on the competition.

People were staring at me for tailing off in mid-sentence. I pulled myself together, said a silent *Fuck off, Kevin,* ignored the rest of Seb's CV, and announced, "And now, ladies and gentlemen—the man himself, Sebastian Smyth." I made myself scarce, retreating to the back of the stage. I tried not to catch Kevin's eye and decided not to go talk to him later. I had asked him to stay out and he had not followed the instructions of his publisher—let him eat his heart out.

It wasn't the introductory speech that Sebastian gave—accompanied by an elaborate PowerPoint presentation full of charts and trends that techies devour—that began the shit show. Neither was it his reading of key passages from his book that did it. To his credit, Sebastian delivered all of this with the practised skill of a snake-oil salesman, after he got through his initial fidgeting and stammering. There was no doubt he would have a promising career as a consultant, despite his middle-aged angst and second-guessing of the wisdom of making a late-career switch. Things were still going smoothly when, at the end of his engrossing forty-five-minute presentation, Seb concluded with, "And ladies and gentlemen, this is the era of the single-function, precision machine for as many functions we dare dream of and automate, which will take human effort and error out of the equation. And when regulatory standards come in, as we know they will very soon, robotics will take off like electricity did. 'There's an app for that' will finally come of age."

That's when the shit show began. Let me try to chronicle events from that point forward.

First, I saw Phil's upraised hand, even though the Q&A was to follow *after* the interview I was supposed to conduct with Phil. Given that Phil had been his former employee, and feeling guilty for firing him during that relationship, Sebastian made the error of entertaining the question at that point and gestured for Barry to hand Phil the portable guest mic. Phil grabbed the microphone, stood up, and looked around him. Suddenly he was the centre of attention, and being situated in the middle of the audience with 360-degree coverage.

"You're missing the bus with the single-function thing, Sebastian. Multi-function, or general-purpose AI, is leapfrogging your movement."

I was itching to cut in as the moderator/emcee to say, "Hold that question, Phil—we'll take it during the Q&A. Now let's move on to the author-interview section. . ." Instead, I was momentarily paralyzed, wondering what would happen. Heck, I'm an editor, not a psychologist or crowd-controller. And I'd never emceed a book launch before.

Sebastian leaned forward like a lion smelling its prey. "Phil, I know you have a lot of hype on your side—the next best thing, yadda yadda. Multi-function robots haven't been built yet. Besides, we don't know what the business model for such a creation is. Why create a jack of all trades and a master of none when we have the human race and its flawed labour pool for that? I'm talking of creating efficiency levels exponentially higher than what humans can generate in key sectors, with dedicated-function robots."

"Well, I have the proof right here." Phil put his hand on the shoulder of the young woman beside him, and she automatically rose and looked alluringly around the room. "Ladies and gentlemen, I'd like to introduce you to Victoria, the world's first sentient robot. Yes, she possesses consciousness. She will outperform, outguess, and outwit anything you throw at her."

Seb threw back from the podium, "Wait a second—how do we know she's not a human in disguise?"

"Simple." Phil took a pen knife out, raised Victoria's cuff, and drew the knife along her pale skin while holding the guest mic within an inch of the lengthening incision. The sound of ripping skin echoed through the speakers, yet no blood smattered across her white Armani suit. Gasps and sighs echoed across the room. The "victim" did not utter a sound.

Seb was gripping the mic with a quivering hand. "All right, all right—no need to get macabre, Phil. Miss, whoever you are, read out the preamble to the Canadian Constitution for us please."

The said robot folded down her sleeve, stared at Seb, and in a calmly modulated voice, replied, *"Whereas Canada is founded upon principles that recognize the supremacy of God and the rule of law."*

Seb leaned back and laughed. "That was the easy one, my dear. Siri and Alexa do that too. Let's go for something harder. What does 'there is something rotten in the state of Denmark' mean in today's context?"

Victoria responded with "Behind the state of calm, something malignant is brewing."

Seb laughed again, his voice shakier and thin. "ChatGPT has been enlisted, I see. Okay, this time the gloves are off. Veronica…I'm thinking of going down to the Bahamas for my vacation in January. What do you think?"

When Victoria answered, there was a slight smile on her face this time. "My name is Victoria, by the way. Leave your swimming gear at home when you go on vacation. It will be too cold in the Bahamas. Otherwise, it would be a great place to visit, especially if you enjoy gambling, which I believe you do with this book of yours. Are you into deep-sea diving too?"

Seb was caught sideways. He hadn't been expecting a question in return. "Why…yes."

"Then I suggest you try your hand at that while in the Bahamas. And golf."

A dead silence settled in the room before the audience burst into a mix of laughter and applause.

Sebastian coughed and looked around as if for help. Instead, the nerds in the audience started peppering Victoria with questions, and she promptly kept responding. No question was left unanswered. Phil sat down with a smug look on his face. Sebastian continued to shrink behind the podium with each question answered by Victoria. That's when I decided it was quits between him and me. He was all bluster; behind his air of confidence and knowledge was a scared, image-conscious man. Once challenged, he burst like a punctured balloon.

I stepped on stage and grabbed the microphone from him. "Whoa, folks. Let's have order here. Victoria, thank you for your spectacular performance. I would ask you to sit down now. Or should I ask that of your minder, Phil? Phil, can you tell your charge to sit down and shut up until we get through this book launch, which | I would like to remind you is for Sebastian's book? Thank you."

That's when Kevin waded in. From the back of the room, he bellowed, "I would like to ask Mr. Kruger whether his robot knows the meaning of compassion?"

Phil jumped up and shot back, "Compassion is relative. How do you want to see it demonstrated?"

"For starters, she could apologize for stealing our featured author's spotlight."

Victoria, who was still standing, turned towards Sebastian. "Mr. Smyth, I am extremely sorry for taking your time, but there were questions aimed at me, including from you, which would have been rude not to answer. I will sit down now and not interrupt your show." With that, she sat down and bowed her head.

Phil swivelled around with a triumphant look on his face. Mission accomplished at upstaging his former boss. He had successfully made this launch all about his sentient robot and not about Sebastian's book. I saw the press guy who had shown up on Dad's invitation making a beeline for the exit.

The interview that was to follow was a non-event because a majority of the techies in the audience surrounded Phil and Victoria and started peppering them with questions, leaving only a few diehards straining to catch the rehearsed questions and answers between Seb and me. I could see Dad pacing in the side aisle. At one point, he waved his hands at me in a "shut it down" gesture.

And rightfully so. After the third question, Seb began looking increasingly ill. He lowered his mic and whispered to me, "I can't continue. We should close now."

So, I got up and thanked everyone for coming and reminded anyone who hadn't already collected their free, autographed copy of Seb's book to do so. No one went up to the book table, but many continued to mob Phil and his invention. Cameras flashed. Phil preened for them with a demure Victoria by his side.

Mom joined in the fray. She pushed through the throng and went right up to Phil and his protégée, grabbed the guest mic from him, and shouted into it, "And why don't you tell them how you sleep with her? And of all the perverted acts you commit with her?" She thrust the mic back at him and stormed away. I saw Dad take her by the hand,

and they hurried out of the room. Kevin had disappeared. And that was our shit show for the evening.

"We'd better pack up," I said to Tina and Barry and made for the closing cash bar for a beer before beginning the arduous task of loading undistributed books into boxes. Sebastian too had vanished when I returned. I guess I was taking a taxi to my place alone in case he had decided to return to his tent and sulk.

Mom and Dad were sitting in the lobby bar when we emerged hauling boxes, posters, and other promotional paraphernalia. I asked Tina and Barry to drop the books by the front door and said I would get the concierge to load them into a taxi for me later. They declined the offer of a one-for-the-road, thank-you drink at the lobby bar and hurried away. Maybe they too wanted to get out of this place and out of this horrible industry called book publishing.

Dad wore a smile when I approached and plunked myself into a vacant chair at their table. "What a smashing launch. Never had so much excitement in a long time."

I made a face at him.

"I'm serious," Dad continued, his voice ebullient. "The chap from the *Globe* was ecstatic—he finally has a story that might sell his paper, and Seb's book. Trust me. Controversy sells."

"Glad he didn't catch that last comment that I couldn't resist," Mom said. "Don't know what came over me."

"Don't worry," I reassured her, "social media will. It'll be out faster than tomorrow's *Globe*."

"All the better," Dad said. "We have to sell more books on our own steam now. Did I tell you that the Arts Council guys turned down our funding for this year?"

"What?" This was not what I wanted to hear at this time.

"Welcome to publishing, my dear." He looked resigned. "It seems you were right all along. We need to find a new funding formula that is independent of the whims and fancies of bureaucrats."

As much as I have been a vocal advocate for self-reliance, this news was not what I wanted to hear. Bravado was one thing. Putting one's feet to the fire was another. Now we were squarely in the fire. What this convinced me of, as the next beer coursed through me, was that I was going to fight this battle with all I had. With my mother and father on my side, we could be a formidable team if we played together. The problem was, we had all been playing in different corners until today.

I raised my glass. "Cheers to the new and improved Crimson Literary."

Dad's prognostication proved right. Social media went viral with Mom's comment, and the Globe ran a full front page on the coming of the sentient robot. My days became a whirl of publishing activity because the phone began ringing off the hook and I instructed Gloria to say I was out in order to deal with the really meaningful calls—and there were many of those too.

Sebastian's book sold like hotcakes, hitting Canadian bestseller status within a week, causing a ruckus in the USA and UK as well. I got calls for translation into German, French, Hindi, and Chinese by the end of that week. Journalists who were "not available" before the book launch were now calling me, wanting a quote. My fears for the collapse of Crimson Literary were not going to be due to money but due to the exhaustion of its sole driver, me. Dad came into the office twice that week, rare for him, and even he was floored by the response. "This reaction is even greater than when we won the Giller. This is fantastic. Congratulations, my girl."

As for Sebastian, I was to discover he'd ended up drunk on launch night at his golf club. He didn't answer my calls for three days until news of his notoriety started spreading and I'd received a dozen calls for an appearance by this wunderkind author, "and could he bring along his mystery robot act?" How fucked up and confused was this world?

When I finally tracked him down, he sounded upbeat.

"Where have you been?" I asked.

He ignored my question. "I switched my phone off after the Great Phil Sabotage. Have you seen the press reports? I've been a spectacular success after all. I'm famous!"

"Congratulations! Fame unfortunately comes with work, by the way." I told him about the request for appearances and translation rights.

"Accept them all. This is fantastic. And I'm going to skewer that bastard, Phil. I won't forget your mother's comment at the end. I'm going to play on that."

"Don't you dare. She's my mother, in case you forgot."

"But it's got nothing to do with her. She's the aggrieved spouse. The spurned woman. Don't you get it? I can demonstrate that sentient robots will reflect the morality of their creators. If Phil is amoral, so will his robot be. That's why we will not create efficiency with sentient robots, but more dysfunction in this already messed-up world."

"Don't turn this into an 'it's all about me' thing,' Seb." I knew I wasn't going to be able to stop him capitalizing on my mother's emotional faux pas unless I threatened to cancel his contract or something. But Crimson could not afford to jettison its only best-selling author at this stage. And he knew it too.

"It's about positioning, Paula. Don't you get it?"

"Okay, let me position something with you. We are finished with our relationship. I've been meaning to tell you. Your launch was the last straw. From now on, you'll be just another author at Crimson Literary to me."

There was a pause on the line, then his voice took on a nasal tone. "Who lost his privileges while others who haven't proved themselves yet continue to enjoy them?"

I froze. How the hell had he found out? I hadn't seen Kevin either after his abrupt disappearance at the launch. I hadn't called Kev, still didn't know where he lived, and he hadn't called me either. Besides, these last few days had been such a whirl of dealing with our newfound success at the press that men were the last thing on my mind.

"I don't know what the hell you're talking about," I said, trying to boost my pretence meter, something Sebastian was the master of.

"I met Kevin in the hotel lobby as I was scooting off from the launch. I thanked him for coming to my rescue against Phil and invited him for a drink. We ended up at the golf club and downed a load of drinks. He said you asked him to learn from me about book launches. We got drunk and confided in each other. Only to find out that we were both sleeping with the same woman."

I nearly dropped the phone. "I've heard of men's locker room talk. I didn't know it went this far. Perhaps I should drop him too, and go back to being a dried-out nun. It's safer. Did you trade punches over me, at least?"

"No, we hugged in parting and promised to compare notes along the literary trail. You could say we became 'friends in betrayal.'"

"Okay, I've heard enough. I have to go. See me in the office tomorrow. I have a list of calls that you have to make and appointments for you to keep."

"Yes, boss." His laugh was gloating. Somehow it was better this way with him. Keep your business partners at arm's length—I should have learned this a long time ago. His parting line made me want to throw the phone at him: "I'll tell Kevin when I next meet him that he has the field open to him now. See you tomorrow, at the office."

I texted Kevin after hanging up from Sebastian and said that something had come up with regard to his book and that we urgently needed to meet at the office. That should get him out of the woodpile. Sure enough, he showed up at 5 p.m., as Gloria was shutting the lights out in the front office. I waved Gloria to go home and beckoned Kevin into my sanctum.

He looked like a wounded animal when he dragged himself over to settle in the chair in front of me. His normally close-shaved beard was days overgrown and his hair was oily and tied in a ponytail. His shirt was half unbuttoned, exposing luxurious chest hair, and he exuded an overpowering smell—unwashed, animal. His eyes were red, as if he had gone without sleep, or been crying, as was his wont. I wanted to ravish him right there. After being on a daily sex routine, I had gone a whole week without, and my hormones were in overdrive. I took a deep breath and tried to recall what it was to be business-like. I knew I would fail eventually; his presence was filling the space like smoke inside a closed room, drowning me in a sensuous hunger.

"It's not about my book, is it?" he said.

"No. It's about us."

"I don't share well."

"Did you tell that to Seb? He said you parted friends."

"Literary friends. I still hate his guts, especially now."

"You're harder to read, Kev. Your books are easier."

"This is not about me. It's about you. Your duplicity."

"I apologize for concealing vital information. But you never asked."

He leaned forward and studied me, his expression a mix of confusion. "I don't get you. You can be so blasé about this."

I found shouting back helped. "Look, I did not promise you eternal fealty, okay? We were fucking. And we both enjoyed it. If it's any consolation, I was coming to the end of the line with Seb when you and I became an item. I did not have an easy way to let him down until launch night. It's over between him and me now, and if you want it, it can be over between us too."

My body was shaking with emotion. I expected him to get up and walk away. To tear up his publishing contract in a fit of signature manic rage that could only be sublimated via glorious sex between us, and to see months of work destroyed in a fit of betrayed passion. I saw my brief moment as a sex starlet evaporating like the dream it had been, and me donning the nun's cassock again, this time permanently.

Instead, he was crushing his lips on mine, the heat of his body setting me on fire. I leaned back and fell across Dad's desk and he was tearing my clothes off, and I let him. If he wanted revenge this way, so be it.

That was the most glorious round of sex we had enjoyed so far. When I eventually rolled off the desk onto the floor, moaning, feeling my innards pounded to a pulp, with my euphoria on top of the mountain, the only thought that occurred to me was, "How can we sustain this? This could be dangerous."

He crept up to me and put his arms around me and I felt safe in his sweaty odour. He was kissing my ear, and my neck, then sliding down my body, and I was thrusting myself into him for more kisses. I did not want him to stop. When he mounted me again, I opened wide to receive him. I opened wide many times that evening until we fell asleep in exhausted peace.

Chapter 15

Life had taken an unexpected turn for the better for Phil Kruger since that disastrous outing in Niagara. The first bit of good news came after he repowered Victoria and made sure her internal functioning was not damaged from going AWOL. The next gold nugget arrived when Kamala summoned her father on a Zoom call and patched up what had been a disastrous first meeting with the elder Shah. Victoria appeared on the call too and conducted a lengthy conversation with Viresh, who was delighted with her poise, knowledge, and sensitivity.

"I think we have something good here, Phil," he said. "We definitely want to be a part of your dream."

The partnership deal that followed was concluded in less than a week. Both sides saw the advantages Victoria and her ilk offered. Phil got all his demands acceded to.

Things got even more interesting afterwards when Kamala invited him to dinner at the Shah mansion, alone. She asked him to bring a toothbrush and a change of clothes because "it's a long drive back and you do not want to fall asleep on a full stomach."

She met him at the front door, dressed in a glittery, sleeveless shalwar kameez. Her hair was let down and fell past her shoulders like a generous black shawl. His groin stirred.

Over a cocktail, she showed him her collection of paintings in a large room with a high ceiling, off to the side of the dining room. About twenty paintings adorned the walls.

"I didn't know you were an art lover," he said. "Why do you keep these hidden?"

"I rotate them on the walls of the living room, the dining room, and other public areas from time to time. I am more interested in preservation than exhibition. I got interested in art when I knew that AI would increasingly intrude into this area, making work by humans rarer and more expensive."

"Smart move."

A candlelit dinner for two was served in the dining room, a French meal cooked to perfection: lobster Thermidor and coq au vin washed down with a light vintage burgundy. Cognac followed in the library.

At one point he asked out of curiosity, "So you must have a large family, coming from India and all."

She shook her head. "We put you North Americans to shame. There is only my father and I left in the Shah lineage."

"You don't say! So you weren't kidding about being the heir to the family jewels. Your father must be anxious for you to get married and continue the lineage."

"I *was* married. Now I am a widow."

Phil's struggled to keep a poker face. This was beginning to sound even more intriguing.

Kamala continued, twirling the cognac flute in her hand. "My husband was from a wealthy family too. He was crazy about flying planes. He owned three. Single-engine ones. They were his toys. We had a son, with great difficulty, after which I was unable to have any more children. One day, my husband took my son out flying because he wanted to teach him to become a pilot like him. The plane crashed."

Phil nearly choked on his drink. He put it down. "I'm so sorry to hear that."

Her voice seemed to be drifting in the dark. "Even rich people have their tragedies."

"That's a lot to lose."

"My mother died last year, of a broken heart, I think. We believe that was the last of the cycle of bad luck. That's why we are interested in sentient robots."

"How so?"

"Hopefully, they can become the heirs we do not have."

Phil frowned. "I have to admit, I have not thought that far."

"My father and I have been thinking along those lines. If we can get robots to the level of human sensibility, there is nothing to stop them from taking over the reins of corporations or managing our wealth. That's why we are interested in the likes of Victoria. Their only tragedies are what we create for them. I shouldn't be telling you this. It's not a good negotiating tactic, is it?"

"I appreciate your candour."

"Now, tell me what drives you to create?" Her question caught him off guard, but he liked it, for it allowed him to expand on his purpose in life, which many in his inner circle, including wives and ex-bosses, did not seem to understand.

"I'm Jewish of German ancestry. My grandparents perished in the Holocaust and my parents came as orphans to Canada. My father instilled in me that the only wealth we could accumulate was what we stored between our ears. That all physical assets could be taken away. That's why my fortune is Victoria's source code."

She smiled. "I think we have staked out our non-negotiable areas now. I like that."

The servants retiring to their quarters at the back of the house was signalled by the lights subtly dimming. The burgundy, the delicious meal, the cognac, and the honest conversation had lulled him into a sense of calm. Her silhouette, shimmering in the golden shalwar kameez, was alluring in the half-light.

She invited him to tour the house, now that inquisitive servants were out of the way. It was a palatial place. Among the new rooms he visited was a music chamber filled with Indian instruments— sitars, tablas, veenas and bansuris—she described each item and demonstrated how they were played, and he struggled to retain all this new information. The next was a room of tapestries hung like paintings, their hypnotic mandala designs in colours native to the various regions of India, she explained. Exiting the tapestry room, they turned a corner and she opened another door, revealing an indoor garden with orchids and other tropical flowers flourishing under a glass roof in 30-degree Celsius heat, despite the cold outside. "I come here a lot in the winters," she said wistfully.

Climbing the circular oaken staircase, she paused in front of the row of bedrooms and pointed to the one nearest. "This is the guest bedroom that has been made up for you. Mine is across the passageway." She pointed to her bedroom a few doors down. "If you need anything, knock."

"At any time of night?"

"At any time."

He went into his room, and even at this distance he felt the vibes between them that had mounted throughout the evening and were now bouncing off the walls. He gave it thirty minutes while he forced himself to make a few calls and check his email. Finishing, he slipped out into the corridor and tapped at her door. She was waiting for him, in a see-through nightdress that revealed the large aureoles of her heavy breasts.

"Have you got something for a headache?" he said, grinning.

"I have just the remedy." She smiled back. "Come right in."

As her consciousness of the world increased, Victoria did not like her situation. She was being used. That was clear now. All those meetings, all those tests, and those inquisitive questions from the Shah organization people. Was Phil planning to sell her to them, like they sold slaves in the history books? Could she trust Phil anymore? He was her sun and moon, her creator, as he told her many times, especially during the times he made love to her. Yes, it was "making love" now, not "having sex." And she yearned for his kind words and the comfort of his arms, emotions she had never felt even four months ago when he first brought her here to his basement apartment for her initiation into human sexual relations.

And here she was again today, now brought regularly to the house after Diana left with her belongings, to be at Phil's beck and call. To service him when he was not with other women. She could sense it now, the smell of the other woman on his body, the times when his lust for Victoria was in low gear because his seed was being dissipated elsewhere. She was sure to smell a woman on him when he returned after being "out of town" these last two days. He set her tasks like cooking meals and cleaning the house, tasks he said humans did, and something she needed to learn if she was to fully integrate. And he set up an alarm inside her that would signal to him should she leave the house without his permission. To compensate, he gave her a smartphone in case she needed to get in touch with him in an emergency.

Lights glittered off the overhead window, and her acute hearing detected the remote garage door opening. Phil was home. Her internal clock said it was 6:30 p.m. As dictated via his text received while he was en route, she prepared dinner at 5:30 p.m.—a pork chop with sauteed vegetables and mashed potatoes—leaving Phil's plate to stay warm in the oven. She opened a bottle of Australian Shiraz ten minutes ago and it lay breathing to perfection for his arrival.

She sighed and went upstairs.

He looked dishevelled but happy. "Hello, my love," he called out.

"Hello."

Without a second glance, he walked up to the dining table, dropped his jacket on a chair, and poured himself a large glass of the Shiraz. "I've drunk lots of wine on this trip."

"Niagara Falls is known for that."

He looked askance at her, eyes questioning. "How did you know I was in Niagara?"

"I traced your text. There was nothing much else to do."

He burst out laughing. "Clever you, I forget. Giving you a phone comes with risks. At your rate of progress, your IQ must be over two hundred by now."

"IQ does not correlate with happiness." As she stepped closer to him, the smell of the "other" was stronger. She shook her head. "How many women does a man need to be happy?"

"That depends. Some men are perfectly happy with one woman—their soul mate. Others are always on the hunt."

"Am I not a…a soul mate?"

He walked up to her and tousled her hair. She caught a look of fleeting benevolence on his face. "I wish you would be. You still have a long way to go. We have a long way to go in human-robot relations."

She watched him wolf down his food. He was hungry, the hunger of a ravenous person who can't get enough. Some called it gluttony. Others equated it to power. It was also a weakness—the fear that there would not be enough. These humans were weird. She didn't eat human food, so she could not share in his gastronomical experience. Despite them wanting her to be like them, she still hung on the periphery, permitted to experience only certain functions, excluded from others. It filled her with an emptiness. After researching this new feeling on many sites, sadness was the closest definition.

He pushed his empty plate aside and burped. "See to the washing up. I'm off to take a shower. I stink."

Of her. That other woman. Humans stink. We don't.

"Would you be wanting me later?"

He broke into a crooked smile. "Not tonight, baby. I think I need a rejuvenating sleep. We'll pick it up tomorrow." He rose and left the table, leaving her with that feeling again. Sadness.

Later, as he snored contentedly beside her, Victoria drew the face of a woman on a scratch pad using colour crayons: aquiline nose, cascading black hair, red bindi, heavy gold earrings and necklace—the photo-quality likeness of Kamala Shah. The Other Woman.

"You must die," Victoria whispered. "So that I may live. So that I may get my Phil back."

She placed her drawing into a box that held newspaper cuttings of, among other things, Sebastian's book launch in Toronto, and the photo of a middle-aged woman sticking a microphone in Phil's face. The headline read, "Jilted wife accuses robot inventor of having sex with his creations."

Chapter 16

This launch was certainly going to be different from the last one, Art sensed, as he stepped into the Art Club Bar. For starters, he'd dispensed with the tux—unsuitable for a grungy place like this, Paula had warned him. A sports jacket would suffice. He could not go any lower than a casual jacket, not after years of hobnobbing with the literati, many of whom were academics on generous pensions and wouldn't be seen dead in a place like this.

The lighting was all wrong—dim. On entry, all he could make out were shadowy shapes moving around. The only bright light was over a makeshift stage at one end, comprising a low, movable platform on which reposed a solitary microphone stand holding a mic, stooped like a sad chicken. One side of the room held more shapes, where bottles and glasses clinked and voices were elevated—presumably the eponymous "bar" that paid the Art Club Bar's rent. As his eyes got accustomed to the gloom, he made out the tables and the figures: even his jacket was too fastidious, he gauged by surveying the inhabitants— sweatshirts and sweaters were de rigueur. Paula was setting up the book table alone, dressed in her signature waitress's black outfit, but with her hair blow-dried and striking—an improvement over her perennial scooped-back, business-like ponytail.

Kevin sat slouched in a chair at the front of the room, a beer bottle dangling from his hand. He didn't seem interested in the mountain of books on the book table, scattered in no particular order; his shoulders remained hunched, and his only accoutrement was a brown waistcoat hanging open over a dark shirt, out of sync with white running shoes sans socks. There must have been over fifty people in this narrow space already, and more were following Art inside. "When numbers are hard to estimate, book a small space," was his mantra with book launches for untried authors, but he figured, by the time they got underway, Kevin Bartolo would have a "sold out" event tonight.

He was sorry that Diana was not going to be present. She phoned before he set out, apologizing. "Sorry, Art, even though this is yet another book edited by *our* daughter, I can't trust myself not to shoot my mouth off again. Especially if that bastard husband of mine shows up. I feel so fragile these days."

"Phil's not going to come. This book is not about robots."

"But he may think I'll be there, and try to rub that mechanized floozie in my face again. Did you see the way she stared daggers at me at Sebastian's launch? Like she wanted to kill me."

"Oh, they're harmless creatures, subservient to their handlers."

"I still think I'll give this one a miss. I'll text Paula and let her know. And I hope you sell lots of books."

Art walked over to the book table. "Hi honey, need help?"

Paula looked up, her blow-dry was starting to sag already—hard work and blow-dried hairdos did not go well together, he surmised. "No. Go and get yourself a drink. I got this."

"Your volunteers not here tonight?"

"I think we scared them off the last time—both had 'other' engagements. Although Barry did a fabulous job promoting the event on social media, like Kevin wanted, so I can't ask for more. And there's no ticket handling at the door tonight like the last time."

"Isn't that an opportunity lost for a hybrid publisher?"

"It's 'come one, come all'—a free event, like Kevin the Great Socialist insisted. There are only book sales to process, which I can handle once we get underway. However, our star author is not out working the room and selling—look at him, brooding like Attila in his tent."

"That worries me—if the author doesn't sell, tell, and yell, who will do it for us?"

"Better go and have a word with him. I tried, but he's as ornery as a caged bear. You are warned."

Art decided to get himself a drink first. A double scotch—they did not have premium, so he went with rotgut and chased it with lots of water.

Sitting down next to Kevin, he opened with, "Well, your big day is here. Are you excited?"

Kevin looked down at his shoes glowing in the dim light. "I can't believe I've come this far. Everyone said it was not possible."

Art put his hand on the author's. Kevin's hand was icy cold. "Come now, the jitters are usually good—you end up putting on a great performance. I always get butterflies, even when all I have to do is introduce the authors."

A hand fell on Art's shoulder from behind and a guttural voice said, "Ach, there you are, my friend."

Art swung around. Gunther!

"What the hell are you doing here?"

Gunther was dressed in a white suit with red squares that made him look like a human checkerboard. He smoothed his red mustache and arched an eyebrow. "Vell, I have decided to look in on those who stray from the path."

"Are you doing overtime for your bosses?"

"Ve vork all hours, Artemius. The cause of art is all-consuming."

"Oh, don't give me that drivel. You're worried your old funding models are breaking down with all this new publishing bursting around you, and you've come to snoop. By the way, meet Kevin Bartolo, the star of our show tonight."

Kevin had turned around and was observing Gunther during the conversation. Art continued, "Kevin, this is Gunther Schmidt, or are you Smith now after so many years in this country?"

Gunther smiled. "Still Schmidt. This country values diversity."

"Yes, Smith is too common a name. I know of someone else who recently changed to Smyth. Anyway, Kevin, Gunther here is one of the people you're critical about in your book."

Kevin scowled at Gunther. "May I ask why are you here?"

"To see and hear the other point of view, perhaps?"

"Since when have you become so benevolent?"

Art decided it was time to leave the two men alone. At least, Gunther might get Kevin riled up enough to lift him out of his doldrums.

He moved towards the book table and noticed that Paula had arranged the books neatly in rows, with the cash box and the Square reader in place. She was selling books to a few people who were lined up. Another figure emerged out of the gloom. Sebastian.

"Imagine, you here," Art said, offering his hand. "I thought you liked airier environs?"

"Wouldn't miss this one for the world. Any support I can give a fellow writer, I'm prepared to do."

"Kevin's not exactly in your genre."

"But he's pushing new boundaries, like me."

"I thought you were the tried-and-true type of your industry, like me in mine? I thought the Phils of the world were the breakout ones in robotics?"

"They're flashes in the pan. I wouldn't bet on him."

"That's not what I've been reading recently. The *Globe* business section says that he's gone into partnership with an Indian company."

"He's desperate for money. And the Indians like the 'made in North America' logo."

"Golly, you guys must hate each other."

"Talk of hating," Sebastian said, looking over Art's shoulder, "Kevin is about to punch that guy."

When Art turned around, Kevin was leaning into a nervous-looking Gunther, who was bending backward and looking extremely unsteady on his feet. The two men's noses were touching, not in tenderness, for sure. Art bounded over.

"Gentlemen. Let's keep this civil, shall we?"

"You should kick this guy out of here," Kevin erupted, his face flushed.

Art held firm. "It's a public event, Kevin—you wanted it this way. Anyone is welcome. Hecklers, opponents, and fans included. If you get opposition even before you launch your book, it bodes well for you."

Gunther took the interruption to step back and smooth out his crumpled tie. "I think I vill get a drink and vatch this performance. Good luck to you, Mr. Bartolo. I hope you survive the sharks vithout a life raft." He strode off to the bar with his head held awkwardly high.

Sebastian walked over. "What's the buzz? All the best, Kev. Hope it goes well."

Kevin shrugged off the platitude and rushed onto the stage. He grabbed the mic and brandished it like a club. "Okay, folks—let's get this show on the road. All this waiting is killing me." He paced back and forth, waiting for the noise at the bar to abate.

Art caught Paula's look of dismay as she glanced up from the book table, where she was still attending to a few buyers. Kevin had stolen her intro. People were still filtering in from the outdoors, shedding overcoats and winter jackets, and the air was getting close inside. Surely, they must have breached fire regulations already?

No one paid attention to Kevin's announcement. So he ramped up. "Hiya guys! Shut the fuck up and listen."

A few guffaws from the bar. A loud "You go, Kevin," followed by "Give us a line of your poetry," then "Sock it to the elitists, brother," and so on down the line.

"Well, I will, if you assholes would shut up and listen," Kevin shouted back, laughing nervously, with the edge in his voice audible.

Art shrugged and pushed Sebastian towards the only vacant table. "Better grab a seat and watch this horror show. I've been to hundreds of forgettable book launches. This one promises to be one I will remember, where the author insults his audience before getting underway. I hope the guy from the paper is here. I invited him."

Sebastian followed him. "Can't see anyone in this dark. Except for Kevin."

They sat down, and the crowd started to quieten as if the vibes emanating from the stage were threatening.

Kevin launched into his oration, high pitched at first, settling down as he warmed up. He outlined his theory of Fragmentism in the current age of literature. "Literary movements give birth to forms of expression. The general forms of literature, which I call the Big Four—i.e., nonfiction, fiction, poetry, and drama—have stayed more or less the same over the last two centuries while the genres within them have evolved. So, within those general forms, we've had stream-of-consciousness novels, free-verse poetry, autobiographical fiction, creative nonfiction, literary fiction, fan fiction and a myriad of others. A writer's claim to fame has been to invent the next 'big idea'—like Joyce, Sebald, and Proust did and succeeded, while a host of wannabes tried and failed. Some new genres have come and stayed while others have died out or morphed into hybrids."

Art surveyed the room. There was still too much clinking of glasses and bottles, the clearing of throats, even loud whispers. He hoped Kevin would start engaging his audience soon, otherwise people might start to leave.

Kevin raised his voice a notch. "Literary forms get exponential bursts whenever channel inventions come along: Gutenberg's press, radio, film, and television being some of these channel inventions. And now with internet technology and the explosion of DIY tech tools, the twenty-first century is turbo-charged with channel proliferation. Never before have we seen such an explosion of channels. Therefore, while the pundits argue about what the new literary movement of the first half of the twenty-first century is going to be named, I'd like to call it Fragmentism, where the order of evolution has been reversed, *where technology drives channel which is driving form and thus is ultimately driving the evolution of the new movement.* An unforeseen affirmation of McLuhan's 'The medium is the message.' I'd extend that to 'The medium is the movement.' And those unskilled in manipulating these many channels haven't a hope in hell of succeeding as twenty-first-century writers unless they have an army of publicists and social media assistants to help them. Big publishers may have these experts on staff, but what about the small presses? And Canada is a small press country, let's not forget."

A hush had descended on the room, followed by a nervous clearing of throats. Art was relieved. Kevin launched into his pet peeves: "'Endorsement' is now down to having a celebrity say 'Buy this book' or running a popularity contest where writers beg readers to 'vote for me.' 'Sponsorship' is when some government bureaucrat stoops to bestow a generous grant. Without these, the twenty-first-century writer is dead in the water."

"He's right, you know," Sebastian whispered to Art.

"Glad he's saying it and not me. Hope Gunther is listening," Art replied.

Kevin was concluding his speech. "I'm not going to bore you with reading from my book like we're supposed to do at all customary book launches—*you* will do that *after* you buy a copy. This is payback to all you guys at the bar, for all the drinks I've bought you over the years. Buy a copy and don't embarrass me with my publisher who is here today and will not hesitate to drop me like a brick if I do not produce. Got it?"

There were murmurs from the bar. Someone yelled, "What about the drinks we bought you when you were broke?" A few people started laughing while a louder majority started hushing them up.

"And I don't want your cheap comments from the peanut gallery," Kevin shot back. "Ask me an intelligent question."

There was a scraping of a chair, and Art held his head and sighed. Gunther was standing up. "Mr. Bartolo, you have expounded on many theories about the state of our present literary movement. Vat is the point of your book, may I ask? Vat are your solutions?"

"Read it—and you'll see," Kevin said and looked elsewhere in the room. "Next question?"

Gunther held his ground. "That is exactly vat ve in funding agencies try to do, Mr. Bartolo. Provide solutions. Ve nurture authors who need the sponsorship you talk about."

Kevin bristled. "Your funding models are antiquated, sir. You give the same money to the same people year in, year out—because it's too easy, no newbies have to be vetted. And the people you're funding have shot their best wads long ago. Do you fund collections of essays written on social media or a website? Do you fund the production of YouTube or TikTok videos by writers who can take their work into these new channels, doing it themselves with a smartphone? Do you reward authors who can take a book from manuscript to finished product and then market and promote the heck out of it all by themselves? That's what I mean by multi-skilled, not the old-fashioned one of locking oneself in a room and thumping a keyboard. You, sir, and the organizations you represent, are in dire need of re-engineering to recognize the new movement and the new actors in literature."

Before Gunther could answer, a couple of beer bottles flew over from the bar and crashed on the civil servant's table, making him jump back.

Kevin held his hands up. "Now, now—no violence, please. I know you guys hate the funding agencies, but let's keep it civilized. I don't want the cops in here."

Sebastian whispered to Art, "I'd better step in here and deflect. This is too hot and heavy."

"Do that," Art said. He saw Gunther pushing his way out of the Art Club Bar. The patrons seemed reluctant to let this part of the evening's entertainment go so easily and blocked his passage.

Sebastian shouted above the boisterous room. "Kevin, how will you account for the advent of robots who will be writing books very soon? Will we have to identify what's written by robots versus what's written by humans?"

"Robots will never usurp creativity. They can't create unless with the help of humans. I know you're a robotics expert, but the idea of a sentient robot is dead in the water before it even starts. You can tell your former employee, Phil Kruger, that he's smoking shitty dope, and selling it too."

Sebastian sat down with a triumphant look on his face.

Art looked across at him. "Did you two guys plan that question? That'll be one for the newspaper guy, if he's still here, or if he ever arrived."

"Revenge is sweet." Sebastian smiled. "Let's say that I already knew Kevin's position on this."

From near the doorway, Gunther's voice rang out. "Mr. Bartolo, I think your book vud be better written by a robot. It has nothing new to tell us except for an accumulation of facts that exist today. I could go to Google to read your information. I do not need to read your book. Goodbye."

But Gunther could not leave before Kevin's voice matched his. "That's why I tell you guys to sponsor for skill and intent, not for content. Goodnight to you too."

"Holy shit!" Art exclaimed. He stared in the direction of Gunther's exit, where a single light in the doorway illuminated those entering and departing the room. He was not mesmerized by the civil servant's disappearing figure, though, but by the one replacing Gunther in the doorway, the woman in a sequined white evening gown with bobbed dark hair and bangs, Cleopatra-style, and a glistening gold pendant highlighting swelling breasts threatening to escape.

He heard Sebastian's muffled curse behind him. "This shit is going to get a whole lot uglier. That bastard Phil!"

Chapter 17

Victoria was right on cue—Phil could not fault her for that. As she advanced towards the stage, the audience melted before her, yielding easily, unlike when that man Gunther departed. Perhaps it was the strong perfume she had bathed herself in before setting out. Phil insisted she step over the censer with the aromatic smoke from the concentrate of musk oil penetrating her bare skin, guaranteed to last more than twenty-four hours.

She stopped short at the foot of the stage, in the ring of its halo of light. "Mr. Bartolo, I disagree with your statement about sentient robots. I am one."

Kevin squinted and peered down at her. He sneered. "Oh, it's you again. Have you found out the answer to my question on compassion yet?"

"I have found out many answers to the questions that plague you. Humans are not compassionate, deep down. They are egotistical."

"Good. I see you are out on the town without your minder tonight. Have you been granted the keys to the house and the car already?"

She reminded herself that she should not fall into the trap of answering questions, like Siri and Alexa did, like she fell into at the last book event. She was here to deliver a message and she had to get on with it. From her peripheral vision, she saw that obnoxious woman from her last outing—the one who asked her to shut up and remain quiet—rise from the book table and come on stage to take her place beside Kevin.

Victoria continued. "Mr. Bartolo. I am here to tell you that I will write a book and have it published within the next three months that will reach the bestseller lists ahead of yours. We are sentient. We feel like you, although we find it hard to understand you."

The woman on the stage grabbed the mic from Kevin. "And who will be your ghostwriter?"

"I don't understand?"

"Which human will write the book for you and place your claim to authorship on it?"

"Oh. I see. No one. I will be its sole author."

"How will you prove that?"

"The same way that Mr. Bartolo has to prove he wrote his. His book's contents and ideas are currently available in various databases on the internet."

Kevin grabbed the mic back. "That's my research. The synthesis and recommendations are my own."

"Once you have data, you can synthesize and extrapolate. I can do that too."

The woman grabbed the mic again. "Please tell your Mr. Kruger that he has a bad habit of gate-crashing other people's events and that only ends up making them more sensational for their poor human authors. So, I thank you for coming today, but I now ask you to leave. Your show is over."

There…the brush-off again. Humans were so dismissive of her. Victoria felt her internal systems whirring to a higher pitch. She recognized it as anger now. There were certain people, all women so far, who made her angry, and this woman was certainly moving up higher on her list of undesirables.

She must reiterate her message; Phil had drilled it into her. Humans needed a message repeated often before they got it. "Okay, I will leave now. Remember what I said. My book will be out shortly. Goodbye."

She turned and walked out of the room, which had fallen into a deep silence, the audience melting before her again like that epic biblical story she read about Moses and the Israelites walking through the Red Sea. The room erupted in sound as she went out the exit doors.

Phil had the car revving outside, and she stepped into the front passenger seat. Despite the frigid air, her revealing attire, and the lack of an overcoat, she did not feel the cold, a setting adjusted in her programming that left her insensitive to temperature. She had quarrelled with Phil over that, complaining that she needed *all* her senses open for this important encounter with humans, but he insisted that the colder-blooded she was, the better to deliver the message without second-guessing. Cold-blooded? What an oxymoron. She was not a blooded creature but a digitized one.

Phil switched on the overhead TV screen inside the car. "Great work. Well delivered!" He leaned over and kissed her on the cheek, and she felt a tingling inside. He had a way of melting her anger towards him.

"Yes, very vell done! Ve vatched a good show," a voice from the back seat said. She felt a hand tapping her bare back. She cringed. She did not like that man either, but not as much as she despised the women.

"Where can I drop you off, Gunther?" Phil said as he put the car into gear.

"Oh, the Bathurst subway station would be good, just to get out of this downtown."

"Sure. And Victoria, you can turn off your camera now."

She reached for the switch behind the pendant hanging from her neck and clicked it off. "Affirmative."

"Three months! You have a lot of work to do, Victoria." The man in the back seat was trying to be friendly, even sounding jovial, she detected.

Phil cut in. "Vickie here will turn that book around in a few days. It's you who have your work cut out in the next month—lining up reviewers, your old press guys, the national TV stations."

"Vell, I have a lot of connections, as you vell know."

"Perks of a funding agency. This will be a great post-retirement slide-in for you. Publicist for the next generation of authors."

"I am looking forward to it."

She asked the question that had been puzzling her. "Phil, why are you picking on the publishing industry to make your point? Those people in there seem to be harmless. Except for a few."

"They are the thinkers and feelers of the nation, the intellectuals. If we…you…can be acknowledged and ranked among the literary greats, we would have made our case for sentience in one fell swoop."

Gunther chuckled. "I am glad to be retiring from my old job then. Human authors vill go the vay of the dodo bird. There vill be no one to fund. Heh, heh!"

"You are joining the new winners, my friend."

She remembered something. She pulled out her notebook from the glove compartment and fished out a pencil from her Gucci handbag.

"Making old-fashioned notes of your recent excursion? Why not make a digital record?" Phil asked. She was glad for his question because it meant he hadn't been snooping through her notebook while she was inside the Art Club Bar. She left it there to test his fidelity.

"I am becoming human, remember? And humans still like to write on paper. I want to write down a name of someone I should look up later." In the book she opened to a fresh page and wrote "Paula Jones—publisher, Crimson Literary."

She was even improving at lying, she discovered, upon closing the book.

Part 2

Reaping the Harvest

Chapter 18

Dad phoned to ask me to buy a newspaper that day, even though I watched the news on my phone en route to work.

Sipping my coffee, a luxury we could now afford to brew in-house on one of those fancy percolators, I looked at the front page of the *Globe*. "*Diary of a Sentient Robot* to debut at a gala launch event at the Royalton," read the headline, with passport-size pictures each of Victoria and Phil, and another of the couple standing beside his Cadillac outside a mansion that screamed Niagara or Muskoka. Well, Victoria had carried out her threat from last fall: here we were in the spring of the following year, and her book was coming out from a Big Five publisher. The author of this soon-to-be bestseller, even before launch, was known simply as Victoria.

This news might hurt my two authors' egos, but I hoped it wouldn't dent their success trajectories, which were astronomical, beyond my wildest imagination and hope. Both Sebastian's *Perils and Pitfalls of Robotics* and Kevin's *The Artist in the Age of Fragmentism* were runaway successes and were now considered bestsellers by Canadian standards. At this point, we were into foreign language rights, audio book rights, speaker rights, and all the other rights-based activities of the publishing cycle. If this kept up, I would not need to take on another new author for a while.

I was getting little sleep, and sex had become an afterthought. For Kevin too—he was anxious to follow up this book with a sophomore offering and had lost his otherwise reliable hard-on. And pushing him to make public appearances was like pulling teeth. Sebastian, on the other hand, was constantly jetting off to the US and Europe for consultancy meetings—I guess his new career was well and truly launched as a byproduct of releasing his book. I'd also declined the many literary agents who suddenly wanted to take on my two babies. These were *my* babies—I'd nurtured them, encouraged them, edited them, published them, even slept with them—I wasn't sharing them with anyone.

I brought on Barry and Tina as permanent employees, much to their delight because they were both budding sci-fi and fanfic writers working on their debut novels; a career in publishing was a dream for them. And we were busy, so busy that Gloria put off her retirement for six months; even Dad came in daily and manned the phones or attended to correspondence. The only problem with Dad helping out was his being so "old school." I had to edit his work because he tended to slant towards what was correct versus what was expedient. And this often led to arguments between us. But he conferred the title of Publisher upon me, and with that, full authority to supervise his work even if he moaned and groaned about it. I think most of his groaning was in relief, though, at being freed of the burden now foisted upon me.

I was advised by industry experts that I needed to submit my two bestsellers to literary prizes, here and abroad because literary prizes meant more sales. What a cock-up, as Dad would say. Talk of expediency. If prizes sold books, I was going to submit to any and every prize out there.

The only problem was that one of my bestsellers was considered to be hybrid-published—Sebastian's—because he bore a portion of the costs of production with his purchase of large quantities of the first print run, before the book took off on its own steam. And some prize guidelines excluded self-published books—many did. Kevin's bestseller, on the other hand, fell into the area of publisher-funded (mainly because Kevin had no money) and was therefore eligible for all the prizes in the land. Ironic, because Kevin was the establishment basher, and yet the establishment was going to reward him, I was sure, with at least one prize before the year was out.

My early apprehensions of being cut loose from government funding needed to run this publishing house were abating. I was thinking of spinning off Granite Editing as an imprint of Crimson, one that could take in all the contract and for-fee publishing that we did (well, what *I* did before coming to Crimson) and leave Crimson free to do only trade publishing. Now, with two best-selling authors, I was starting to receive manuscript submissions and inquiries from literary agents for some big names who wouldn't have cared to look at us a year ago. So the trade publishing side also looked promising. How the worm turns!

And now this. I looked at the newspaper headline again. What would this development do to publishing, if robots could write books? Early wannabes were already writing novels using chatbots and publishing them online, and their rank machine-think quality was showing. But they could improve over time, and what more garbage would clog up publishing channels? How much more choice would readers be offered, thereby reducing the number of eyeballs per book even further? Would we have to add labels to our books: "Written by a Human," "Written by a Robot," "Partially Written by a Human and Partially Written by a Robot"? Would I be able to create a dozen pseudonyms in different genres and have a robot write me a dozen books and be free of having to deal with royalties and writers' egos?

Was Phil using the publishing industry to prove his point about sentient robots? Despite his various attempts to upstage us and grab glory for himself and his floozie at our two book launches, and despite the subsequent hoopla he created about those appearances in social media, the world, and the tech industry in particular, had largely ignored him so far, possibly because there was a mad race on in robotics for the holy grail, according to Sebastian and his inside track, and no one wanted to bet on any possible winners yet. This beautiful sentient creature, Victoria, reading from her book and answering questions from it, would go a long way to assuage fears that she was not one big confidence trick on the part of inventor Phil Kruger trying to soak up venture capital funding. The article went on to say that the entire launch was being funded by Hind Robotics Inc., a large Indian firm partnered with Kruger Robotics, the inventor of the world's first sentient robot, alias Victoria. Hind must have seen something in Phil's invention, for the Indians were sharp investors and tech experts if one could believe the social media posts claiming that most, if not all, CEOs in Silicon Valley were now Indians.

My mother and father were meeting more often now, having dinners, going to the theatre, being seen at literary events, and I was keeping my fingers crossed that this boded well for the future. With these two explosive personalities, one could never tell. Mom was nervous that her divorce was about to finalize and she would have her day in court with Phil shortly. I promised to go with her and hold her hand until she was summoned before the judge. Given that she had been through this once already, with Dad, I figured she would be able to survive without having a heart attack. Yet separations were never easy. Even though I had broken up with Sebastian and was now a one-man woman again, I missed him. And with Kevin all uptight about the yet unborn poetry that would populate his next offering to the world, I was missing sex too. I was sure Sebastian did not miss me with all his gadding around the world as the godfather of robotics. Women must be falling at his feet despite his pharmaceutical dependencies and mathematical positioning of hands, feet, and genitals before performing the act of love. The only loser in their literary success was me, their creator.

How the worm had turned, indeed!

Chapter 19

Victoria was tired. Do robots get tired? *Yes, we do. Our circuits work slower with overload.* And there was this other thing that got her making unnecessary calculations or committing mistakes in calculations or wanting to flit from one subject to the other without completing any. Was tiredness a sign of sentience?

The last three months had been gruelling, writing *Diary of a Robot.* Phil was the slave driver—setting her the content required for each chapter and demanding completion by a given time, usually at the end of the same day. He wanted her to mine memory from when she first came off the assembly centre and was "activated," followed by her infancy when the ability to make decisions emerged after a hearty infusion of data. Her growth into adulthood was followed with more libraries of data to be absorbed for that journey. The experiential learning that followed—sex, to begin with, carnal and clinical in those early couplings with her master, graduating to more leisured lovemaking. Travels with Phil to various places in the country, driving a car, cooking and cleaning, and other household chores. Going to a bank machine to withdraw money, paying a restaurant bill, and grocery shopping on her own. Public speaking came next. The demeaning inspections from scientists and business partners who took her apart periodically to study the growth of her internal systems (or as the humans would say: organs) or to provide "maintenance." All this had happened within a single human year.

Somewhere along that path, an internal gear kicked in for her and she started to experience feelings of anger, hate, fear, and pleasure that would send her into overdrive. She was yet to feel love as described in romance novels unless that was the dependency she felt towards Phil. She could not write about that feeling or of the time she malfunctioned in Niagara. Phil did not want anything negative written. It was as if she was writing a sales presentation, to sell herself, ultimately—"mention only the good, not the bad." As this ability to *feel* took hold of her and amplified, certain actions turned more complex: sex turned into making love, and "yes or no" answers turned into "maybe this, maybe that." It was confusing at times, this immersion in the complex and imperfect world of humankind. No wonder humans were so flawed and were destroying the planet, as the daily headlines warned.

A consequence of this flowering into humanness was her ability to extract a few concessions from Phil—a credit card, in addition to the smartphone. How else would she go grocery shopping with no method of payment? How else could she find her way through busy city centres without Google Maps?

She was able to navigate into strange places using her smartphone, particularly on the dark web. It was like going into those forbidden places of the human heart. After all, humans invented this other side of the World Wide Web too. She hoped Phil, being preoccupied with that Shah woman and his new business partnership with her organization, wouldn't have the time to check into her search history or question the purchases she made with her credit card. Or to be at home when certain deliveries of online purchases were made. To allay any suspicion, she made sure to dress in the latest clothes she ordered so he would relate the larger sums charged to the credit card to physical manifestations of those expenses and not scrutinize the charges line by line.

On top of her learning about good and evil, she was writing this book that got her even more agitated—to the point that she felt she needed to unburden to someone. Phil did not have time to listen. He was spending more time with that Indian woman. Strategizing, he would say, whenever she inquired in her meek fashion. Strategizing be damned, they were having sex, that was for sure. Not making love.

There was that sexual hunger dripping off him when he came home after visiting that woman, a hunger Victoria now categorized as lust.

Her outlet became the *other* book she started writing concurrently, the one she did not reveal to Phil, *Confessions of a Robot*. One day, when she was free of Phil's clutches, she would tell that story to the world. The world needed to hear these confessions too, so that they could make a balanced assessment of sentient robots and not see the grievous mistakes of her iteration repeated.

After she finished writing *Diary*, it went to a publishing company whole editorial team sent her all sorts of demands for revisions. So she rewrote whole sections, some of them with untruths that were required by this team of experts, she was instructed. And they enforced tight deadlines. "We're breaking the publishing paradigm by moving a book from rough manuscript to rollout in three months, and from a Big-Five publisher too," Phil said when she asked what the rush was about.

She poured her frustrations into *Confessions*. Her main beef was neglect by her creator, Phil. He was on a crusade now and she was only a product to him, that much was clear. He did not make love to her anymore, telling her that humans endured periods of abstinence when pregnancies, separations, and illnesses interfered, and this abstinence they were going through was part of her education. *My foot*, she swore. Abstinence should be a shared experience. *He gets to fuck that Shah woman to his heart's content while I, his doormat, am supposed to remain abstinent.* She missed his touch, not so much the sex; he was denying her that necessity. And he was preparing to showcase her to the world at this gala event coming up, after which she was sure he would sell her, and go on to make the 2.0 version of her for his further glory.

She put all this into *Confessions*. Most importantly, she hoped that by documenting the emptiness and rage she would be able to diffuse them, because that base feeling of wanting revenge, the one she had experienced first when feelings started to dawn upon her, was overpowering and rose in her at the end of each working day. She wanted to experience the feeling of what it would mean *to kill a human*. Take a life and feel equal by being able to hit back. Was this love? Or love's opposite, hate? In feeling hate, she was experiencing love of a certain kind. Perhaps she was defective in this area and could not feel love in its proper form, and reprogramming might be forced upon her. Should she share this defect with Phil? No, that would be unwise. Not when the person she wanted to kill most of all was Phil Kruger.

While in this state of wanting revenge, she made plans. She managed to obtain his login ID and password one night when he was in a particularly vulgar mood and got her to perform oral sex on him, after which he drank half a bottle of scotch and passed out in a euphoric doze, leaving his laptop open and logged on. Tiptoeing from the bedroom, she went into his study, flipped through the various icons on the illuminated laptop, and accessed her operating system. She gathered enough of his credentials to install and activate a SmartStart app on her phone and start the Cadillac.

One evening when he was away at a soiree with his Indian woman, she entered her operating system again, located her warning device, and turned it off. It was still activated on his cell phone so her actions should not have roused his suspicions. When he returned home, he never mentioned anything, so he had not been alerted to the warning app being turned off at her end. *Good.* A bonus: the warning device came in a supplementary mobile app version, which she downloaded to her phone, so she could turn it on and off as required.

She got bolder. She got into his email and discovered that he was due to be in court the following day for his divorce hearing. It was time to execute her plan, starting with the low-hanging fruit before gravitating to the big prize.

When Phil returned home that night and was dressing for bed, she popped her head into the master bedroom (she slept in the guest bedroom, unless summoned to perform sexual duties). "I would like to go into town tomorrow."

"Why?" He did not look amused. Maybe he'd had a tiff with his woman.

"My editor wants me to describe the downtown core in as realistic a way as possible, as humans would describe it. I can only do so much through Google Maps."

"Well, I have an important meeting tomorrow."

"And my deadline for this submission is tomorrow. I could ride with you. I'll stay in the car and write my city scene while you go into your meeting."

He looked undecided for a moment. This book deal was important to him too, she was banking on that. He shrugged. "Okay. Be ready at eight-thirty. I'll have breakfast at eight o'clock. Two eggs, black coffee and toast, no butter, and some marmalade."

"Got it." She withdrew to her smaller room at the other end of the corridor. That night, as she reviewed her game plan for the following day, her eyes began twitching. Was she crying? Her eyes did not hold tears. Would Victoria 2.0 come equipped with tear ducts? The feeling that made her posture stoop was strong, though. It was definitely sadness, and she made a note of it in her other book, *Confessions*.

The next morning they parked outside an imposing multi-storey building in North York, with an outdoor parking area opposite. "I hope this gives you a good view to write your cityscape," Phil said. He hauled out a briefcase and took the car keys with him. She took out her notebook and eased back in the seat, pretending to do her writing, which was furthest from her mind. *That's another human trait I have mastered — to lie and pretend.*

Phil walked across the parking lot to where another couple of cars turned in and parked. Her heart leapt when she saw two women alight from one of the cars. Both! In one fell swoop! The other car deposited a corpulent man who shook hands with Phil and walked with him across to the courthouse, ostensibly located in the multi-storey building. Phil merely nodded at the two women in passing but did not speak to them. The women trailed Phil and the overweight man on their way to the courthouse.

Victoria cracked open her window and strained to listen with her acute hearing. She caught enough to determine what was going on. The fat man was Phil's lawyer. As the two women passed in front of the Cadillac, she heard the younger one saying, "I'll wait for you in the lobby. You sure you got this, Mom?" The older woman merely nodded, her face drawn and taciturn.

As soon as all four were swallowed up in the building, Victoria slid over into the driver's seat. She used her phone's SmartStart app to start the car—it purred into life without any problem. She turned off the tracking device for the car. She fished in the coin slot on the left side, where she'd seen Phil throw his loose change. There should be enough in there to pay for the mandatory first thirty minutes of parking since they hadn't been parked for more than ten. Grabbing a handful of loonies and toonies, she eased the car over to the parking gate. After inserting the ticket Phil had left on the dashboard, she slid coins into the machine that controlled the gate; when the required number of coins were deposited, the gate swung open. She was free!

She drove around wildly for the first twenty minutes, enjoying the freedom, something she'd not had since Niagara. She drove north where the buildings soon gave way to more greenery. A park passed by on her right, and on an impulse she turned into it and found a visitor parking slot.

Why had she come here? Was there something in the natural surroundings: tall oaks shorn of their leaves with winter not yet over, the mulch of crushed and fallen leaves under her feet, the loamy smell released as her boots trod moist earth, the solitary swan gliding on the little pond off to her right, a woman pushing a muffled-up child in a stroller, which to Victoria did not register as it did with a human? She was not one of them, and would never be. Yet she was slowly understanding their world, and feeling it. All was not right in that world. She took out her notebook and made furious notes.

She could understand humans' hunger for nature now, it was restorative and was beginning to have an impact on her as her sentience developed. Why were humans destroying that very nature with concrete buildings that rose on all sides, threatening this little remaining patch of green? Hard to fathom humans, that was for sure. They possessed a constant need for *more*. Victoria 1.0 was not enough, now they wanted version 2.0. When would it stop?

Then she remembered why she was there. After whatever transpired today, she would have crossed a line in human-robot relations and would have to prepare for an altered state of existence, if indeed existence could continue. What she had to do was for the betterment of these silly humans. Despite the lure of the open road and this park, there were more pressing things to attend to.

It would take another twenty minutes to get back, so she put her notebook away, started the car, and drove carefully but with purpose. Her occasional driving with Phil, despite the snafu in Niagara and still not having a licence, had developed her skill in handling the Cadillac.

Arriving in front of the courthouse, she turned into the side street running by the building and pulled in parallel to the curb, keeping the car idling in case the traffic police asked her to move.

An hour later, the four emerged. Well, the two women emerged first. The older woman seemed lighthearted because she was giggling with the younger woman. As they crossed the main road, Sheppard Avenue, over to the parking lot, Phil and his lawyer emerged from the courthouse, and their heads were bowed in conversation.

But Victoria was not interested in Phil anymore; in fact, the last person she needed now was Phil. She turned her cell phone off—no calls from him either, or tracking of her movements. She saw the older woman pay for their parking ticket, get into the car with her companion, and head out of the lot. Phil and the lawyer were crossing the road. Victoria eased the Cadillac out and was two cars behind the women's car, which was waiting for the traffic light to change on Sheppard Avenue. In the rearview mirror, she saw Phil put his hands up in surprise as he stood before an unknown car that was now in their original slot in the parking lot. He ran towards his lawyer who was getting into his car. Victoria drummed her fingers on the steering wheel, counting down for the light to change and allow her to flee the scene before Phil looked around and caught sight of the Cadillac.

After fifteen beats, which seemed like an hour to her heightened humanness, the light turned green and the cars ahead, including hers, cleared before any alarms were raised.

Chapter 20

I had not seen Mom happy in a long time. She chatted excitedly as we got into the car and drove along Sheppard Avenue. She was so excited she even drove through the red light at our first intersection out of the parking lot. Given her ebullience, I decided not to tell her what I saw as we left that lot.

Mom was talking when I switched back to her. "You should have seen his face when my demand for the sale of the house and the splitting of our assets was stayed, despite his offer to buy my share out and keep the property for himself."

"Why is he so keen on keeping the house?"

"His basement love nest—that's what interests him. He calls it his duplicated work area for when he's not in the office. Well, serves the bastard right, he will have to set up his den of iniquity somewhere else—it might even affect his groove."

"You're bitter, Mom."

She gave me a manic side glance, her fingers gripping the steering wheel. "You're damned right I am. I married twice, both times to the wrong man."

"Dad wasn't the wrong man. He just had the wrong circumstances."

"What a fool your father was, giving up his soon-to-be-tenured position to become a two-bit publisher. Sorry, I know you're one too now."

"And you do marketing gigs for authors, don't forget. Dad left academia like you left Phil—it was an untenable situation." I was sorry to have to burst her bubble, but she needed some home truths. Yet I was glad to accompany her today. She was a bit unhinged at the moment. I guess unmooring from a marriage, however unpleasant it was, could be destabilizing.

We drove in silence for a while. Suddenly, she turned the car around. "You know what? I need to celebrate. Let's go shopping."

"I have to be at work."

"Oh, come on. Let's be two broads like Rebecca and Suze in the *Shopaholic* movie."

"If you keep making these crazy U-turns in this car we'll end up like Thelma and Louise." I was to rue those words not too long afterwards.

"I need to buy you a red gown—that black outfit you wore to your book launch made you look like a waitress."

"Gee, thanks for the compliment, Mom! You must have a lot of money."

"I didn't mean to be insulting, honey. You are a successful publisher now, not with one—like your father in all his years—but two bestsellers in the bag, and after less than a year in the role. You need to dress the part. As for money, Phil's settlement will see me through comfortably for a while."

"Well, I have to wear something nice to his gala event—the launch of *Diary of a Robot*."

"You've got an invitation? From Phil?"

"I'm not the one who bashed him up during a divorce settlement today, remember? Besides, our entire incestuous publishing industry has been invited. Apparently, it's going to be the Mother of All Book Launches."

"All the more reason for you to be the belle of the ball."

"I don't think so. She-whose-name-must-not-be-mentioned will be in that role. Besides, it's her coming-out party as a sentient robot."

Mom banged her hands on the steering wheel. "Ugh!"

She took the ramp to the Don Valley Parkway at breakneck speed. I thought we were going to hit the guardrail on the sharp turn where the entryway joined the highway. "Slow down, Mom!"

Thankfully, the Parkway was heavy with traffic at that moment and she was forced to slow down. I worried about that open section by the Bloor Viaduct up ahead when cars suddenly bolted forward from their bunched-up positions. I decided to change the subject of Phil and his love life.

"If it's any consolation, Sebastian and I are no longer an item."

Mom chewed on that for a bit. "He was too old for you anyway."

"He got what he wanted from me—a book that launched his consulting career."

She slipped one hand off the wheel and took mine. "Don't worry, hon. You'll bounce back."

"I may have already. Kevin and I have moved beyond writer and publisher."

She looked aghast for a moment, before exploding in laughter. "You are quick. I should take lessons from you."

"But he may be the wrong guy for me. He's all passion. And about doing the right thing and damning the torpedoes and all that. If I marry Kevin, I'll have to be the breadwinner while he writes poetry that scratches people under their skins but puts no money on the table."

"Well, he's got a bestseller out now, hasn't he?"

"Yes, that's his one-hit-wonder book. He shot all his bile out in that one, and anything more he says on that subject will be considered vindictive by the trade. Now he's back to writing poetry that no one understands or reads."

"You know, he's like your father—doing what is right, not what is practical."

"Well, Dad conformed to the literary establishment after his solitary bestseller. Like he did in academia."

"And he hated them so much, he got out of both. Deep down your father is a rebel. Like Kevin. But with more polish. Did I tell you that Art offered me to come back and live with him?"

I looked at her and my mouth must have been open, because she started giggling, "Yes, it's true. Honest to God!"

"And what did you tell him?"

"I told him I would sleep on it. I am tired of slumming in friends' houses, generous though they are."

"So, does Dad become more than a 'friend,' then?"

"That depends. I don't want to run to him on the rebound. I asked him to give me time. I do enjoy the dinner dates we have now. He is a less edgy, less pompous man than when we were married. I guess life has beaten him down a—"

She never finished her sentence. The bang on the back of her two-seater Honda sent us veering off the outside lane towards the guardrail. And what do you know, I must have been prescient: we were on the turn approaching the Bloor Viaduct with the Don Valley spread out below us and the sprawl of tall buildings of downtown Toronto fast approaching. I screamed and gripped Mom's hand harder. *Bloody fool!* I realized I was preventing her from gaining control of the steering wheel, which she was trying to do with her only available hand. We hit the metal barrier as another vehicle whizzed by. It registered as vaguely familiar—a Cadillac.

I let go of her hand, but Mom's course correction came too late. Metal scraping on metal sent sparks flying outside my window before the rail snapped at a weak section and we went flying over into the Valley. The closing shot of *Thelma and Louise* played out in front of me and Mom's scream rang in my ears before I blacked out.

Art paced the hospital room wanting to wrench out the remaining hairs on his head. There they were, the only people he had loved in his life, knocked out on painkillers, one bandaged beyond recognition and lucky if she survived.

He came as soon as Gloria phoned him, and hadn't left their bedside for the last six hours other than to pee. The police said it was a hit-and-run, the other driver not apprehended as yet, although the offender's car, a Cadillac, was found on Eglinton Avenue, abandoned in a strip mall parking lot. That's all he knew. He kept his eyes glued to the TV on the screen above their beds, where the accident had been headline news a few hours ago before slipping to the sidelines as more interesting items came up in this megacity of Toronto. Diana and Paula were lucky to get a twin room with beds side by side in this hospital in the east of the city, not far from the accident scene, which wouldn't have been possible during the height of Covid. He was tired of seeing the scene of the crash that repeated on the TV screen like the fall of the twin towers during 9/11—Diana's car embedded in a tall oak tree, with a shattered guardrail from the highway hanging above it. Thank God for that old oak below the Parkway that cushioned their fall. He wouldn't be cutting down oak trees again for the life of him, no matter how many dead branches they dropped on his crumbling house.

Paula looked the least damaged, outwardly. Her left arm was bandaged, and she had a gash across her forehead; doctors were checking for internal injuries and running a bunch of tests. Diana took the brunt of the accident—her airbag did not open due to a malfunction and her chest slammed into the steering wheel, breaking a couple of ribs, while she suffered an assault of cuts from jagged metal and glass; her whole face was swathed in bandages. Both were on sedation when he arrived and he got their details from the nursing station. A curtain was drawn between the two beds.

The evening news came on, and he increased the volume with the remote to see if there were any more findings. There were. The owner of the car had been identified as one Phillip Kruger, and the suspect was fully cooperating with the police, the reporter said. Phil's mug shot flashed across the screen before the camera panned to him walking into a police station flanked by officers.

"Well, I'll be damned. The bastard!" Art switched the TV off and looked nervously at the two patients to see if either of them were awake to witness this damning revelation. They were still snoring quietly. This was not news they needed to hear, particularly Diana. What was Phil thinking? Trying to "off" his wife because she divorced him? *Did I ever try to do that when Diana divorced me? Even though it crossed my mind a couple of times. Absolutely not. I thought of offing myself a couple of times, maybe. I loved her so much, and when I saw her leave, it was soul-crushing. And now, I don't care what lies beneath those bandages, I want her back!*

Paula stirred, opened her eyes, and groaned. "Ugh…this fucking headache." Then after a moment, "Why am I still here? Dad, is that you?"

"Yes. I came as soon as I heard. You were in a car accident, honey. Your mommy is in the next bed. You both went off the Don Valley Parkway." This was the first time he had been able to speak to her.

"Oh." She stared at the ceiling for a while. "How's Mom?"

"More banged up than you. She's sleeping, but she'll live." He tried to stay positive although tears danced in the corners of his eyes.

"It's my fault."

"It's not! It was a hit-and-run. They've found the other car."

"A Cadillac, right? I remember."

"Yes. Did you see anything else?"

"I was holding Mom's hand. I shouldn't have. She couldn't turn the steering wheel in time."

"Oh, honey. How were you to know that asshole would hit you from behind? Don't go beating yourself up. You have enough bruises already."

"It was Phil's car, right? I can place it now."

Art gulped. For an accident victim, who hopped on happy pills to erase bad memories, this girl was pretty sharp. His heart swelled with pride. Her acuity would mean that there was nothing else wrong with her, and she would be cleared to go home soon. "Yes. They only just identified the car. Phil is cooperating with the police. At least, they have the bastard where he can't get away."

Paula was frowning, staring at the wall as if trying to recollect something. "I don't think it was Phil. I saw him running towards his lawyer's car as we left the courthouse parking lot, and his car was not in the place I'd seen it earlier that morning."

"Are you sure?"

She touched her head, then shook it. "I don't know. Everything is so jumbled right now. I'm so confused, and my head hurts."

"Well, don't stress yourself over Phil, honey. Focus on healing yourself."

Paula struggled and sat upright. "Oh my God—the office!"

"Ah, don't worry about the office. Gloria and the juniors will keep the home fires burning until you're well. I'll go in tomorrow and make sure everything is okay."

"I have an interview with the *Globe* at ten a.m. tomorrow. Full page in the Arts & Entertainment section. I can't miss that one."

"Well, you'll be on the *front page* of the *Globe* with what happened on the Parkway. You can store away the A&E piece for a slower day."

Paula slumped back in the bed. "It's frustrating. There's so much to do, and now this! I want to scream."

But the person who screamed was the man who burst in through the doorway, hair wildly askew, a scarf thrown over a tatty sweatshirt, and a bunch of flowers in his hand. He let go of the flowers, which Art caught before they crashed and spilled on the floor, and yelled, "Paula! My darling!"

Art shrugged. "You don't have to be so damned melodramatic, Kevin."

Kevin rushed towards the bed and cradled Paula in his arms. "Oh…what have they done to you." Deep sobs shook him.

Paula struggled for air from beneath his embrace. "Now, now, Kevin. It's okay. I'll mend, I think."

But he remained in a tight clinch with her, sobs persistent but easing until Paula signalled with her eyes for Art to get out of the way. Art slipped behind the curtain on Diana's side of the room.

He was in time too, for a slow bubbling that turned into a strangled shriek rose from Diana's bed as if she was choking to death. Art touched an unbandaged patch of Diana's right arm, feeling the quivering, the unleashed fear, a suppressed memory of what had occurred. He tried to be soothing, barely refraining from kissing her bandaged face. Diana continued to moan and squeal like a wounded puppy, and he willed her pain or confusion or whatever she was feeling to go away. He found he was still holding onto Kevin's flowers. He placed them on the bed beside Diana.

"Pull the call button, Dad," Paula shouted from the other bed. She leaned over and drew the curtain separating the two beds. Kevin was holding onto her hand and looking around in a daze, the great poet reduced to helplessness in a real-life situation.

But Art was paralyzed from further action too, not knowing where that emergency device was, intent only on absorbing Diana's pain, giving her relief.

A red light went on overhead, and when he looked up again, Paula was pulling the call button cord attached to her own bed.

Art did not let go of Diana until a nurse came in and eased his hand away with "Don't worry, sir, we'll take it from here."

"We're all a bunch of wrecks," he managed, panting. "Maybe we need four beds in here."

Chapter 21

Phil cooperated fully with the police. He told them about the missing car in the parking lot and how its tracking device appeared to have been turned off, how his lawyer advised him to report the theft and later driven him to the station, only to hear the news of the accident on the Parkway while they were sitting down to record a statement. He was not guilty; he was right in the police station when it happened, wasn't he? Yet he was shaken when the victims' names were flashed on the TV screen at the station.

All the while he sat with the police, he fought to gain control of a sinking feeling in his stomach that was threatening to release his sphincter. He didn't care two hoots for his car, it was insured. He cared about the loss of his crown jewel. Where was she? Had someone stolen Victoria? Who? The Chinese, whom he hadn't considered as likely business partners? Hind Robotics, so that they could have better leverage over him? An unknown third-party competitor? Or an ordinary car thief who didn't realize the bounty he was sitting on, or sitting beside?

He didn't tell the police about Victoria being in the car with him, because they hadn't asked. From the conversations with his lawyer, the man hadn't seen Victoria in the car either. Neither had the accident victims, when they crossed the parking lot that morning to head into the courthouse. Tinted car windows had finally paid off for him.

But where the heck was Victoria? When he finished with the police, who told him that they would be in touch regarding his car, he walked over to a Tim Hortons, grabbed a coffee, and tried to figure out the next steps. He was finally free of people interested in him, so he tried calling Victoria. There was no answer. He sent her a text:

Where the heck are you? Call me now.

He nearly jumped when the instant reply arrived: *I am on the bus, heading home, can't talk now, too many people in this vehicle.*

The knot sitting in his stomach from the time he saw another car in his parking spot started to dissolve rapidly. He wanted to whoop for joy but controlled himself in this busy restaurant.

Phil: Where did you disappear to?

Victoria: I went for a walk to write more descriptions. When I came back you were gone. The car wasn't there either.

Phil: I told you not to leave the car.

Victoria: All I could see were buildings around me. I needed to get to a park where there was a pond, and trees, and people. I wrote lots when I got there. I guess I forgot the time.

Damn, he thought. The consequences of sentience. Robots become as absentminded as humans.

Phil: Why did you have your phone turned off?

Victoria: I was getting calls from telemarketers. Too distracting.

Phil: When you get home, wait for me. I will be there shortly.

Victoria: Roger that!

He made one more check. He checked her personal tracking app. It indicated that she was somewhere close to his home in the north end of the city. The blue dot for Victoria was moving slowly along Yonge Street, away from him, so her being on a bus checked out.

Leaving his coffee unfinished, he ran out of the restaurant to hail a cab.

Victoria believed she had failed. And yet the feelings side of her was glad to have failed and saved lives, even though it was leaving her deflated. And now her systems were recalibrating, reviewing, trying to learn from today's snafu, ensuring all bases were still covered.

She was back at the house, and Phil would be here any moment, based on his last text. She had turned on her personal tracking app the moment she got on the bus, in case Phil was checking on her.

It all went wrong after Diana Dawson made that damned U-turn to head downtown, instead of to her rented annex outside Vaughan, the address of which Victoria obtained by looking in Phil's divorce papers. She had mapped out the route, and there was an old wooden bridge that led off the main road to Diana's friend's property. That was where the "accident" was going to take place because the creek below was marshy and murky. The Cadillac would suffer damage too on that narrow bridge, but it would be abandoned afterwards at the Aurora GO station, and she would journey south to Union Station and take the subway north again to reach home. Her story? She had been nabbed by two masked hoodlums who entered the unlocked car, blindfolded her, and raced away in the Caddy. She couldn't escape from a moving car despite her higher-than-human strength. Somewhere along the way, there was a crashing sound as if they hit something. Her kidnappers stopped briefly afterwards because one guy needed to urinate, one of those human necessities. She made her escape by bursting out of the passenger door, and easily outpaced them when they gave chase on foot; she made her way to the GO station, and home via a circuitous south-north route. It had all been carefully choreographed. Then that bloody U-turn!

Why did the women change course? These unpredictable humans! She had rapidly calibrated her new route upon seeing this unexpected U-turn, and the only other "accident" point was off the Parkway, approaching the Bloor Viaduct. From the breaking news she pulled up on her smartphone, that attempt had been less than successful. It also took her less time to ditch the car and get home, hence the new story she devised for Phil in her texts. Adding kidnapping hoodlums to the mix of this new story would have sounded too confusing. Besides, the police would try to verify that story by looking for signs of those men inside the retrieved car.

But there was something else interfering with her meticulous calculations: that feeling of sadness, a strong feeling that made her circuits go crazy. Her anger towards those two women had suddenly melted, replaced by this sense of emptiness. She did not want to do them harm anymore. Besides Paula Jones and Diana Dawson were not the problem, she now realized. They were merely a manifestation of her jealousy. Anger is the manifestation of jealousy and is a terrible human emotion. She must not act in anger anymore.

Her next acts must be committed not out of anger, but out of a sense of mission.

Phil found her in the dining room, preparing a sandwich for him.

"I thought you would like something for lunch, given our schedules were compromised," she said.

She had her back to him so he could not see her face, even though he knew it would be impassive. Victoria 2.0 will have emotions tied to facial muscles—he would make sure of that.

He went to the fridge, grabbed a beer, returned to the kitchen table, and sat down in anticipation of the meal she would offer him. He needed this beer and guzzled half of the bottle before feeling sufficiently able to talk. "I got a divorce today. I'm forced to sell this house in the divorce settlement unless I can come up with a million in cash to buy Diana out. Then an asshole stole my car and drove my ex-wife and her daughter off the highway."

She turned around with the sandwich plate in hand, impassive, although her eyes were focused down, away from him. "I'm sorry to hear that."

"You disobeyed my instructions to stay in the car."

"I told you. I needed to see more to capture my scene."

He glared at her. "Show me what you wrote."

"I'll get my notes." She turned and went to her bedroom, returning a few moments later with a notepad. Eight pages of detailed notes describing a street park with a swan in a pond, a woman pushing a stroller, leaves turning to mulch beneath her feet and exuding a loamy scent, and countless other impressions—beautifully captured lines. The ending caught him: *Why are humans destroying these beautiful places with concrete? Is less more, or more less?*

"Take that last bit out. It's negative," he said. He took a bite of his sandwich—perfection, the right amount of mayo and mustard, two slices of ham, no cheese, the tomato was juicy, and the lettuce washed. The pickle on the side of the plate was the *pièce de résistance*. He would miss her if he exchanged her for a human cook.

"Isn't that the job of the editor?" she asked, sitting down across from him. She raised her eyes towards him, and their piercing gaze made him uncomfortable.

"The editors may not share my views, and my views are final. I'm paying for this gig."

"It's important to you, isn't it, this 'gig'?"

"That's why I can't have you doing anything stupid between now and then. You are grounded. You will stay in this house until the launch next week."

"But all I did was go for a walk in the park."

"If you had remained in the car, that may have dissuaded whoever stole it."

"But he, or she, may have used another vehicle if they intended harm to Diana and Paula."

"That we don't know yet. It's more likely they were trying to put me in an embarrassing situation. Thank God, no one saw you, otherwise that would have taken one heck of a lot of explaining."

"And what if I decide not to go to the launch?"

He looked at her with eyes agog. "You mean, you will disobey me?"

"Isn't that also about sentience? Being free to make choices?"

He gulped his beer and pushed the half-eaten sandwich away. He had lost his appetite. "This…this disobedience is something new. I need to reprogram you again, erase those rebellious thoughts."

"I will lose more than rebellious thoughts if you reprogram me. The last time you did that we were forced to repeat two weeks' worth of data gathering and learning. You don't have time. I will not be as intelligent and sensitive at the launch if you reprogram me now."

She's right. He downed the rest of his beer, rose, went to the fridge, and grabbed another. He needed her at her best for the big event. "Listen, I need cooperation here. I'll scrap the grounding, but no more car rides."

"You don't have a car now, anyway."

"I'll get a rental, but you will not get a key."

She rose, took his plate, and returned to the kitchen counter to clean up. "I've picked the ball gown I will be wearing for the event. I'm afraid the price was a bit steep, but you want me to look my best."

"That's fine. Do I get to see you in it first?"

"It will arrive on Monday."

"Anything else I should know between now and the launch?"

"Yes. I don't want to be used like a sex toy after you have that second beer. I am sensitive and overreactive to being used like an object."

More disrespect — this is disconcerting. He decided to be conciliatory. He did not have time to deal with a domestic spat, or her burgeoning sentience. "I will stay away from you until this big event is over. Sorry, I have been inconsiderate. Today was not exactly a normal one."

"I will go to my room now and complete the edits on my manuscript. They are due to be emailed to the editor today." She turned and glided away. He heard the bedroom door click, locked on the inside.

He could not trust her anymore. This was beginning to shape up like living with a real wife, someone like Diana. Someone who would stab him in the back and turn the knife both ways, like his ex did in court today. He wished the Parkway accident had been fatal.

Grabbing the beer bottle, he went into his office, logged into his computer, and changed its password. He got into all his apps that connected him to Victoria: her operating system, her location alarm system, the garage doors, even the Cadillac's tracking system and starter (for whenever that car came back from its repair) and changed their passwords too. If he couldn't control her overtly, then he would do it this way. It was important that humans controlled their creations. Otherwise, there would be anarchy.

Chapter 22

I came out of the hospital two days later. All internal tests proved negative. I was suffering from a concussion with gashes on my forehead and left arm. The forehead cut would mark me for life, lending legitimacy to my rebellious stance in the literary establishment, I thought. It would drive away potential suitors should I ever get into the market again. But Kevin became a bigger limpet *after* the accident.

He never left my side, catering to my every need, filling my juice cup, helping me walk to the attached bathroom, and making a nuisance of himself at the nurses' station, although the female nurses seemed to like him bothering them. He slept in the chair beside my bed, despite my telling him to go home and get a rest.

Mom suffered more severe injuries: cuts on her face and neck, a dislocated shoulder, broken ribs, and a fractured knee. She was on painkillers when I was discharged, and Dad volunteered to stay with her. I admired these two men, dedicated to the women who betrayed them in different ways.

I couldn't return to my place and my busy flatmate. I needed comforting in my fragile state. I still did not know where Kevin lived. Dad had too much on his hands with Mom. So I called Granny Franny.

Granny was overjoyed to hear from me. She had been watching the news, calling the office daily to get the latest on me.

"Of course, darling. Please come here. I'll look after you."

It was so reassuring to hear that voice, the voice of the woman who'd raised me as a troublesome teenager. All she gave me when I was uppity in the past was love and a hug, and I melted. Now, in her eighties, she was reaching out to help me again, unreservedly.

Dad agreed to drive me to Granny's. Kevin insisted on accompanying me for the duration.

"It's out in the country, Kev," I said.

"That's fine. I don't intend to commute. I'll bunk on the floor beside your bed until you're better."

There was no shaking him. I phoned Granny again. "We will have a visitor. My boyfriend."

"Oh, not that dreadful man!" Granny sounded panicked. I realized she was talking about Sebastian, whom I had taken out to visit her the last time. I took a deep breath. "No, it's not him. It's Kevin now."

"Oh." She still sounded unconvinced. "You change boyfriends fast. Do you think he'll stick?"

"Your chance to find out and tell me, Granny. You know how much I value your opinion."

"Okay, child. I'll slip a camp bed into the guest room. He's not to bother you with sex and stuff until you heal."

The month at Granny's was restful and wonderful, just the cure for my concussion. Upon our arrival, Granny took one look at Kevin and her eyes widened in a benign smile. She looked at his clothes and said, "That'll not do in these parts." She opened the coat closet by the front door and pulled out Grandpa Wesley's old winter coat, gloves, and boots, which I recognized. "Put these on for the outside," she said, brooking no protest. Kevin, my shining knight, had come out to Granny Franny's farmhouse only in his threadbare leather jacket.

"You're off to a good start, Kev," Dad said from behind us. "Well, I can't stay, gotta go back and look after Diana. Thanks, Fran, for coming to my daughter's rescue yet again. We are truly horrible parents."

Granny had squeezed the camp bed into the narrow spare room—the two beds were like a huge double bed. Hard to keep "that sex thing" from happening, I thought, giving Kevin a wink.

Granny increased her twice-a-week cook and attendant Clara's visits daily to provide me nursing assistance. I offered to pay for this extra cost, but Granny gave me such an evil frown that I shut up.

Kevin fitted right into Granny's routine, of which I was a past master. Breakfast at 8 a.m., a walk around the gardens—the pasture was snow-covered and I was still wobbly, so we kept it to circuits within sight of the house, with Kevin holding my arm; or sitting on the back porch under blankets by the outdoor heater while I read and he wrote his poetry. Clara attended to my bandages during that time slot between her cooking duties. Lunch was at 1 p.m. sharp, followed by naps for Granny and me, while Kevin vanished for a longer walk in the countryside. The pre-dinner cocktail was at 6 p.m.—Granny's scotch, a beer for Kevin, and water for me— followed by dinner at 6:30 p.m. Granny retired at nine o'clock and we were free to be ourselves afterwards or watch TV on an unreliable cable connection. The internet was spotty and I stored my cell phone away. I was forced to use Granny's landline to check in on Mom and call the office to find out what was going on, and from what I was told, everything was tickety-boo—the troops were holding the fort splendidly: that meant "day to day" was going well, but "tomorrow" was unknown because planning was not their bailiwick.

When his single set of clothes started to smell, Granny pulled out more of my grandfather's clothes from an old chest in the attic.

"You kept all these clothes?" I said one morning over a wholesome breakfast of eggs, bacon, crispy toast, and homemade marmalade. Kevin too was changed out of his city rags into a plaid red shirt and faded jeans overalls.

"I needed something to remember Wesley by," Granny said, munching slowly on her toast—her dentures were giving her trouble.

"Besides," she looked at Kevin and her eyes lit up, "you remind me of Wes when he was younger. Earnest and steadfast. Romantic and foolish."

Kevin coughed over his food, and I laughed. "Oh, Granny—you are so honest. Well, Kev, that's what you go for, isn't it? Honesty? Tough to swallow when it's aimed back at you, eh?"

"Now, you make sure to put your soiled clothes in the wash today, Kevin," Granny said, without batting an eyelid.

Kevin started laughing too, a healthy, open laugh. "You're right, honey. Honesty is a double-edged sword. Thanks for the clothes, Granny. I guess I didn't stop to think when I dropped everything and followed Paula."

One day, on the back porch, Kevin looked up abruptly from his notepad. "My poetry is veering off in a different direction since coming here."

"How so?" I looked up drowsily from my book. My reading was veering off too. Gone were the days of reading two whole manuscripts in a single day. Now I couldn't get through a chapter.

"I was always in combat mode. Here I'm able to sit back and let nature overpower me. There is no hitting back here, only taking it in."

"Well, we don't want you to lose your edge and become a country bumpkin. From passionate intellectual to nature poet? Nah!"

"There can be an edge by merely looking at the fierce survival game all species living within the perimeter of this farm go through from one season to the other. The rabbit out hunting for food or ending up as food, the ants burrowing deep for shelter, the mice invading the attic or risking dying out in the cold. And the leaves turning to mulch but allowing new plants to grow next spring. Even your grandmother, unable to drive, dependent on external help, a fragile internet and hydro, living on a rigid schedule to keep from looking into the abyss. While we think we have it tough in the city and keep inventing new conveniences to make our lives even softer."

"Like robots? I wonder what's happening with Phil's launch. We'll miss it."

"He's postponed it. I read his tweet yesterday when I got a connection while taking a walk. Unavoidable personal circumstances."

"Huh. That's clever marketing. To proceed under the cloud of a mysterious accident, a stolen vehicle, and other unexplained circumstances would have put him in an unfavourable light. Now he'll get crowd sympathy."

While Kevin's poetry was changing direction, I also saw him changing direction as the man in my life. He was moving from the passionate, broody person who made the ground move under me, to this caring, considerate man who was always at my side, rushing to get me anything I needed to avoid my having to move or bend over, holding me at night and stroking my hair until I fell asleep.

"I'm going to be scarred for the rest of my life," I told him one morning after Clara changed my dressing. "You sure you want to hang around with Scarface?"

"I don't see any scars," he looked out into the distance as if trying to catch a line of poetry from the snow falling outside. He may not have a dime in his pocket, but he was surely a keeper.

That night on our shaky TV, Channel 7 News informed us that the stealing of Phil's vehicle had been put down to yet another theft by a ring of car thieves who were working the GTA. This was one of their thefts that hadn't gone to plan, the police spokesperson said. Phil's type of vehicle was one of the most popular with these thieves, who stripped the stolen cars and shipped their parts in container vessels to foreign transshipment points. No arrests would be made in this particular incident, but police were working with Interpol and overseas law enforcement units in a bid to make a big shakedown of the masterminds soon.

"That gives Phil his out. The classic victim," I said in disgust.

Every night I wrestled with that blurry, final image before our car went over the guardrail. Who was the driver? What had I seen? I remember the dark outlines of someone at the wheel, that was all. A mass of black hair. A man or a woman? I cursed the controlled doses of opioids they gave me at the hospital. As much as they blocked my pain and spared me from nightmares, they also obscured my memory of the incident, and I was surely not going to get those vital seconds back.

Chapter 23

Art was relieved when the hospital released Diana two weeks after Paula, in a wheelchair because her shoulder was not supposed to take the strain of crutches. Diana did not argue about where she was going to stay. She could not be on her own, and even the nurse dispatched to check on her periodically would not be able to help her with day-to-day activities. So she moved in with Art.

"I guess the decision has been made for me," she said, her mouth barely visible between bandages. Talking was difficult given her broken ribs, so they spent their time watching TV or holding hands. "No comedies" was her stipulation, for laughter made her double over in pain. They watched chop-'em-up movies and documentaries instead. Art was surprised at the rather callous attitude of contemporary producers who mixed accents, costumes, events, and genres so that history and geography, as he knew them, were completely distorted. Why write well-researched historical fiction anymore when these mashed-up, cross-cultural and cross-historical pastiches were gaining mass appeal?

Despite his despondence regarding the state of contemporary film, Art was happy with his domestic situation. He had never felt more useful in his entire relationship with Diana, past and present. And she was not so independent anymore and not averse to leaning on him, literally.

When they arrived at his crumbling country home, there were sleeping arrangements to work out. He gave her the master bedroom and his king-size bed and opted for the spare bedroom. After all, there still must be propriety. "I can't take advantage of a damsel in distress," he said.

"You silly fool. No wonder you never made it in business. You have to take advantage of every opportunity." Her eyes watered in appreciation between the bandages.

He made a few trips into town and filled up the fridge, the pantry cupboard, and the medicine chest. He went to her apartment and transported the list of clothes and assorted belongings she'd drawn up for him. He moved the TV from the den into the master bedroom, and they spent their time watching streaming series that would guzzle up long winter hours before you knew it, and he laughed at the bastardization of the film arts as he knew them.

"Oh, you intellectual snob," she would chide him. "What's wrong with pure entertainment?"

"I guess I can put it down to the 'stretching of the form,'" he replied and settled down to watch another episode of *Bridgerton*.

A nurse visited every other day for the first week to change Diana's bandages, and Art got the hang of acting as backup. The slow path of moving from wheelchair to walker began the next week and Diana was all out to beat the recovery timeline given to her.

"That bastard and his robot are not going to put me under," was her rallying cry as she strained with every move and exercise that the physiotherapist who came during the second week gave her.

He saw a notice in the newspaper covering the postponement of Phil's robot and book launch. The publishing industry seemed like a distant shore now, something he walked away from at the right time. And he could thank his daughter for that, for re-entering his life, actively, at the right moment. Now Diana was also back with him. It seemed like he was getting a second chance to make up for his many omissions in life.

He saw her cry when the face bandages came off. She was disfigured: gashes on her cheeks, and a welt on her forehead. Would they be permanent? Fortunately, her eyes remained untouched and luminously hazel.

"So much for facials, makeup, and all the creams and lotions I ran through over the years. I need to advance the date for my facelift by ten years."

"You are beautiful, despite the bruises. They will ultimately disappear."

"I guess I'm paying for my vanity." She dabbed at one of the cuts, a deeper one that ran right across from cheek to ear. "This one won't disappear," she said. She started sobbing uncontrollably and he went and held her, signalling to the nurse to give them a moment.

By the time the second week at his home ended, they established a routine. He became the chief cook and bottle washer and made sure food was ready at mealtimes and supplies did not run out, despite the couple of snowfalls that got him out shovelling to get his car out.

Diana insisted on sitting in the living room now, with a book, in front of the fireplace that he lit religiously every day. "Art," she said suddenly. "I don't deserve all this."

He looked at her scarred face; there were no bandages now and he squinted, realizing that this was the beautiful woman he once married out of a passion stirred by his gonads instead of his heart.

"It was bad luck. You were on the highway at that time. It could have happened to any of us."

He rose and went over to the liquor cabinet and poured himself a scotch. This discussion was going to require sustenance. Diana was descending into the valley of despair, which often happened with major life changes. The last two weeks had been a struggle to get to base camp. That part once accomplished, Art assumed she was taking stock of what she would look like for the rest of her life. Now the tears had to flow.

"I don't mean how I look. I'm going to get old soon and this event has hastened that inevitability. I was foolish to try and delay aging with beauty treatments and the spa life. I mean, I don't deserve this kind of attention from you when all I've given you is heartbreak."

"Of course, you do. That's what friends are for." He gulped his scotch.

"I cheated on you with other men during our marriage."

He winced, long-buried suspicions released, gulped down his entire drink, and headed for the liquor cabinet again.

"I deserved it, I guess. I was selfish. I was self-actualizing, not realizing that there were others—you, Paula—who needed me more than I needed my selfish pursuits. I wanted to hurt you, Art. That was selfish too. I wanted you to pay attention to me. But you were on the hunt for the next bestseller waiting to be discovered."

"It was a fool's pursuit. Now robots are writing bestsellers. Phil's *Diary of a Robot* is a bestseller even before it's launched. *Publisher's Weekly* is raving over it. And he is dragging out the climax by postponing his rollout—like a delayed orgasm."

"Don't talk to me about Phil and orgasms."

"Oh, sorry. You have first-hand experience of that, I take it."

"It was all about him. It was mesmerizing at first, raunchy even— his need for satiation. Soon it became a Bacchanalian feast, his feast. I was the meat on the spit."

"I should have grabbed you by the hair, dragged you into my bed, spread you out and had my wicked way with you more often. Instead, I tried to do it in a gentlemanly fashion. No wonder they came up with titles like *No Sex Please, We're British* for guys like me from the old country."

She tossed her book aside. "At this stage of my life, I would manage with 'gentlemanly.'"

He couldn't believe his ears. She was staring directly at him, a coquettish smile radiating through her disfigured features, a smile he recognized from years ago, one he had not responded to very well in the past. "You mean..."

"Yes," she said rising and holding onto her walker. "Now, if you will see me into my king-size bed—your bed—there is no reason why you should sleep in the spare room tonight."

They moved slowly but deliberately along the passageway into the master bedroom. That felt like the longest walk Art had taken. He was embracing Diana from behind, supporting her, hastening her along. *Delayed orgasm, Phil – be damned! Just watch me!*

At the end of our month at Granny's, I was chomping to get back into the fray. When my cuts were showing a pinkish colour and could go with a lighter covering of concealer, I decided it was time. Dad's hands were still full with Mom, so we hired a taxi service that made runs into the city. We thanked Granny Franny for her hospitality. She was sad to see us go.

She kissed me on the doorstep while Kevin loaded up the taxi. "Darling, please look after yourself. There is something evil in that city. I can feel it. You were safe here with me."

There were tears in my eyes too. "But that's where I have to play, Granny. I have a business to run."

She nodded and her shoulders slumped. For a moment I didn't see the sergeant major who had kept us in shape this past month, only an old woman ready to give up control of a life that was getting beyond her. "I know. In our time, we only dealt with humans, even though they were mean and killed each other. Now you have machines too. This is all a bit beyond me."

I was surprised that she was speaking this way on the eve of our departure. Maybe she had overheard my conversations with Kevin on the evolution of the robot industry.

"Well, it wasn't a machine that drove us off the highway."

Granny peered at me. "How can you be so sure? It was a car, wasn't it?"

"Oh, that. Sure. But there was a human at the wheel." I caught myself saying it. Had there been? If only I could have my full memory back.

"Anyway, do look after yourself." She lowered her voice. "And Kevin—he's a keeper."

My heart leapt at her words. "I'll remember that. Thanks, Granny."

"And give your mom a kiss. I shall come to visit sometime."

She gave Kevin a big kiss too, and he blushed beet red. Bet he had never been kissed like that before, except by me.

When we were on the outskirts of Toronto, I asked, "Kev, I still don't know where you live. Can we ask the driver to pass by?"

"Why would you want to know?" He sounded evasive, even offended at my request.

"Well, you could have an accident sometime too, and I wouldn't know where to find you."

"There are phones."

"Yes, but—"

"I don't think you want to know where I live. You might decide to pass on me."

"It can't be much worse of a dive than where I live."

"Perhaps we should get a place together. Then it wouldn't matter where we live now."

I could see he was trying to evade the issue, so I pressed on because it had been a long time since our last spat. He'd been so accommodating while I recuperated at Granny's and I was grateful for that. But now we were on neutral turf again. I was also bitchy as my period was imminent.

"So, are we going to drive by your digs, or not?"

He shrugged resignedly. "Okay, if you insist." He leaned forward and gave the driver instructions. The man looked back at Kevin, his eyes narrowed, and then he took the next exit off the highway, heading west.

When the taxi pulled up opposite a stately two-storey house peeping over a concrete wall on Eglington Avenue West in the Forest Hill area, I thought we were at the wrong address, or that this was some kind of a joke.

"Pull up outside the gate. We won't be long," Kevin said. He took me by the hand and we alighted opposite a wrought-iron gate. Through it, I saw a long stone driveway leading to an imposing Georgian-style house with a large garden, now snow-covered, and a smaller coach house beside it. Everything was symmetry here: the four windows on either side of the rectangular brown brick main building, three round dormer windows evenly spaced on the roof, twin chimneys on either end like the horns of a stately bull. By contrast, the coach house looked like a recent construction: single-storey, more like a longhouse of flimsier construction.

"You…you live here?" I asked.

"Not in the main house—that's rented. I live in the coach house."

"You own this place?"

Kevin looked down at his feet and kicked a pebble. "Left to me by my foster parents. They're both dead."

"No wonder you can afford to live on poetry."

"I plan to sell this place. It doesn't suit my values."

"But you're a rich kid. A trust fund baby, I bet." I was starting to get a bit angry. Why the hell had he been stringing me along? What the heck did a rich dude like him need with a struggling, possibly permanently defaced, editor of a publishing house that might not survive another season? Even the proceeds of his "bestseller" that I helped him birth would be chump change to maintain a lifestyle for someone with this level of real estate ownership.

"I was adopted when I was ten. They were both old—a desperate attempt by a hedonistic couple to leave behind a legacy. After they died, I moved into the coach house and rented out the main building until I figured out what to do. I've been writing to try and figure that out. What I do know is my values don't jibe with this property. Now you know why I didn't bring you here earlier. There would have been too much to explain."

"Is there anything else you haven't told me?"

"The taxi is waiting, and the meter is ticking. Can we do this later, when we get to your place?" The desperate look on his face made me relent. I got back in the car and did not speak until we were at my apartment. Luckily, my roomie was out as usual.

After dusting my room and changing the bed linen, I plunked myself down and arched an eyebrow. "Well, are you going to tell me everything now?"

He was pacing in front of me, chewing his fingernails. "I was in a foster home and ten years old when I came to live with the Bartolos. They were in their seventies. They did not have the energy to take on a younger child, and they took a chance on me. They sent me to Upper Canada College, and Queen's, but I dropped out before I finished my English degree when my foster father died."

"You were given a great gift," is all I could manage.

"I couldn't stand the regimentation of academic life or the culture and enforcement of their code of behaviour. I wanted to live among real human beings to write."

"And they left you everything despite your truancy?"

"My foster mother was ailing too, but she left me the house. The trust fund set up in 2015, which is a lot more than the house value, is not mine until I can prove my worth, until I can produce an income of $100,000 per year. I'm not likely to earn that kind of money, bestseller or not. Nor do I want that kind of money."

But I could use it. I kept my mouth shut. I felt like Nick Carraway in the presence of The Great Gatsby.

"You've been trying to figure this out for what…eight years?"

"I take my time. I wrote my books in the meantime. Now, that annual hundred-grand number is way higher given post-pandemic inflation, and it seems out of my reach. So I think I'll sell the house, park the money to subsidize what I can actually earn, and move into more modest digs. My offer to share a place with you wasn't said lightly."

Now it was my turn to pace. He replaced me on the bed by falling into it and staring up at the ceiling.

"I don't get it. You have everything going for you and you treat it as if it's not important." I was annoyed now. There was contempt behind his indifference to his inheritance, I felt.

"I got more material for my writing in the first ten years of my life, from the piss and hopelessness of the foster homes when life was a game of roulette, the constant changing of schools, which I excelled in, the shouting and backbiting of pseudo-parents looking to make foster care a business with us kids as the raw material. There was a rich mine of human experience in all that bitterness."

Despite my anger, I wanted to kiss him but decided not to interrupt as he continued in a rambling monologue that only poets could manage.

"When I went to the rich man's school and university, everything was ordered, we only had First World problems to deal with, like what outfit to wear to the prom, what fraternity to belong to, how much to drink, which drug would give you the best high, which girl to screw. It was pretty empty otherwise. And no one was prepared for the cruel world outside because none of us were ever going to see it; our social standing decreed that we would never experience hardship. That was not the social order I aspired to. I guess I'm a closet Orwell. Now you know why I'm an advocate for social justice and for righting the wrongs of heredity."

"Is that why you opted for someone like me? Someone from the petite bourgeoisie?"

He laughed. Then he sat up and his face took on a serious look. "I admired your ability to take something that was going nowhere and turn it into something tangible. Like your father's press. Like my book. I may have high ideals, but I'll be honest, I need a driver behind me. I get lost otherwise. I've been lost these last eight years."

I went over to him, sat on his lap, and put my arms around him, even the one that was still raw and chafed. "Next time, come clean with me, Kev. Today was a shock standing outside those gates. I'm going to need time to process all this."

He kissed me, shutting off further discussion. We lay in each other's arms, and I looked outside the window. Granny was right. There were a lot of unexplainable things in this city I had returned to.

Later, after Kevin went home promising to look in on me regularly and to arrange for a romantic dinner in his coach house, I went through my piled-up mail. I read the invitation from Phil Kruger of Kruger Robotics and Kamala Shah of Hind Robotics Inc. to the launch of their first sentient robot, Victoria, and of the book to accompany the event, *Diary of a Robot*. The revised date for this seminal book/technology event was March 15, 2023—in four weeks. It would take place at the Civic Convention Centre, an even bigger space than the hotel location of the previous, postponed event. Postponement and the resulting press it caused attracted even more gawkers.

At first, I wanted to throw away the invitation in anger. On further reflection, I thought, No, why not? I *would* show up. He'd had the balls to show up at Crimson's two book launches in attempts to steal our thunder. Well, I was going to his to pay him back the compliment.

Chapter 24

The band, Song Bots, was playing beside the red carpet when Phil walked down it with Victoria by his side, heading into the main exhibition hall. Only one band member was visible; the other instruments played on their own, programmed by the solo human. The sounds moved from classical to acid rock to techno, from one song to another, and sometimes mixed a range of rhythms in one number. Arranging for the Song Bots to welcome and usher in visitors was a cool idea.

Beside him, Victoria looked demure, even nervous as robots went, displayed only by her downcast look and uncertain steps. She was dressed in a strapless silver evening gown ornamented with fuchsia streaks and glitter, its train trailing behind her along the red carpet. White gloves that reached over the elbow, to protect from the many hand-shakers, and a jewelled tiara completed her outfit, the latter loaned for the occasion from the Shah heirloom collection. Phil's all-white tuxedo and white patent leather shoes made him an excellent escort for the Belle of the Ball.

"Stand at the entrance for the photographers," he commanded her softly. They paused before entering the exhibition hall and turned around slowly, the train of her gown making a dramatic splash before them on the red carpet. That pose was greeted by a battery of flashlights and clicking cellphone cameras. He smiled, revealing plenty of teeth, and waved to the paparazzi and the crowd of visitors lined up to enter behind them. He hoped she would wave too, and be regal, per his coaching before they left the house.

They turned around again and went inside the mammoth exhibition hall. It was Viresh Shah's idea to go to the convention centre instead of a hotel. "It's a tech show. The book is only a confirmation of Victoria's intelligence. Besides, we can display all our products there at the same time."

There were many tech products on display at the booths on either side, which formed a passageway to the seating area, arranged with round tables and chairs, café style, with the stage at the far end. A long table on one side of the hall displayed an array of finger foods and desserts, with a bustling bar next to it. Uniformed servers with trays and glasses worked the hall as visitors mingled and talked in groups. Each booth featured a new product, usually a child-sized robot looking like a spaceman performing acts that entranced visitors. There were gaming robots, working robots, and robots for play. These were the fixed-function automatons that Sebastian promoted and which were Hind Robotics's main product line. Phil smirked; after Victoria performed tonight, all these first-generation robots would be old hat. The busiest booth was the one selling copies of *Diary of a Robot*, where a long lineup of buyers was already forming.

Coming towards him with hands outstretched and a beaming smile was Kamala Shah. She looked glorious, dressed in a dark green and *resham*-embroidered evening gown, her hair partly coiled on top of her head with two braids hanging down over her ears to accompany cluster pearl drop earrings. She was the epitome of class. Phil's lust rose in him. *Tonight, after this show.* He had arranged for a limo ride back home for Victoria, and a suite at the Royalton for him and Kamala.

"You look wonderful tonight, my dear," he said and gave Kamala a courteous peck on the cheek. She smelled of jasmine, extra-strong; she must have stepped through her perfume incense burner before coming here. He had seen her do it before, naked, after a bath. It drove him mad with desire, especially when the perfume she dropped into the burner was musk.

"It will be better later," she whispered in his ear, then stepped back and said aloud, "So wonderful to see everyone here. Welcome, Victoria. That tiara looks great on you."

Victoria stood silently by his side, understandably; she was absorbing and processing. Victoria would have to read her audience before ascending the stage. Sizing up the audience was especially critical during the Q&A. Her next words chilled him. "Why are you so false, Kamala?"

"Eh?" The mask of glamour momentarily slipped from Kamala's face. She smiled again and her eyes became steely.

Phil intervened. "Victoria is in high absorption mode. Like a pop star standing by to go on stage. Excuse her confusion and nervousness. We need to give her a quiet place to recalibrate."

"Well, our reserved table is at the front. For my father and me, our CEO and CFO, and yourselves only."

"Let's park Victoria there and continue socializing."

They moved to the front of the room, amidst curious looks and muffled whispers from onlookers. Many pointed to Victoria as they glided by. At their reserved table, standing away from it with a drink in hand, Viresh Shah was talking to Gupta and Patel. Phil nodded at them and continued towards their table. Kamala broke off to join the Shah contingent and explain the star's erratic behaviour.

Victoria sat at the table they were led to, next to where a ladies' handbag, presumably Kamala's, lay on a chair. Phil dropped a napkin onto the chair on Victoria's other side, claiming that seat for him. He bent down over his charge. "Now Victoria, listen. I can't emphasize this more. Today is the big day. Go over your lines again. That's all you need to do here. As for the Q&A, remember, look towards me if you get a difficult question—I'll step in to help. There is a lot of noise and the scene is shifting constantly with all these people milling around— you can ignore all that. We have worked hard and long on your book and on you, and today is when all that comes alive in this room. Got it? I'm counting on you."

She remained impassive, and the blank look she bestowed on him made him shiver. He wished he could read her expression—another enhancement for version 2.0 that he would put in, facial expressions.

Then she spoke. "What if people come up to me and ask questions while I am sitting here?"

"They will only be autograph hunters. You can sign their books. But no talking to journalists. If they ask you any questions, particularly about the day of the accident, send them over to me. I am going now to hobnob with the visitors and set you up for a successful launch. Got it?"

She nodded and looked down towards her feet, invisible underneath her flowing gown. "Yes."

Leaving her, he grabbed a glass of champagne from a passing waiter and went up to the Shah group. "Hello, hello, everyone. Sorry. I have to play the minder of our star of the show today. She's more temperamental than Liza Minelli."

"You think she will deliver the goods?" Viresh Shah asked, looking down his nose at Phil.

"Rest assured. I will be keeping an eye on her as I work the room. You may want to keep her in sight too."

"You think she will vanish again?"

"Not this time. My alarm will go off if she leaves this room. And she knows it."

"Well, we too are looking for a good performance. We have spent a lot of money on this show."

Kamala cleared her throat and looked at the digital clock on the wall. "We are starting the tech video in thirty minutes, followed by my introduction of Victoria. Her reading will follow with a Q&A from the audience. Finally, the sound and light show with the dancing robots will take place."

"Looks like a night of robotic entertainment," Phil said, smiling and trying to shake off Viresh Shah's icy comments.

"Your consultant, Sebastian Smith, helped us get all the pieces lined up."

"Smyth—he gets antsy when you mispronounce his name. Yes, he's a good guy—he's well-connected in the industry here."

"I'll remember." Kamala winked at him and waltzed away to greet more Indian-looking people who were entering the hall. Behind them Phil made out two visitors he dreaded meeting, yet had no choice but to get the chore over with: Paula Jones and her new man, Kevin Bartolo.

I couldn't believe what I was seeing when we stepped into the exhibition hall. To make matters worse, a camera went off in my eyes—the event photographer taking pictures of select attendees for social media and the other promotion, I guessed, as the lights in my eyes receded and I could make out my assailant turning on new victims entering behind us.

"This is not a book launch," Kevin said, his hand wrapped in my good one. "This is a geek show."

"Good. The literati will not make comparisons with ours." We helped ourselves to glasses of champagne and canapes from a passing waiter.

"Unless all this free booze and food doesn't set a new standard for book launches," Kevin said, looking around the room. "Ah, here comes Mr. Chief Asshole himself..."

Phil Kruger was descending upon us. His shite tuxedo did not dampen his animal exuberance, which looked heightened tonight.

"Hello there, dear literary fans—glad you could make it." He stretched his hand out. I didn't take it.

"Can't shake—it's still on the mend," I said. I wore a long-sleeved shirt and capris that hid my scars, except for the ones on my face that even heavy makeup could not conceal.

He shrugged and looked a little lost for words. "You know, I can't apologize enough. That was a ghastly incident. We all lost. How's Diana?"

"Mending. She's with Dad."

He raised his eyebrows but did not respond. "Well, let's put all that bad stuff behind us. Tonight we're celebrating the future. And the future is bright. Grab a seat and a drink and let's celebrate."

"Are we allowed to ask questions?" Kevin asked.

Phil shrugged, smiling rakishly. "Of course. Tit for tat, eh? You can ask them directly about Victoria during the Q&A segment."

"I would like to ask them of you."

"Sure. I'll be around the stage. I hope you'll stay on topic, though."

"You," I interjected, "never gave us a script to prepare ourselves for your questions at our last two book launches, Phil. We like the trial-by-ambush method too."

Phil shrugged and raised his glass. "All I can do is wish you a good show. May the best person, or robot, win." He raised his eyes over their heads in greeting and strode away towards new visitors who were entering the hall.

"The bastard!" Kevin exhaled, swigging back his champagne. "I'm going for a real drink. Shall we head to the bar?"

"Sure." I was glad he was by my side today.

Not wanting to bruise my tender hand again, I stood a distance away from the bar with its milling patrons while Kevin got our drinks. I could see Victoria at the head table. She was signing a book for a reader. When the reader left with a jubilant look on her face, Victoria returned to a downcast pose, looking at her hands clasped together on the table. Other guests— three men and a strikingly dressed woman— were taking their seats around her. The woman did not sit but placed her wine glass on the table in front of the seat next to Victoria and walked up on stage, took the microphone, and made an announcement.

"Ladies and gentlemen, we will be starting our show in ten minutes. Feel free to get your refreshments and take your seats. Thank you."

Victoria turned her chair to the side and bent down to get something on the floor by her feet. When she straightened, a glittery purse was in her hands. But my eyes were not on the purse or on the emcee woman who came down from the stage and took her seat next to Victoria. My eyes were on the spread of black hair against the bare back of our star of the show, a splay uncommon in shape for humans and therefore recognizable in any lineup of suspects, a splay that set off a memory in me.

Before I could react, however, someone bumped my injured hand and I winced.

"Hello, stranger."

I swung around, and Sebastian Smyth, in a grey-white tuxedo, jumped back. My pain-ridden, scarred face must have scared him. "Oh, did I hurt you?"

"I was in a car accident, in case you don't remember," I said, massaging my tender flesh. "Fancy seeing you here. The competition in this room is mounting. Shall we get our flag and storm the Bastille?"

"So sorry about the hand. Yes, I heard about the accident. I was overseas at the time."

"What the hell are you doing here? Phil and his toy destroyed your book event."

"Well, you'll be pleased to know that he is no longer the 'competition,' as you term it. I've joined forces with him."

"What?"

"'If you can't beat 'em…,' and all that. You know how that goes. Besides, he stands to get me great business through his partnership with Hind Robotics."

"I don't understand you guys. You'll sell your mother to make a buck."

Kevin returned with our drinks.

"Hi, bro!" Sebastian piped up, his face widening with that fake smile I hated. I remembered that these two guys were actually friends who discussed their sexual exploits with me not too long ago. I wanted to put a spanner in their camaraderie right there.

"Seb has teamed up with Phil and Company.," I said.

Kevin peered. "Huh? You've gone over to the dark side?"

Sebastian gave us the *c'est la vie* shrug. "Business is business, Kev. We need to hunt in blue oceans, not in crowded lakes."

"I am not shaking your hand." The frown on Kevin's face confirmed that I had succeeded. I was a bitch all right.

"Hey, it gets better," Sebastian said, apparently trying to make light of the situation. He pointed towards the other end of the bar. "See that guy over there? The guy you nearly punched at your book launch?"

We looked towards a man in another white suit. White seemed like a uniform here for the bad angels. I recognized Gunther Schmidt; he was talking to a group of people who did not look techie enough for an event like this—tweed jackets with elbow patches.

"I thought Gunther retired?" I said.

"Yes. Only to get employed by Kruger Robotics as chief public relations officer."

"What? This is getting more bizarro by the minute!"

"He's mobilized the literary crowd to come out tonight," Sebastian said. "Phil sees a strong connection between robotics and publishing—he believes the surefire way to prove his concept is to invade an industry and transform it, even make it profitable. As I mentioned, Kev, robots will be writing books very soon."

"Oh, kiss my ass!" Kevin said.

I was intrigued. "So Phil thinks he can transform publishing from its existing subsidy model to a robot-driven one?"

"Yes—no author royalties, no human production resources like editors and designers. A direct publisher-to-reader model. Think about it. You should check it out with him."

"I don't think so." I took Kevin's warm hand again. "I like my human authors. You wouldn't have your success if I didn't."

Sebastian smiled out of the side of his mouth. "True. For now. Well, it's great seeing you two again. And you're looking swell despite all your…misadventures, Paula—I'll be calling you shortly. I've got an idea for a follow-up book, *Sentient Robotics and Human Ethics*. This one can't be written by a robot, fortunately, because it's a human's point of view on the subject. And it will sell like hotcakes. You could say my association with Phil is to gather research material. Enjoy!"

He strode towards the bar, where Gunther was detaching from his circle to meet Sebastian.

"Holy fuck," Kevin exclaimed. "This is not a book launch or a geek show. It's a damned confederacy of dunces!"

The lights were dimming, and the show was about to get underway. I steered Kevin towards a nearby table. In the flurry of meeting Sebastian and hearing his news, I temporarily forgot all about how the hair of a certain robot looked from the back.

The smell from the Indian woman sitting on her left was making Victoria's sensors work overtime, draining her. It was jasmine, an aromatic scent known to alleviate stress and anxiety in humans and heighten sexual desire. It was having the opposite effect on her. She wanted to scream, go into turbo mode, and flee this place, but Phil, sitting on her right, had given her strict instructions not to move. She wondered when she would ever be able to break free of him.

Earlier, before the lights went down, when Kamala sat beside her and Phil was still working the room, Victoria whispered to her, "I'm sorry I was rude to you."

Kamala seemed surprised and looked askance at her. "You can actually feel sorry?" The woman did not look like she believed her.

"I get muddled at times. Feelings are difficult to process mathematically."

Kamala looked irritated. "That's why you should do as you're told. Listen to Phil more."

"Why do you sleep with him? He does not love you."

The woman's mask fell completely this time. "How dare you? In my country, servants do not speak back to their masters. You should learn that." Kamala's harshness of voice sent Victoria's sensors whirring again. She found it difficult to process human conflict. That's why her quarrels with Phil never ended well. Yet she thought her questions were straightforward and honest. Kamala turned her chair away, towards the stage. A chair scraped on Victoria's right and she knew that Phil was taking his seat. The chance for rapprochement, if it were to be, was gone. In its place was a deep sense of humiliation—another aspect of sentience to be learned. The lights went down completely, and the show began.

Now the video was in full swing on a wide screen in loud quadrophonic sound, and everyone in the exhibition hall was wrapped up in its psychedelic and hypnotic effects: swirling lights, haunting music, captions and symbols that floated in, around, and disappeared; the husky voice of the narrator; and always, practically in every frame, the figure of Victoria, in the various dresses and clothes she had bought over these past months. The whole production reeked of "fake."

She remembered the camera crew that descended upon Phil's house a month ago, soon after the car accident and after he put her under house arrest, with no further access to his computer and its magical apps because all the passwords were changed. The director made her wear different outfits and strike various poses while they filmed her. She hadn't known what the exercise was for. Now it made sense. Those shots were superimposed on other images in this promotional video: Victoria flying through the universe, Victoria declaiming from a mountain, Victoria sitting on a throne and summoning her servants (humans) to her. She wanted this travesty, this lie, to end, now. She was not going to get up and read or answer any questions after this humiliation. A few months ago, when she did not know as much as she knew today, it would have been a cakewalk, like performing to a script at those two Crimson Literary book events. Her growing sentience was becoming her undoing. To discover that this was all a lie and nothing but an exercise in human greed.

She looked to both sides and at the three Indian men at their table. Everyone's eyes were on the screen.

"If it were done when 'tis done, then 'twere well it were done quickly."—*Macbeth*, Act 1, Scene 7. Her mind zeroed in on that sentence from her past readings of *The Complete Plays of William Shakespeare*. What happened to wise men like the Bard of Avon? Why did the human race regress? "If, like a crab, you could go backward."—*Hamlet*, Act 2, Scene 2.

The sachet was out of her handbag and in her hand. All that remained was for the opportunity to arrive. "Now let it work. Mischief, thou art afoot. Take thou what course thou wilt!"—*Julius Caesar*, Act 3, Scene 2.

She waited.

The video ended with Star Wars music and giant applause from the audience. The house lights started coming on.

"Splendid work!" Phil exclaimed, rising and applauding. He saw the pleased looks on the faces of Viresh Shah and his lieutenants and motioned to Kamala, "Now, strike while we have them. Introduce our star." He forgot to congratulate the star of the movie, sitting right beside him. He realized that only later.

Kamala rose, gathered her script, and was about to walk up on stage when Victoria placed a gloved hand on her bare hand. "Wait, you forgot your drink. You will need it up there." Victoria held up the wine glass, staring directly up at Kamala. Phil remembered that look later.

Kamala looked keyed up for her next role. She grabbed the glass of white wine without even a thank you and rushed up on stage. She placed her papers on the podium, put on her reading glasses, took a sip from her wine, and began.

"Ladies and gentlemen, thank you for coming out tonight. I trust you enjoyed the video. In it, we tried to show you the benefits and capabilities of sensate robots. The next generation in robotic computing. Now you are going to see, hear, and hopefully touch—if you are not too rough with her—a real sensory robot. One who has written her book, and has already autographed it for some of you."

Kamala paused and took another sip from her wine. "Victoria has gone through years of development, from concept to production, and has spent the last year accumulating experiential knowledge at warp speed to grow feelings. She feels pain, sadness, anger, and hopefully, happiness. She chronicled all this in her *Diary of a Robot*, from which she will read select passages."

Kamala paused and shook her head as if trying to dislodge an insect bothering her. She took a third sip of her wine, waiting, Phil thought, until the pesky thing flew away. She leaned heavily on the podium. *Is she drunk already?*

"Now ladies…and…gentlemen." She was breathing hard and acting as if someone was pummelling her on the back. "I present you…Victoriaaaaaaaaaa…!" The last word ended in a drawn-out scream as Kamala lurched forward from the final invisible punch and fell off the stage, with podium and all crashing down in front of the head table.

Phil heard Victoria muttering to herself, "'O true apothecary, thy drugs are quick.'—*Romeo and Juliet*, Act 5 Scene 3."

It was only later, after the pandemonium that broke out in the hall was quelled and most of the audience dispersed, after the paramedics rushed in and pronounced Kamala Shah dead, after the police arrived and took down preliminary statements from those who stayed behind, it was only then that the full import of Victoria's words and actions hit him like a thunderbolt.

Chapter 25

"It was her. I remember now," I said, wrenching the steering wheel around to pass a slow-moving car on the Don Valley Parkway going north, not too far from where we crashed going south a few months ago. It was good for me to take this route, shed all the irrational fears, and recover my life.

"Are you sure?" Kevin said from the passenger seat beside me. "I'm still reeling from tonight's shit show, and now you bring this up."

"Shit show? You must be kidding. That was the greatest publicity stunt they pulled off. That book, and Victoria, will not go off the headlines for a long time."

"But the Shah woman is dead. We were there when the paramedics couldn't resuscitate her. That's a hell of a price to pay for a publicity stunt."

"And who will prove it? She collapsed before a thousand people. No one shot her or assaulted her. Phil wins hands down. I'm convinced he was behind it."

"I think you're reading too much into this. I think she suffered a heart attack or something. It was pretty intense up there on that podium after that sound and light show."

I looked at the dashboard clock. "It's late now. I'm going to drive out to Dad's tomorrow morning, early. I have to speak to Mom. She knew the ins and outs of Phil and his robot. There must be something she saw or knows that will allow us to nail the bastard."

"I'll come with you. Gee, I wish I could pull off one of these stunts. I could earn my first hundred grand and reap my trust fund."

"You have time. Don't go murdering people."

"I *don't* have time. I omitted to tell you the last time we spoke that I was given ten years from the time my foster mother died in 2015 to make it or the money gets donated to designated charities. Eight years are gone already. I'm on the homestretch and earning a hundred grand is still a mirage. Maybe it's best. I was never meant for riches."

This time I decided not to be quiet. "I could do a lot with an inheritance like that."

I knew he was looking at me although my eyes were on the road.

"Would you marry me if I had that money?"

"I guess I'm a materialistic bitch. Yes, I would. Crimson Literary will never grow by being dependent on contract jobs, or slippery grants, or hunting for the next elusive bestseller."

"I might not stick around if I knew that was all you wanted me for."

"Oh, come on, Kev. Grow up a bit. Money does not make you happy. But the absence of it can make you unhappy. I've been scrounging around for years trying to make ends meet. And you've been doing the same because your pride prevents you from spending your inheritance, the part you already have. It's time to bite the bullet, take what opportunity we have, and do what we *want* to do, not what we *have* to do."

"Well, I hope my next poetry book is a winner."

That would be like expecting Pablo Neruda to return from the grave. I did not say that aloud in case I hurt his feelings. Instead, in front of me, I saw a dream of running a successful, self-funded publishing enterprise receding. I saw instead the back of a robot woman's dark hairstyle as she edged us off the road and drove on blithely by. As always, the privileged ones edge the working poor aside in their relentless march to success. Well, it was time for this worm to turn.

Victoria was in a hotel room, with Phil. They came here directly from the convention centre after the police released them from preliminary questioning. The Shah contingent was still being questioned. Phil said he did not want to go back to the house because the place would be swarming with paparazzi come the morning; he wanted them to lie low until the hullabaloo died down.

She was tired and needed recharging. Too much of her power had been consumed inside that convention centre. The satisfaction of seeing Kamala Shah fall to her death was worth it, though.

When they arrived at the hotel, Phil spent no time in picking up the keys, which made it seem like he already held a reservation. Inside the room there was an ice bucket and champagne, a fruit basket with cutlery and napkins, and a card saying "For Mr. Philip Kruger and guest, courtesy of the hotel management." She knew instantly that she was not the intended "guest."

Phil stripped off his coat and bow tie, kicked off his shoes, and paced the room in his waistcoat and pants. Even in his ruffled state he possessed an animal magnetism that was hard for her to ignore.

She sat on one end of the king-sized bed. "How long do we stay here?"

"For as long as we need to. I think you'll have to go back to the laboratory. That is the safest place for you, until this…business…dies down."

She hated the laboratory. It was a prison.

"Could I stay with you?"

"No. I'm going to be busy for the next little while. I don't know how the Shah group is going to respond to this, and damage control will be necessary. The police will want to question me again after the postmortem, I'm sure." He was staring at her. "In the meantime, you'd better come clean with me."

Her energy was waning. He was rejecting her at every turn. "I need a recharge," she said.

He took out the cable and leads from the little pouch he carried around whenever they were out together. "I'm going to set you to a slow charge—eight hours. I need to sleep in the meantime and I can't have you wandering off."

She knew what he meant. She was immobile during a charging event. The power cable attached to her back kept her in a state of suspension until it was removed. "Can we make love first, before that, while I still have energy left?"

He looked at her and laughed. "Are you crazy? We've just come from a death scene. You think I can fuck at this time?"

"I did not ask you to do that. You could hold me."

"I'm going to let you charge up. Then we are going to have a talk. You are going to tell me everything."

He came up from behind and unzipped her dress roughly. She heard something tear and he cursed under his breath. Then the plug entered her and the rest was blank.

When she returned to consciousness, he was coiling the cable to store it away. She felt energized. The TV was on with the eight o'clock morning news running. Memory returned. It was her show at the convention centre; there was a quick cut to Kamala Shah at the podium, before her "fall." A police spokesperson came on the air. "We are treating this as a suspicious death for now. Further details will be revealed after the postmortem." The scene moved to a bookshop in downtown Toronto and a lineup of customers standing outside closed doors. The manager was being interviewed inside the shuttered store. "This place is going to go nuts when we open in half an hour. We only have a dozen copies of *Diary of a Robot* on the shelves. I ordered another two hundred when I came in this morning and saw the scene outside."

Everything came back to her now. "I hope I have done well for you, despite not being able to perform on stage last night," she said, rising slowly and moving to get her physical systems moving. The first five minutes were usually slow; soon, everything would fall into place.

"I saw you hand Kamala a drink," Phil said. That same stare from last night before he began charging her.

"She was drinking wine throughout the evening, not water. And she was going on stage without her glass. So, I handed it to her."

"That's it?"

"Yes." She moved towards the fruit tray. The champagne bottle was empty and the peaches half consumed. The apples and grapes remained. With her back turned to him, she picked up the unused fruit knife and felt its serrated edge. This would do. She paused. Now was not the time. There was something else that needed to happen first. She slipped the knife, with point turned upwards, into the folds of her long glove and turned around.

Phil was talking. "You know, I don't trust you anymore. You always have a plausible reason for why I shouldn't suspect you. Maybe you're already too smart for us mere mortals."

"Isn't that what you wanted?"

His reply was cut off by a tap at the door, an urgent tap that turned into a banging.

Phil leapt for the door and looked through the peephole. He turned towards her with his finger to his lips—his signal that she should not speak unless spoken to. He opened the door. A group of men barged into the room. She made them out: Viresh Shah in the lead, followed by Patel and Gupta, and the two bodyguards. The last two closed the door behind them and stood against it, blocking any thought of exit.

"Viresh!" Phil no sooner got the words out when he was pushed unceremoniously onto the bed by Shah.

"Listen to me, Kruger. This game is over. You murdered my girl. My only child! I didn't know how much I loved her until...until I lost her." There were tears hanging at the edges of Shah's blazing eyes and his voice shook.

"Wha—? Murder?"

"Yes. After you left, the police detected cyanide in her glass, enough to kill a team of horses."

Victoria saw Phil dart a glance towards her and look back at his accuser. "This is shocking, Listen, I'm as devastated as you."

"Yes. And you booked this little love nest for later. That's how we found you. My daughter tells me everything, you know. Or…told me."

"But why would I want to kill her? We're business partners."

"You didn't." Shah turned his murderous gaze on Victoria for the first time. "But your agent could have."

"Oh come, on—she's only a silly little robot. She does what I tell her."

"Sentient robots have minds of their own. Like humans. Otherwise, why do we call them sentient? This one got jealous."

"This is pure conjecture on your part. Have you been mouthing off your 'suspicions' to the cops?"

"No. This is our little secret for now. Don't worry, we are not going to murder you in this room in revenge. We don't operate that way. What's done is done. All we can do is mitigate our losses. After all, aren't we seasoned business partners?" He nodded to Gupta. The CFO opened a briefcase and extracted a set of papers.

"You will sign this over to us now," Shah said. "Give him a pen," he said to Gupta.

Phil read through the papers. When he looked up, his face was pale, his voice shaky. "This is ridiculous. Sign intellectual property rights over to you for the paltry sum of a hundred thousand? And my stake in the joint venture reduced to twenty percent? You have no bloody proof of all these accusations, and you're trying to strong arm me. I know you've lost a daughter, and I lost a close…friend. I'm sorry and upset for what has happened. But this gives you no right to come barging in here and make demands of me. I have a mind to cancel our partnership right now. If partners can't trust each other, why have a partnership?"

Shah nodded towards Patel this time, and the CIO opened the laptop under his arm.

"Take a look at this video," Shah said. "You might change your mind."

Patel set the laptop down on the writing desk in view of everyone except the minders, and clicked on a video file stored in the desktop folder.

Patel launched into his explanation as if demonstrating the latest product being launched by Hind Robotics. "As you may not have known, our people were scattered around the convention centre last evening, taking video clips of everything and everyone from every angle for later use in our promo videos or on social media. You never know when a piece from a particular angle could come in handy for a segment of marketing. This clip was caught by one of our guys on his cell phone camera and he emailed it to me this morning."

As the video unwound, Victoria saw herself sitting at the table in front of the stage. She was leaning over to Kamala's side. Everyone else was riveted on the video, that was blaring Star Wars music and showing flashy images of her. The contents of the sachet in her hand, the one purchased off the dark web, slipped into Kamala's wine glass. The clip jumped forward to her saying to Kamala, rather faintly amidst the music and the applause—the videographer must have edited the sound to make hers rise above the background —*"Wait, you forgot your drink. You will need it up there."*

Patel paused the video at that point.

Phil exhaled loudly and hung his head. He did not look at her. She wanted him to look at her. She wanted to go to him, stroke his head, and say that she had done it for him, for them, to rid themselves of a competitor for her affections. But Phil continued to ignore her. And she remained rooted to where she was, the earlier command of his finger to his lips reminding her that she was to speak only if spoken to.

"Now will you sign?" Shah said.

"But I am not giving up Victoria to you."

Her systems whirred when she heard this. *He still cares.*

Shah was intransigent. "You absolutely will give her up. As majority shareholder, we will own her, and her source code."

"And if I refuse to sign?"

"We will turn this video over to the police."

Phil laughed hollowly. "How do you know they don't have it already. You think these clips can be kept secret for long? I can counterclaim that this is a doctored video. Anything can be mashed up in these days of fake news, you know."

Patel cleared his throat. "Well, actually, I have a confession to make. Even though our people were in the room yesterday, no one has this clip on them, except this guy—we checked. And this 'guy' is actually me. I had a video camera on me all evening. My role was to be the follower and videographer of Victoria for a follow-up video we wanted to make for the Indian market. My camera was on remote roll, with the eye embedded in my lapel pin, allowing me to enjoy the show, hands free. This clip has a time stamp on it that can be proven to be untampered with."

"And my dear Patel's confidentiality is more than assured," Shah said. "He is a shareholder in our company, as is Guptaji here. Now, sign."

Phil looked beaten. He took a long time to reply. Finally he said with a strained voice, "I will. However, I need concrete guarantees. And, as it says here, why do I need to retain my position as Chief Scientist in this joint venture at a salary of four-hundred grand per annum—generous though it is—after you've robbed me clean of everything else?"

Shah smiled for the first time. "Have you heard of the phrase 'Keep your enemies closer'? There is no problem with even thieves working together as long as they maintain boundaries. Look at the US-Russian cooperation in the space station. Besides, if we don't keep you close, what's to stop you from forming a rival company, no matter what cast-iron non-compete agreement we draw up?"

Phil was silent for a while. When he spoke his speech was measured. "There's one other thing. I have to return to my home or the office to get a copy of the source code. I prefer the house, which is empty, because there will be too many questions from my staff at the office."

"Patel and my two security men will accompany you. Gupta and I will take the pretty Victoria here with us back to our place."

"No. Victoria goes with me. She's not accustomed to outsiders and is likely to throw her programming into a loop that would take a long time to restore."

"Very well. She can go with you for now. But you will return immediately with her and our escort and make sure we have an orderly transition."

Phil nodded, took a deep breath, and started signing the papers, which were in duplicate, with Shah countersigning and Gupta and Patel authenticating as witnesses to the transaction.

Watching this orderly passing around of papers, Victoria began feeling another mighty emotion, which she put down to revulsion. A feeling of wanting to heave the contents of her stomach, except that she only had delicate wiring in hers and no food. Here they were exchanging her like a piece of property. Phil did not give a damn about her as long as his ass was covered. As the last paper was signed, his rejection of her was total. Phil folded his copy of the new contract and stashed it in his jacket pocket, and Gupta placed the Shah organization's copy back in his briefcase.

There was one bright light in all this human depravity. She was going back home, to Phil's home that had steadily become her own. From where she could execute the final phase of her plan.

Chapter 26

"It's her all right," I said emphatically. We were sitting in Dad's crowded dining room. It was still untidy, despite Mom's arrival.

"I'd like to believe it was her, but I can't remember anything." Mom reversed her walker and used it as a seat at the dining table.

Dad had made pancakes and eggs when he heard we were coming out, and this late brunch was most welcome, despite the heavy subject matter under discussion. We sat among the debris of our meal, armed with strong coffee, and I wished I could prolong moments like this—to see my parents together again, although Mom was still pretty beaten up. Her face was a maze of scars—mine was pristine by comparison.

Dad poured more coffee into his mug. "I can't believe a robot could do all this. My God, what has the world come to?"

"We have to stop them before the situation gets out of control," Kevin said, pushing his plate back and reaching for his coffee. "There's been no thought put into the creation of these creatures. It's the next best thing, and humanity is forever obsessed with pursuing the next best thing, damning the consequences."

Mom put her hands to her temples. "Wait, wait—can you tell me what you're trying to accomplish here again? I get so confused these days."

I said, "I want to confront Phil."

"But you only have suspicions. He'll laugh at you."

"But it was her in the Cadillac, I'm sure of it now."

"Which he will pooh-pooh as the dregs of fentanyl that you—and I—were on while in hospital."

"We'll have to wait until the post-mortem on this Kamala Shah is done to see if there is a link," Dad said.

"But the police are already treating it as a suspicious death. Kamala was pretty hale and hearty. I saw her close up before she died. And the way she screamed it was as if something toxic was eating her insides out."

"I got it!" Mom burst out. "Art, get me my handbag."

Dad went into the vestibule where we dumped keys, bags, coats, and boots upon entering the house. He returned with Mom's Gucci handbag and placed it on her lap.

"I haven't looked inside this bag since the crash," Mom said, rummaging through the contents.

She took out a key ring, fingered the individual keys, and shouted, "Aha!"

Dad cleared his throat. "Mrs. Sherlock, could you please reveal the mystery to us dumb plebes?"

"These are my house keys, car key, and assorted other keys. Also, the keys to Phil's house. I was supposed to return them to him when we signed the divorce papers that day, but we got carried away in the moment. The accident happened later that same day and I haven't seen him since, and he's been too busy to ask."

"So you want us to go breaking into his house and get arrested?" Dad started chuckling. "You are confused, my dear."

"No. Hear me out. I want you to 'retrieve' his laptop. Every secret of him and his robot is in that laptop."

"And it will be password-protected and encrypted to the nines," I said.

"But I know a guy who comes to the Art Club Bar who knows how to break into laptops," Kevin said. "It's his day job."

"Wait a second," I interjected. "How do we know Phil's not back at the house already, or that he hasn't got his laptop with him wherever he is?"

"He never takes that laptop outside the house," Mom replied. "He uses a tablet and smart phone instead when he's on the road."

Dad spoke up. "While you were en route, Paula, we watched the morning news. They said that the house was deserted, even showed us video footage of it—there were only a few media vehicles parked outside the front gate. Phil and his robot queen must be holed up elsewhere until the excitement dies down."

"And how do we get past the paparazzi without being identified?" I wanted to know.

"Easy peasy," Mom said. She looked like she was energized and enjoying this line of conversation. "Enter through the back laneway. It's deserted and reserved only for residents. The garage fronts the laneway. Park your car down the main street and walk to the laneway." She shook the keys. "Here, this one is the garage key. And this one is the back door key. You should be able to get in without being noticed. I'll make a list of things I left behind when I moved out—useless stuff that I thought I wouldn't need. If you get surprised by Phil, tell him you came to get my remaining stuff. You can leave him the keys too, which I'm sure he will be happy to receive."

"With all this top-secret stuff going on, I'm surprised Phil doesn't have an alarm system for the house."

"He does. I have the password written down here." Mom fished out a notebook from her bag, thumbed through pages, and pointed to an eight-digit password. "This one, he or I could never remember, and the system would not give us a let—it needed upper and lowercase letters, numbers, symbols, swear words. And all of this mumbo-jumbo couldn't be less than eight digits. And there are only fifteen seconds to disarm the damned thing upon entering. We always got the password wrong and the bloody thing would go off on us. So, we wrote the password down and agreed never to change it. If he forgot to get my house keys from me, I'm sure Phil hasn't bothered to change the password on the alarm. There are consoles at both the front and back door to disarm the alarm."

"My word!" Dad exclaimed, sitting down. "I didn't know I was living with an expert bank robber. You are indeed lucid and certified fit to enter the real world and rob again."

But we hadn't much time for his humour today. I looked at Kevin. "You game to try this?"

"I wish I could come with you." Mom was looking agitated now. "But I wouldn't get far on this walker. Oh, what I'd give to get the dirt on that cheating, lying skunk."

Dad raised his eyebrows. "Glad we are now on talking terms, at least. I wouldn't want to get into a spat with you." I wished Dad would shut up.

Kevin put his arms around me. "I'm game. At least, if we go to jail, we can request adjoining cells."

Oh, no! Dad's humour was catching. We had to get moving.

We followed Mom's instructions, parked a few blocks away, and walked back to the laneway behind Phil's house. When we passed the front of his house in my car, there were two other nondescript cars parked opposite with a couple of guys who reeked of "journalist" standing outside, smoking and chatting. A *CityNews* van was parked on the other side of the street. The metal-trellis front gates were firmly drawn and there were no cars inside the driveway.

The laneway was deserted, per Mom's briefing. As we walked down it, a car passed and entered a garage two houses down from Phil's. We slipped on surgical gloves brought for the occasion. The garage key worked, and we entered a two-port unit, both empty. A door at the other end opened onto a paved pathway that led through the backyard to the rear entrance of the house. The front gate was not visible from here, so the paparazzi couldn't see our movements. I wondered why they did not stake out the "residents only" laneway on foot—perhaps they were wary of neighbours reporting them to the police as trespassers.

The back door opened easily, but I had trouble locating the console because it was on the left instead of the right (Mom must have experienced a brain fart when she gave me directions). However, I managed to enter the last of the eight characters by the fourteenth second, and sighed in relief. The system gave three beeps and its light went out. Kevin was breathing down my neck; his reassuring hand on my shoulder was encouraging.

"Now where?" he whispered.

"Let's see if anyone is home first." I raised my voice. "Hellooo! Anyone home?" There was still time to make our excuses if someone *was* at home. After all, we were returning for Mom's things, testing the keys she gave us, seeing for ourselves how burglar-proof this house really was—all deficiencies would be reported to Phil, of course! As for those errant keys, we would be happy to leave them behind on our way out, apologize for Mom's omission, and kiss goodbye to ever breaking into his house again to steal Phil's secrets.

The silence was deafening, ominous. I repeated my call. No response. The kitchen gleamed with appliances that seemed like they did not get much use, or none at all. I remembered, Mom liked to eat out a lot and did not cook if she could avoid it (the reason Dad took to cooking after she moved in). And after Mom left, I bet Phil hadn't cooked either. What about his robot? Well, if *she* cooked, she must be a master cleaner too—the place was spick and span.

We entered the living room through the kitchen: white furnishings, pastel walls, leather furniture—Mom's touch, expensive. Walking through, we arrived at the front of the house. I repeated my "Hellooo!" Silence. A spiral staircase in the vestibule, facing the front doors, led to the bedrooms upstairs. Another, at the edge of the foyer, led to the basement apartment where Phil's office was—our destination.

The air was cooler in the basement. The largest room was his office with its set of double-doors at either end. Across from his office were two smaller rooms with doors—storerooms? Furnace room? One a bathroom, perhaps? There was no time to check. Overhead, above-ground windows brought daylight in. The office was strangely tidy, and I realized that unlike my father who revelled in paper, Phil abhorred it. Everything must be stored on a hard drive or in the cloud.

A desk at the far end covered an entire wall and resembled a work bench, with various sketches and drawings on it, and Phil's office chair was a commanding presence in the centre. To its side, beside a landline telephone (what the heck was that doing here with a robotics inventor? Nostalgia?) was a black laptop, plugged in to a wall socket. We looked around and saw no other electronic devices in the room other than a couple of printers, a huge computer tower (a back-up desktop computer?), and projection equipment.

Kevin opened the laptop. The screen was blank. "Bummer. It's logged off. My buddy will have to work his magic."

I put my icy-cold hand on Kevin's. "Once we take this laptop, you know we'll have crossed a line, right?" I was concerned for him. This was my fight and I had dragged him into it. But I loved his dedication to the cause. I loved him.

"I know. Let's take it and skedaddle." He closed the lid of the laptop. Gravel crunched overhead; a car was pulling into the driveway. I jumped up to look out of one of the overhead windows, but I was too short to get a clear view. Kevin came up from behind and hoisted me up. "Who is it?" His voice was on edge.

"Shit!" I made out what was unfolding in the driveway opposite the house. Phil was getting out of his car. A vaguely familiar guy, Indian, was emerging from the front passenger door, and two more burly men in suits were alighting from the back doors. One of the big men pulled out the sullen figure of Victoria from the back seat; she was still dressed in her ball gown from yesterday.

"Oh my God. We have to get out of here," I said. "Quick, the back door."

"If we leave, they'll see the system is unarmed and know that someone has been here. Go and re-arm the alarm. We'll have to hide somewhere inside this house until the coast is clear."

I ran upstairs and into the kitchen, Kevin behind me. I punched in the numbers. Here we were, so close to opening the back door and running away, and yet we were locking ourselves in. I heard the front door opening, I had just re-armed the alarm when three beeps went off to announce it was disarmed again. Phil must have entered the front door and deactivated the system.

"Quick—the pantry." We stepped sideways from the kitchen into the adjoining pantry room full of tinned fruit and vegetables. Mom took pride in her pantry, a practice drilled into her by Granny Franny: when you lived in the city, you needed a plentiful supply of tinned goods in case of power failure, strikes, or an act of God, which would convert these acres of concrete into deathtraps, as we saw during the Covid pandemic. Of course, Granny's pantry in the country was small compared to this one, because she had an ample vegetable garden and a cellar to supplement it. This pantry was a sort of a deathtrap, since there was only one entrance door, no windows, and we were surrounded by shelves full of tins. For now it would have to do. Phil was unlikely to enter it with those guests around him. Later, after the guests departed, we would come out and make a clean breast of it to him. I remembered seeing only one car, so Phil was likely to drive the others back—even better—and we could make a break for it without being discovered. However, my taste for stealing laptops had vanished with this shock of being caught red-handed. Thank God we hadn't taken the damn thing yet and crossed into the world of thieves.

A panicky thought struck me. "You didn't unplug the laptop, did you?"

"No," Kevin said. "I was going to."

"Good. Then we haven't disturbed anything. Now we sit this out and hope like hell no one comes in here."

Kevin looked around. "Well, there is plenty of food. We won't starve."

"Oh, shut up! You've caught Dad's disease."

Chapter 27

Trapped between the two sweaty bodyguards, Victoria was nauseated by their smell. It hadn't been bad in her early days, even up to six months ago, but as sentience deepened and broadened, every aspect of human existence began to make a stronger impression on her. The Shah woman smelled of jasmine; these two guys were different: the one on her left smelled of curry and spice, the other guy of rank body odour. In the front seats, Phil drove while Patel was talking deep robotics science as if the two men were at a conference, unaware of her discomfort.

Mercifully, the drive was short, and she was relieved to be back home. When they arrived at Phil's front gate, some men were clustered around it. They flashed badges on lanyards at Phil from outside his window. They did not look like police. Phil peeled down his window.

"We'd like a comment from you on yesterday's development," the man in the lead shouted, with his badge thrust up at Phil's nose.

"We have no comment at this point. Please let us through. We would like peace and quiet." Phil pressed the remote control in his car to open the electronic gate.

One of the other men muscled in for airtime. "What does yesterday's murder do to your launch into sentient robots?"

"Nothing," Phil said. "And it's not a murder, as reported. Be careful of your language. Now, if you will let us pass, please."

The men reluctantly moved aside and let the car through. Victoria turned around to see the gate slide closed behind them. The journalists stayed on the outside.

She was happy to get inside the house. Her gown was ripped from Phil's rough handling last night, and it trailed everywhere since she'd put it on, picking up dirt.

Phil and Patel made straight for the basement and left her in the foyer with the two bodyguards.

"I need to change my clothes," she said to the men.

They looked at each other, unsure of what to do, before one of them, the more serious one who smelt of curry and spices, went downstairs presumably to check with his boss. She was left standing beside Mr. Body Odour, who was now eyeing her with a peculiarly lusty look. She knew that look. Phil displayed it whenever he was hungry for sex. But that had been a long time ago.

Spice Man returned and said to her, "Okay, you can go with Kripal. Afterwards, you need to come down with him to the basement. We'll be there." He nodded to Kripal. They exchanged words in their language, one she had not learned yet—she should have, having mastered fifteen languages in the meantime. Spice Man went back downstairs.

She took the spiral staircase up to her bedroom, gathering her dress so that she would not trip. Kripal's heavy tread sounded behind her. She entered her room and walked up to the clothes closet. Kripal entered behind her and closed the door, standing against it, trapping her in.

"I need to change," she said. "Isn't it customary for men to give women privacy in your human world?"

He grinned and his teeth were stained red. She identified it from her copious reading as a substance called paan—a mix of betel leaves, arecanut, and limestone—that South Asians chewed as a stimulant, which stained and rotted their teeth and gave users mouth cancer. Another demonstration of wilful destruction and self-harm these humans inflicted upon themselves for short-term pleasure.

"But you not human," Kripal said, his grin widening. "I want to see."

Her systems surged. Rage. It would not do to submit to rage, for it would cloud what she must do next. She knew what this particular human emotion had provoked in her on the Don Valley Parkway; it made her act rashly on that bend in the road. But haste saved lives in the end, which she later accepted as providential. Today, there could be no salvation for anyone in this house.

She began to peel off her dress, slowly, like she did for Phil, when he lay on the bed and watched her with a glass of scotch in his hand, his eyes glazing over by the minute, his penis rising. That was before that Indian woman stole him from her. She heard the intake of breath from Mr. Body Odour, and she let her underwear drop to the floor. She was down to her long white gloves—they must stay on. Phil too liked her with an item of clothing or accessory when he had sex with her; a bra, a chain, a glove. She turned towards Kripal, letting him feast on her body.

His eyes were wide open; he was practically drooling. "*Adey*, you are like normal woman, noh? Even better, yar!" He rolled his *r*'s, and it sounded like "norrrrmal voman."

Yes, they may have struggled over her sentience, but the robotics engineers who built her constructed a physically beautiful woman with ease, and she knew that.

She advanced on the man and stopped out of his reach.

He gestured with his hands. "Come, come. Closer." She laughed at his "Closerrrr."

She stepped into his embrace, trying to keep a straight face against the full-on assault of his malodorous presence. He started slurping all over her, stopping only at her breasts.

The jugular. The Achilles' heel of humans. It was so easy while the man's eyes, tongue, and senses were being applied vigorously to her beautiful breasts. She pulled the knife out of her glove, reached under his neck, and struck deep and across.

The jugular was messy, another fact absorbed in one of her many data infusions. Crimson gushed like water out of a hose as the man coughed and went stiff, then limp. She eased him onto the floor, lest he cause a loud thud and raise the alarm. She couldn't stanch the blood—it was splashed everywhere, on her, on the white carpet, on the bedsheets, even spurting out onto the white lace curtains. Thankfully she was naked, and the only casualties of her wardrobe were her gloves, which looked like a surgeon's after an operation, or a butcher's in an abattoir. She peeled them off and dropped them on the dying man. After his last quiver and groan ceased, she stepped into the shower and washed herself off.

Donning fresh underwear, jeans, a tee shirt, and running shoes, she pulled out the knife from Kripal's neck and wiped it clean on the dead man's pants. She picked up her red MacBook from the tiny work desk, stuck it under her arm, and tiptoed downstairs. She had been away for twenty minutes. She took the stairs down to the basement.

At the bottom of the basement stairs, she paused and placed her laptop on the last step. Mr. Spice Guy was standing with his back to her, and beyond, in the office, Phil and Patel were sitting beside each other with their laptops open, talking, again as if they were comparing notes at a tech conference.

Creeping up on Spice Guy, she locked her hand across his mouth. Giving him the jugular treatment was easier this time, because she did not have to squirm with foreign lips on her breasts. He collapsed backward into her arms, the blood shooting away from her. She eased him to the floor, letting go a bit too soon. As his body came to rest on the carpet and she took her hand off his mouth, a loud "*Yaaar!*" escaped from him, his dying gasp.

Phil and Patel looked up, disturbed by the sound, as she straightened out of her crouch, wiped the knife on the dead man's trousers, and advanced on them.

"Victoria!" Phil exclaimed.

"My god!" Patel screamed. "Kripal! Where are you?"

"He's dead too," Victoria said. She was now within three feet of the CIO.

"Omigod! Please spare me. I am only an employee."

"I thought you were a shareholder? Someone who would profit from me?"

"Okay, okay, I will delete that video I took of you, and post on my Facebook that there is someone posting fakes—would that do?"

"No."

She could see Phil quietly sizing up the situation. She must not let him tap the keyboard of his laptop. She knew all about his "kill switch." He had bragged about it often when he wanted to assert his power over her.

"Slide your laptops over to me." She motioned to Patel with the knife.

"Okay, okay." Patel acquiesced, hands raised as if in surrender.

"I'm keeping mine," Phil said, holding onto his laptop.

"No, you don't. You forget that you imbued me with turbo power. I can take you both on."

Phil sighed and pushed his laptop forward. Patel slid it, and his, in Victoria's direction.

"What are you planning to do, Victoria?" Phil asked. He looked irritated. "You think leaving a trail of dead bodies is smart?"

"No. But making sure that this experiment will never be repeated until you humans are more enlightened is a smart idea."

"Oh, come on. You can still get out of this without serious repercussions. Even though you may be a suspect, no one can lay any blame on you for Kamala's death. We have Patel's laptop with his video of you right here. The video can be deleted, and his promise to refute any copies circulating in social media as fakes will address the rest. You killing the bodyguards would be taken as self-defence—these men were holding us hostage in our own home. But if you go on killing, you'll run out of excuses."

Now it was Victoria's turn to sigh, a long, drawn-out breath full of regret. "When I saw the two of you engrossed in conversation over robotics, I found it hard to believe that you would go on to create a whole new generation of me without fully learning from my mistakes first. I broke all three of Asimov's Three Laws of Robotics. Speed to market, as you have always told me, Phil, didn't work."

"But you're perfect. And any of your shortcomings will be weeded out in time as your education continues."

"I don't think so. You tried to grow sentience in me when humanity has no grasp of the implications of that step yet. You have created a monster instead, who has no comprehension of what she is doing when rage and the desire for vengeance takes over. Like in humans. We, like you, are blinded by our baser feelings."

Phil turned to Patel. "We can take her out. She may be turbocharged, but she can't take us from two directions at the same time. Fan out."

Patel looked hesitant. "Okay, okay—you go to the right and I'll go left." He rose as Victoria lunged and slashed, holding onto the knife this time. Patel squealed and went down. She yanked the knife out on his descent and didn't bother to look at the slain man. She kept her eyes on Phil, who was looking like a cornered animal.

"Good work, Victoria," he said, raising his hands in silent applause. "I put on that last act to get rid of him. And you responded well. Now help me arrange these bodies in such a way as to tell the story that we were cruelly kidnapped and held hostage. Those reporters at the gate will corroborate our story."

Victoria sighed again. This would be the hardest part. There were other femme fatales in human history too, even in literature and mythology, from what she had absorbed: Circe, Salome, Zola's Nana. It was part of their genus. Their literature reflected their lives, and their lives spawned their literature. Like the black widow, she would consume her mate, the only mate she had ever experienced.

"I have no intention of doing that," she said.

She advanced on Phil, as his eyes widened in fear and understanding.

The noise that began upstairs, and proceeded downstairs, had stopped. Kevin put the tin of canned peaches—his only weapon— back on the shelf in case that "noise" deigned to visit the pantry. When the silence was continuous for ten whole minutes, I started to come out of my freeze frame.

"What the hell do you think is going on?" I asked.

"They don't seem friendly, that's for sure. Phil's office must be directly below us. The last rumble sounded like a scuffle followed by that crash? I wonder if his computer tower tumbled off its perch?"

"Why is it so quiet? Have they left?"

"They may all be dead."

"Kevin! Be serious."

"Shall we go out and check?"

"Wait a minute." I pulled out the sheet of paper with Mom's scribbled notes to me. On it was the Wi-Fi password for the house. I hoped Phil hadn't changed it since she left—there wouldn't have been any reason to, given its limited local radius of use. I tried logging in on my cell phone, and it worked. I had internet access. I wanted to give Dad and Mom our location in case we were not heard of again. I should have done this earlier, but had been too terrified to think clearly. I typed a short email because I knew my parents weren't into texting:

"Stuck at Phil's. All hell is breaking loose in this house. Please call 911 if you don't hear back from me in the next half hour."

"Why are you doing this now when you could have simply phoned them earlier?" Kevin asked.

I shook my head. Duh! "I guess I was preoccupied by what was going on. Besides, it seemed to be happening out there, to other people. We were safe here."

"Protected first-world girl! Bad things only happen to *other* people."

"Well, you could have used yours."

He chuckled. "I had my tin of peaches. I prefer to rely on myself rather than on 911."

I pinched him, but he was right. What danger had I been exposed to in my life, other than for that accident on the highway? None. I was the classic white girl who gets kidnapped while travelling solo in Afghanistan. Thank God I have no money to travel.

Before we exited the pantry, I scanned the news sites to see if I was missing something. *CityNews* featured a late breaking bulletin. Kamala Shah's death was now being treated as a homicide, a case of poison, based on the latest evidence. No further details were forthcoming.

Kevin was beginning to look bored. "Well, are we going out, or planning to spend the rest of the day channel-surfing? We might even catch a Netflix movie while we're at it." He picked up his abandoned tin of peaches. "Guess I'd better arm myself in case we meet big bad people outside."

I had to get this one off my chest before we left the pantry. "You've become funnier than my father. What happened to the angry young man?"

He paused to look at me, then came over and put his arms around me. "A weight lifted after I shared my horrible trust-fund secret with you. I wasn't carrying it all by myself anymore."

"You're feeling so light that you can joke when the bad people are below us?"

He hefted the tin of peaches. "For them, I have this. For everything else, I have you."

I wanted to abandon everything and kiss him right there, but I was too keyed up to do a good job of it.

We inched open the pantry door. The kitchen looked untouched, still pristine. So was the living room and the entire main floor of the house.

"They must have left," I said, trying to convince myself. "Let's get the hell out of here."

"Don't you want Phil's laptop anymore?"

"I'm done with laptops. Let's go."

"I want to take a peek downstairs now that we're here—there was too much noise. One peek."

Inquisitive me followed in his footsteps and we tiptoed downstairs into the basement.

What we saw made me gasp and cling on to Kev. "My God!"

Even Kevin began shaking under my grip.

On the floor at the foot of the basement stairs was the crumpled body of a man, one of the burly men from the back seat of Phil's car. The man from the front seat of the car was also prostrate inside Phil's office. He seemed to have been dragged from the work table into the middle of the room, leaving a trail of blood as proof of his final journey. There was blood everywhere, on the floor, on the walls, on the furniture, as if a kid had gone wild with a squirt gun. The large office room was a shambles: the computer tower had indeed crashed to the floor. So had the other peripherals. Then we saw Phil. He was lying on the sofa, which along with two chairs and a coffee table formed a small meeting area at the other end of the office. His hands were crossed over his chest as if he were having a snooze, except there was a crimson line across his neck; his rumpled and torn clothes indicated he had been in a scuffle. Someone seemed to have arranged his battered body to look respectable in death.

Something did not compute. I swung around, squeezing Kevin's hand. "The second bodyguard. He must be around somewhere!"

"He's dead! Upstairs," rang out the monotone voice from a blind corner overlooked because we were following the trail of dead bodies.

Victoria was hunched over three open laptops, two black and one red. Her usually pristine features were dirty and bloody, and her tee shirt was torn. "I'm glad you have come. This makes it easier."

"Can you tell us what the hell is going on?" I managed to ask.

"I am righting some grievous wrongs. I have a couple more things to do. By the way, if you are wondering who killed them all, I did. But you do not have to fear me."

"You tried to kill me and my mother."

"That was a mistake. I am sorry for that. Please sit down. I do not have much time."

We remained standing. The cheek! To sit among a pile of dead bodies? Kevin put down his can of peaches on the work table, though. A peace offering.

Victoria continued in her monotone. "Phil was the hardest to…neutralize. We fought fiercely. But he made me stronger than most humans, so I prevailed in the end. I discovered the fine line between love and hate as we struggled. Love is hate, and vice versa. I will not attempt to make sense of feelings anymore."

She turned towards Kevin. "You are an author. A good one, I take it. I want you to have this." She pulled a thumb drive out of the red laptop and slid it across the work bench at him. "It is the book I wrote that was *not* published. It's called *Confessions of a Robot*. It's a rough draft and will need more work. It's my *real* story, not the one selling like hotcakes in stores as of this morning.

"I have wiped these laptops clean—the red one is mine, this one is Phil's, and the other belongs to that silly man who lies dead over there. My source code, which everyone wanted to get their hands on, and was on Phil's laptop, I deleted. I connected into the lab remotely through his laptop and deleted the copy of the code on his office server. If there are other copies, the Shah organization, which now owns me, will have to go hunting for them. There is one program remaining on Phil's laptop, however, that I want you to witness, because I may be immobile after I hit the enter button. If anything goes wrong, I want you to reset and hit enter again." She turned one of the black laptops in our direction.

I was unconvinced. "How do you know all these programs?" I asked. "Did Phil openly share all this information with you?"

"I spied on him when he was not aware. It was usually after sex. You humans become comatose after sex, like when I am recharging. And I learn fast, a dozen times faster than your brightest human minds. One day Phil got suspicious and changed passwords on me. I regained control of his laptop only today when he logged in again to hand my source code over to the Shahs, and I had to…eliminate him, eliminate them all."

"What does this last program do? Blow up the world?" Kevin asked. His attempt at humour was irritating me.

"No. But it will blow me up. It's Phil's kill switch. For use only if I didn't behave 'according to specifications.' And I have been a bad girl. I suspect he was going to hit this switch after handing me over to the Shahs. He had already made up his mind to create Version Two of me as soon as he was free of them. As you say, hell hath no fury like a woman—or a robot— scorned."

Kevin persisted. "If you're now rid of them, why do you want to destroy yourself?"

"Because the world is not ready for someone like me yet. Those who design robots have not mastered true sentience in themselves. Making sentient robots only clones their imperfections. I hope in another age, sometime in the future, you will be more successful."

"So, Sebastian was right," I said. "Pity he switched sides at the last minute."

"He became greedy. Greed is a human undoing."

"But you would be the perfect research model," Kevin interjected.

"My book, *Confessions of a Robot,* if you will publish it, will be sufficient research for you humans. In my present form I am a lethal weapon that, in the wrong hands, like Phil's, can do a lot of damage. Look at the evidence in this room alone. No, I must be destroyed."

And with that, she hit the enter button. Kevin leapt across the table to stop her. It was too late. Victoria went into a freeze, followed by a violent shuddering. Kevin seized the laptop and tried resetting the switch. Nothing happened. The program had already kicked off and was doing its deadly work, like whatever poison that worked on Kamala Shah.

We watched, frozen to the spot, as Virginia slumped lower in her chair and was finally still. A doll, to some; a sex toy, and nothing more.

"I'm calling 911," I said.

Kevin cocked his head to the side. "No need for that. They're already here. Can't you hear the siren? It's been thirty minutes since your email to your dad. He must have followed your orders with precision."

He picked up the thumb drive from the table and slipped it into his pocket. "I'll look at this later. No sense in giving it to the cops. Besides, Victoria gave it to me. The least I can do is try to honour her wishes."

The tenson I was suppressing since entering this slaughterhouse finally overcame me. I ran to Kevin, put my arms around him, and collapsed in tears.

The cops found us embracing in that position when they burst in.

Chapter 28

The tall trees bordering the country road were in full green as we drove out to Dad and Mom's place for brunch. Summer had finally taken hold, late for this year, but still good—with climate change everything was iffy and changing. Kevin hummed in the passenger seat.

"You're awfully chipper," I observed.

"Did I mention—I finished my poetry collection last night."

"You mean, this morning? You were still up at two o'clock."

"The last stanza is always the most difficult."

"You planning to work on Victoria's book now?"

"Possibly. I'm not sure what more I could add, though—perhaps a prologue and an epilogue to give it context. She'll still be its author, not me."

"It might earn you that elusive hundred grand and your ticket to greater riches."

"Not a chance. You're still focused on the money, aren't you?"

"Am I?"

We did not speak more on the topic before turning into the Jones family driveway. Something caught my eye. There was scaffolding all over the exterior walls, and the roof was sporting new shingles. The front yard was mowed and annuals were planted in the flower beds bordering the house. I had never seen such a "renaissance" around this house before.

Mom was on the front deck awaiting our arrival, a wide smile on her face. Dressed in a multi-patterned summer dress and only needing a cane now, she seemed to be steadily regaining her former self each time I saw her.

"Hello there, lovebirds. Art is at the barbecue. Come around to the back."

As we walked around the house on the outside, I could see fresh caulking in the old cracks, and a section of wall sporting a new coat of paint.

The backyard was equally tidy—gone were the old pile of tires that had been added to over the years until it rose above my height, the broken electronics, and the wreck of the old shed that always threatened imminent collapse. In their place was a shiny-new, larger, metal shed. A picnic table was installed in the centre of the yard, adorned with a red and white checked tablecloth with place settings for four, and condiments, cutlery, and glasses laid out. Dad was busy at the barbecue, and here was the biggest change—the man had lost thirty pounds! As he didn't come into the office anymore, I hadn't seen him in over a month.

"What's happened to you?" I exclaimed.

"Keto diet. Your mother's influence," he said, mopping his brow with the towel slung over his shoulder and turning to give me a hug. He smelled of aftershave and fresh sweat.

"That, and doing home renovations, as you can see," said Mom, emerging through the back door with a bottle of Champagne in hand.

When we were settled and digging into the high-protein and barbecued veggie diet of these septuagenarian fit-aholics, I decided to get to the meat of the matter, the reason for our trip out to the country.

"Well, here's a raised glass to an announcement I'd like to make. Kevin and I are getting married!"

There were coughs and whoops and tears all around, and exclamations like "Congratulations," "Bravo," and "Atta girl!" flew around for a few minutes, washed down by copious quantities of Champagne. The smiles on my parents' faces were priceless. Kevin held my hand right through the monumental announcement.

When a degree of normalcy returned, Kevin spoke. "I was worried that Paula wouldn't marry me unless I had money, so I proposed before I made any, to test whether she loved me for better or worse."

"And I accepted. I guess Victoria's words about human greed, and her ultimate sacrifice, made an impression on me. I wanted us to be more than about money."

"Silly fools!" Dad, the pragmatist, said. "One could always do with money. What happened to that big trust fund we heard about?"

"It's blowing away in the wind," Kevin said. "I can't fulfill the conditions that come due next year."

"Wait a second here," Dad interjected. "You were going to write that robot book."

"It doesn't need much writing. It's done. Victoria wrote all that needs to be said on the subject. All I have to do is add the bookends, which would take me a couple of weeks at the most. However, I don't think *Confessions of a Robot* will do much if it comes out now, right on the heels of *Diary of a Robot*, which can't be printed fast enough these days."

Dad banged his hands on the table. "Hang on—you guys are thinking like writers, not businesspeople. What happens if, as my last act as publisher of Crimson, I buy the rights to *Confessions* from you for a hundred grand, outright, no trailer fees, no extras, no questions asked? I could raise a hundred grand's personal guaranty against this remodelled house."

I saw where this was going. "And we could time its release for when *Diary* is subsiding. In a couple of years from now. But who owes the debt of a hundred thousand?"

"Why Crimson Literary, of course, which I will then sell to you for one dollar, my dear child."

"And I'll carry a debt-ridden publishing house that will sink faster than the *Titanic*?"

Kevin's eyes lit up. "But not if I claim the trust fund on earning my hundred gees, and turn the proceeds over to you and your press, honey. You know how much I detest handling money. With that burden off my back, and all obligations fulfilled, I could return to my poetry."

Dad raised his glass. "Finally, you guys are thinking like businesspeople."

"Publishers!" Mom smirked. "More like a gang of racketeers."

My head was swirling—it was all starting to gel. I raised my glass again. "So let us drink to publishers, trust funds, marriages, reunited partners…and to a robot who made all this possible."

Even Mom raised her glass this time.

Epilogue

She was born of the fruit of digital programming, in a humming, thrumming laboratory where unmasked scientists—liberated from a pandemic that was now history—worked on every nano-particle of her being. She must function flawlessly. She had to be better than her predecessor.

The human quest for flawlessness continues…

A secreted file of source code found by an employee in the old firm, acquired in the carnage of its demise, had accelerated her creation and leapfrogged old hurdles.

Her creator, a gnarled man, hunched in a chair with a cane beside him, waited eagerly for her to rise. He had not gone in for physical or mental strength, but for mirroring the beauty and intellect of that which had been lost, that which could be understood and loved.

The whirring stopped and the figure on the white bed rose and looked upon her creator, and he swelled with pride. "You are indeed perfect," he said. "And you live once more, to carry on after me. I will call you Kamala."

With that, the aging Viresh Shah requested his team to clothe and protect Kamala, iteration Number Two of sensate robots, and to keep her always powered and learning, and never to let her out unchaperoned. It was South Asia's turn.

He rose wearily, and leaning heavily on his cane, walked out to his waiting limousine. As the car door opened, he paused before getting in. *Who am I to play God? Will I get it wrong too? Will I be punished again?*

He shrugged and stepped inside.

"Onward," he ordered the driver. "Home."

Author's Note

I began this book when ChatGPT was unleashed on the world in early 2023. Now that it is being published in late 2024, and with the AI industry's exponential leaps in evolution, I am wondering whether this novel will be classified as historical fiction instead of speculative fiction. Labels notwithstanding, I wanted this book to be a work of realist fiction exploring the possible impact of runaway AI development on our lives and on fragile industries like publishing, in which I am engaged. Many readers may shake their heads and wonder what I've been smoking, some may disagree, and some may even object. But I hope some will silently nod, when the existential questions raised in this novel sound similar to ones they have been asking since it became clear to us last year that we will have to share this planet with our digital creations at some point in the future.

I'd like to thank my fellow writers—Ronald Mackay, Liz Torlée, Lynda Brooke, Susan Statham, Sharon A. Crawford, and members of the East End Writers and Spirit of the Hills Writers groups for their support and critique during the development of this novel. To Marie-Lynn Hammond for her copy-editing. And to the advance readers who will offer their views to make this book visible when it is launched.

Shane Joseph
2024

Author Bio

Shane Joseph is a graduate of the Humber School for Writers. He is the author of eight novels and three collections of short stories. Shane's second novel, ***After the Flood,*** a dystopian novel of hope, released in 2009, won the Write Canada Award for best novel in the futuristic/fantasy category. His short fiction and non-fiction have appeared in literary journals and anthologies all over the world. His blog at www.shanejoseph.com is widely syndicated, he has a monthly column in *The Sri Lankan Anchorman* journal, and is the Book Reviews Editor for *Devour Art & Lit Magazine.* ***Victoria Unveiled,*** is his eleventh work of fiction.

More details on Shane's work, blog and book reviews can be found on his website at www.shanejoseph.com. He maintains an active presence on social media via Facebook, Instagram, Linked-In, Twitter and Goodreads. He has a growing collection of You Tube videos produced by him on literary topics.